To Jaque
all be.

Uncle Stan Reynolds

Murder In A
Cold Climate

Stanley Reynolds

**Grosvenor House
Publishing Limited**

The right of Stanley Reynolds to be identified as the author of this
work has been asserted by him in accordance with Section 78
of the Copyright, Designs and Patents Act 1988

The book cover picture is copyright to Carolyn Harris

This book is published by
Grosvenor House Publishing Ltd
28-30 High Street, Guildford, Surrey, GU1 3EL.
www.grosvenorhousepublishing.co.uk

A CIP record for this book
is available from the British Library

ISBN 978-1-78148-634-4

About the Author

Stanley Reynolds, journalist as well as novelist, was born and raised in rural New England but has lived most of his life in the UK. Literary Editor of the late <u>Punch</u> and a long-time humorous columnist for the <u>Guardian</u>, he wrote <u>Better Dead Than Red</u>, a satire on the American extreme rightwing published in England, America, and in translation in Germany and Italy. Michael Frayn called it "a superbly stylized grotesque".

His first crime novel, <u>Death Dyed Blonde</u>, was published by Quartet in 2008.

He lives in the Westcountry in a 17th Century cottage full of dogs and cats.

Prologue

Dr Phyllis Skypeck was getting to be quite a slut.

The clock on the bedside table said four, and at first she didn't know if it was day or night. She was naked in bed in a room that was completely strange. Only her clothes scattered on the floor and the empty browned-out feeling of a hangover were familiar. The curtains were drawn but she could see it was dark outside. "I must go," she said.

Moving to get out of bed she disturbed the man beside her, a stranger too, just like the room.

"What?" the man said. He was still full of sleep.

"I've got to go," she said. "Say, just where the hell am I?"

"At my place."

"Obviously, but just where exactly is that?"

"Say," he said, imitating her off-hand manner of speaking, "you must have really tied one on last night."

"No kidding." She was out of bed, not embarrassed at all by this strange man looking at her naked.

"You know," he said, "you're really good-looking. But I suppose I told you that last night."

"I can't remember."

"Well, I must have, and it's true." He held the bedclothes back, inviting her to return. "It's four o'clock in the morning on a cold winter's day," he said, "come back to bed."

When you go out and have a few drinks you might end up anywhere, she said to herself, putting on her underclothes.

"I've got to go to work," she said aloud.

"At this hour?"

"Well I've got to get home. Just where the hell is this?"

"Springfield," he said, "Springfield, Massachusetts, New England, the United States of America, the Western Hemisphere, the World."

He had a Southern accent. She saw the uniform hanging on the back of a chair. He was an Air Force sergeant from the air base at Westover, that explained the Southern voice being so far north. She couldn't remember a uniform last night.

"Jesus," she said, "Springfield's miles from home. I've got to get back to North Holford."

"North Holford?" he said. "That's funny."

"What's funny about it?"

"Never mind," he said, "but it is."

She had her clothes on, but she couldn't find her winter coat. Her red knitted hat was there, but the big winter coat wasn't in the room.

He got out of bed and pulled on his pants.

"Are you really going?" he asked.

"As soon as I find my coat. And where is my car?"

"Outside. I drove it for you."

He got the keys and handed them to her.

"Thanks," she said, sounding to herself as though she was speaking to a perfect stranger, which she was – except.

In the mirror she looked pale and dissipated. Like a girl who's been on the razzle, she said to herself.

"Where's my bag?" she asked, turning away from the mirror and the offending image.

"You didn't have any luggage," he said, smiling again as if it was a great joke.

"My black bag," she said, "my little black bag."

"It must be in the car. Or else at Fred's."

"Fred's?"

"Sure, the bar we were in. Or maybe it's in the bar we were in before Fred's."

"Oh Jesus," she said.

But the bag was on the floor.

"What the hell is in that?" he asked.

"It's my little black bag, I'm a doctor."

"You really are a doctor? I thought you were only putting it on last night. I thought maybe you were a nurse pretending."

When you go out knocking around just anywhere, she said to herself, you get into these situations.

"If the coat is here, I'm OK," she said, looking around the room to see where she might have thrown it. But it wasn't there.

"It must be freezing outside," she said.

"Here," he said. He took a red plaid lumber jacket from the closet and handed it to her.

"I'll return it," she said.

"Never mind. It doesn't matter. Don't you want a coffee or something?"

He was really very polite. She supposed that must have been one of the things that attracted her last night. And, of course, the Southern accent.

"I don't have time," she said.

"Sure you do," he said.

He went out of the room, and she followed down a linoleum covered hall into a tiny kitchen full of dirty dishes and the floor not too clean.

There was the sound of someone sleeping and snoring, a noise like a small engine, and then there was a sound of bare feet in the hall and a woman came into the kitchen. She had henna-ed red hair with dark roots. She wore a bathrobe but had nothing on underneath. Her red hair was every which way and she ran a hand through it.

"Hi," she said in a sleepy voice. "What's going on? I heard voices and I thought it was more trouble. I thought it might be the police."

"The police?" the man said. "What would the police want here?"

"Oh, you know," the woman said.

"Have you seen the doctor's coat?" the man asked.

"The doctor?" the redhead asked, looking about to see if there was somebody else in the room. "Who's the doctor?"

"She is. Can't you see her little black bag?"

"A doctor?" the girl said and looked at Phyllis as though she were a Martian.

"About the coat," the man said, "have you seen the coat?"

"What?" the redheaded girl said, getting suddenly angry. "You accusing me of stealing a coat?" She wasn't talking to the man.

"She's not accusing anybody of anything," the man said, "but she can't find her coat."

"She's got one on," the girl said. "Isn't one enough for her?"

"That's mine. She's borrowing it."

"A doctor, huh?" the girl said, looking at Phyllis again. "Who says she's a doctor?"

The girl had a Southern accent too, but, Phyllis thought, maybe she had acquired it associating with the Air Force men at Westover. It would be interesting for a girl like that to be someone else other than herself for a while, or at least to sound like someone else altogether.

"She says she's a doctor," the man said.

"Sure she does. I didn't take no coat. I never take nothing that doesn't belong to me. And I don't go stealing fancy identities either, pretending to be something I'm not."

"It doesn't matter," Phyllis said.

"It does to me," the girl said.

"The coffee," the man said, "it's ready now."

"I want a drink," the redheaded girl said. "And a cigarette. You got a cigarette?" she said to the man. "I don't suppose the Doctor smokes. She does plenty of other things, we've seen that, but she draws the line at smoking cigarettes."

"Listen," Phyllis said, "I'd better get out of here." But the man handed her a coffee. Then he left the room and came back with a cigarette for the girl.

"This place," the redheaded girl said to him, "what a dump. I don't mean your apartment, except it comes with Al and he's in there out cold. Can't you hear him snoring? What a Romeo. I mean the city. What a zoo."

"The doctor isn't from Springfield," the man said. "She's a doctor in North Holford."

"Holford?" the girl said, "that's another zoo."

"Not Holford," the man said, "North Holford. It's in the country. It's pretty."

"There's nothing pretty up here," the girl said. "I hate the North, and I hate Yankees."

She strolled round the room blowing cigarette smoke.

"Say," she said, "did you tell her you already got another girl? When you were out of the room I thought I might tell her about Evie, what's Evie going to say about this one?"

The man got embarrassed.

"It wasn't anything," Phyllis said. "It wasn't anything to upset anyone."

"It wasn't, huh? Listen, I seen you, and I heard the noise. It sounded like the sort of noise Evie would sure get upset about, Doctor. It even drowned out Al's snoring. What a romantic creature that Al is."

"I've got to go," Phyllis said.

"I'll bet you do," the girl said. "Have you checked your wallet, Sam? Maybe that's what she's got in her little black bag."

"Don't be like that," the man said.

"Don't be like what? I'm not the one who comes into a bar alone on the hunt, making believe I'm a doctor."

"When I get out of here," Phyllis said, "which way do I go for North Holford?"

"Listen to the Yankee doctor," the girl said, "she can't even find her way home."

"You can't miss it," the man said, "there's a road sign outside for Holford."

"I don't suppose she misses much, except what she wants to," the redheaded girl said.

Phyllis left. The weather was cold as if snow was coming on. Or too cold to snow, she thought.

The car was all right, but her winter coat wasn't inside.

It was a good long drive to North Holford, but she would be there in time to change before she went to the hospital, which was in Holford, which was a mill town and a bit of a zoo like the redhead said.

"I've got to stop this," she said aloud as she drove along the river road, through Holyoke and Northampton, following the river out into the countryside, going North. "I don't know what gets into me. Or maybe I do." And then she smiled, thinking of the raggedy red-haired Southern belle in the dirty dressing-gown, with her boyfriend Al snoring away in the next room and the belle getting belligerent and accusing her of stealing a man from her friend. The man was nice, she wished she could remember him. "It'll come," she said, "later on the sudden horror of memory will descend."

Then she concentrated on her driving. There was black ice on the road. It was dangerous because you couldn't always see it. Then it was too late and you were skidding into a crash and maybe killed.

Chapter 1

It was still afternoon when Hugh Styling, a handsome young Englishman of twenty-three, arrived at the Lake House Hotel in North Holford, but the sky was overcast and it began to snow. The lights were on in the hotel and also at a nearby ice cream parlour which looked incongruous in the snow, or perhaps it looked as though it was the origin of all ice cream. The hotel overlooked a lake which was already partially frozen even though it was two weeks to Christmas. Hugh stood on the steps of the hotel with his bags in his hands peering at the winter scene through large round glasses. The ice cream parlour had a name that appealed to him, for he was a student, among other things, of American literature, and he knew the name of the ice cream parlour, the Emperor of Ice Cream, came from the American poet Wallace Stevens. He thought he was probably one of the few people in the place who did know that.

But something was happening at the Emperor of Ice Cream. From the steps of the hotel Hugh could see a man with a gun in each hand. The man started shooting at the lights in the sign that spelled out the Emperor of Ice Cream. The man was wearing a red cap with long ear-muffs that tied under his chin and he looked rather comic although Hugh could see that the guns were real, the lights in the sign were breaking.

"Are they making a movie?" he asked a pretty girl about his own age in a red-knitted hat and a plaid lumber jacket.

"A movie?" the girl said. "No, it's not a movie, just some local colour to liven up the winter tourist trade."

They moved inside the hotel porch, out of the way of the falling snow and any stray bullets.

Having shot out the lights in the Emperor of Ice Cream sign the gunman in the red cap went into the ice cream parlour. There was much screaming.

On the hotel porch there was a man with field-glasses watching the scene inside the Emperor of Ice Cream.

"What's going on?" the girl asked him.

"It's Joe Prew, he's gone loony again," the man with the field-glasses said. He began to do a comic commentary in the manner of a baseball sports broadcaster describing what he could see inside the Emperor of Ice Cream.

"Jesus," someone on the hotel porch said, "this is dangerous. You read about these crazy bastards shooting up places, see it on TV all the time. Where the hell are the police?"

Because it was a cold winter's day the Emperor of Ice Cream was fairly empty. Joe Prew didn't seem to notice the customers who were there. He shot the bottles on the glass shelves behind the counter, then the glass shelves themselves and the mirrors on the walls and whatever advertising signs caught his eye, anything that would splinter or shatter and make a noise.

On the porch of the Lake House the pretty girl in the red hat said, "What's he got against ice cream?"

"His wife used to work there," the man with the field-glasses said, "then she ran off with a salesman from Hartford."

2

"How sad," the girl said.

There were a number of people on the glassed-in porch now. All but one of them was watching the scene below them at the Emperor of ice Cream. The one who paid no attention to it was a small woman who walked up and down between the tables picking up empty glasses. The gunfire from the Emperor of Ice Cream was loud and could be clearly heard through the windows of the porch but she never once lifted her head. Hugh watched her, thinking it very mysterious. Then he saw the pretty girl in the red hat motion to the woman. The girl made signs with her fingers and Hugh realized that the woman was deaf. Once the fingers told her what was going on she came to the windows and watched with the others.

There was the sound of a siren. A police car drove down to the ice cream parlour. The driver, a uniformed policeman, got out and aimed a gun at the Emperor of Ice Cream. The back door of the police car opened and another man, in the uniform of the local citizens, jeans and a plaid jacket, got out. The man was very tall and thin and he moved as though he never did anything in a hurry.

The man with the field-glasses said in a mocking, comic voice, "Boomer Daniels, our colourful police chief, has got here at last. Look at him, Parker 'Boomer' Daniels, what a clown!"

The tall thin man shouted to the ice cream parlour, "Now, Joe, put down those guns."

"This is terrible," the girl in the red hat said.

"At least it's some action," a blonde girl said. "Nothing exciting ever happens here."

"Maybe you should try doing some work," a woman said to her. The woman smiled at Hugh. She was

3

good-looking, sexy in a cheap way, older but much more attractive than the blonde girl who wanted excitement. The sexy woman wore a short black leather skirt and a tight, white blouse, and looked rather under-dressed in the arctic scene that presented itself in the large windows, but there was a big radiator on the porch and it threw out much heat.

"I wish that crazy Joe Prew would come up here with his guns and shoot you," the blonde girl said in a lowered voice.

The sexy woman heard but didn't say anything. She walked over to the man with the field-glasses.

"Can you see inside, Jack?" she asked him. "What's that crazy bastard doing now?"

"Just shooting aimlessly," Jack said.

There was a sound on the porch as if someone was dragging something. Hugh turned and saw a limping man of about fifty coming out from inside the hotel.

"Hello, Mr Barch," the girl in the red hat said.

"What's going on, Doctor?" Mr Barch asked. "I was down in the cellar."

"It's Joe Prew," Jack said. "He's shooting up the ice cream parlour. But it's all right now, Boomer Daniels is on the scene, he's going to talk to him, he's going to disarm him with boredom. Or perhaps he'll use irony on him."

"I've got a business to run," Mr Barch said. "There'll be plenty of people coming to dinner tonight. The dining-room has got to be made ready." He was speaking to the sexy woman.

"There's plenty of time, honey," the sexy woman said. "We got time, boy do we have time."

She spoke as though she were an actress in a bad play sending up the lines she had to speak.

"She's Pop's wife," the blonde girl said to Hugh. "She's my stepmother, can you believe that?"

It was hard to believe. Mr Barch was small, with the tired look of a man forced to drag a crippled leg about, and Mrs Barch was tall and bursting with sexy vitality, a big sexy woman married to the pinched little cripple. Hugh was interested in <u>film noir</u>, and here he was surrounded by what looked like the cast of one of them.

Outside the Emperor of Ice Cream something was happening.

"Holy Christ," Jack said, "Davy Shea is going to shoot Joe Prew. No, it's all right, Boomer's stopping him."

Hugh stood on the porch trying to take in the scene of the big frozen lake and the people on the porch. He thought he might have an exciting story at last and be able to write a novel that wasn't about himself being unhappy. Better, and more lucrative, he might have a film script. He knew someone in London who said he was thinking of making a movie.

The customers came tumbling out of the front door of the Emperor of Ice Cream. "They all seem to be there," Jack said.

Then the back door of the Emperor of Ice Cream opened and Joe Prew came out and started running into a small wood along the lake shore. The snow was falling steadily and he was a shadowy figure among the trees. They could see his red cap with the ear-muffs no longer tied under his chin. They hung loose and flapped like the wings of a bird running in fright.

"I wish everyone would go back to work," Mr Barch said. "There's work to be done."

"I wish Joe Prew would come up here and shoot you," the sexy Mrs Barch said.

"Stop your kidding," Mr Barch said.

"Who's kidding?" his wife said.

Below them Parker Daniels had a deer rifle and he aimed it at the running man.

"Go ahead why don't you, Boomer?" Davy Shea, the uniformed policeman, said.

Parker Daniels lowered the rifle.

"I don't know why not," he said, "but I can't."

"Oh, for Christ's sake, Boomer," Davy Shea said, "now we got an armed man running loose in the woods with only fourteen shopping days left to Christmas."

Davy Shea raised his .38 revolver and let off a round, and then another one, at the fleeing man.

"I can't hit him at this distance," he said. "Let me use the rifle."

But Parker wouldn't give it to him.

"This is bullshit," Davy said, "we got an armed crazy man running loose and you won't shoot."

People were coming down from the Lake House porch, looking into the woods to see if Joe Prew was down. Hugh came with them. This is exciting, he said to himself, this is America, not in the movies but in real life, and it looked just like the movies.

"There he is!" someone shouted, pointing to the lake.

Joe Prew was running across the ice. The lake was large, many miles long from one end to the other, but only a quarter of a mile wide from the Lake House to the opposite shore.

"He'll go through the ice," a man said.

Evidently this thought came to the fugitive. They could see him stop and gaze down at the ice at his feet.

"It's breaking up," someone said.

Joe Prew turned and ran with his ear-muffs flapping back the way he had come to the shoreline and the cover of the trees.

Davy Shea raised his gun and took another shot.

"Don't do no more shooting," Parker Daniels said to him.

"I think I got him," Davy Shea said. "I'm sure I got him. The bastard dropped one of his guns."

The sexy Mrs Barch, with a coat now covering her remarkable breasts, was standing near Hugh looking into the trees to see where Joe Prew had gone. The blonde girl and the limping Mr Barch came and stood beside her.

"Did he get him?" Mrs Barch asked.

"I wish somebody would get you," the blonde girl said.

"If he's wounded," Mr Barch said, "he'll bleed to death, or freeze himself to death in this snow."

"I wish you would," the sexy Mrs Barch said.

The Barches seemed keen on having each other murdered. Hugh wondered if it was a family joke, but then they didn't seem as though they were joking.

Joe Prew had disappeared in the woods, but there was blood on the snow.

"We can track him," Davy Shea said.

"Not with the snow coming down like this," Parker Daniels said. "You shouldn't have shot him, Davy."

"We're policemen, Boomer, that's what we do. Anyway, I'm certain he dropped one of his handguns. When I hit him I'm sure I saw him drop something."

The people from the hotel were walking through the woods as though everything was perfectly safe now. They wandered under the trees with their heads down as if they were looking for Joe Prew's tracks in the snow.

Parker Daniels was worried about the people making an outdoor activity out of the search for the gunman.

"Watch out," he said, "he's armed and wounded. He might get exceptionally cross and shoot somebody."

"It was here I hit him," Davy Shea said. He was standing where the first patch of blood appeared. The snow was quickly covering it. "Where's the gun he dropped? I swear he dropped one of them."

"Any of you people pick up a gun as a souvenir of the great Emperor of Ice Cream massacre?" Parker Daniels asked the crowd.

No one answered, but then Hugh heard the girl in the red hat say, "If he's wounded we've got to find him quickly, Parker."

"I'd like to, Doctor," Parker Daniels said to her. "It would be the end of a perfect day if I got Joe before Davy could shoot him some more and you could patch him up before he bleeds to death, but it's getting dark."

"It's not a joke, Parker," she said. "It's sad."

"I know, Doctor," Parker Daniels said.

Hugh went back to the hotel porch. The blonde girl came with him in out of the cold. From the way she looked at him, she seemed to be thinking how good-looking he was, a tall dark stranger new to the town who might take an interest in her. Then he said, "Who's that in the red hat?"

"Do you like her?" the blonde girl asked, sounding disapproving. "Is that your type? The pale, brainy kind? She's a doctor."

"What's her name?" Hugh asked.

"Phyllis Skypeck," the girl said, "<u>Doctor</u> Phyllis Skypeck, she thinks she's something, but her father, he's just an old Polack builder. He's doing the extension here.

8

Or he was doing it until the ground froze up. Are you going to be staying here?"

"That was the idea."

"I mean, do you <u>still</u> want to stay, after what happened? With a madman running loose shooting at things and the cops shooting at him? If I were you I'd go to the College Inn. That would be more your kind of place. You're some kind of a classy college guy, aren't you?"

There was the sound of high heels on the porch. Hugh turned and saw the sexy Mrs Barch. Her coat was opened and her breasts were back on display.

"Carmen," she said to the blonde girl, "are you driving customers away? Never mind Carmen," she said to Hugh, "let me check you in and show you your room. God, you bring back such memories for me, memories of England. I lived there for a time. I liked it, it was fun, only the guy I was mainly with in England wasn't no fun at all."

She still spoke as if she were on stage, explaining her character to the audience.

Hugh smiled.

"What are you smiling about?" she said. "I've had a tragic life." She laughed and gave him a shove. It was a roguish shove, Hugh supposed.

There was the sound of steps on the porch and she turned.

"What the hell's going on now?" she said.

There was a large Christmas tree being held by two people, a hawk-nosed thin man and a woman with a big round jolly face.

"Oh, it's you, Ed," Mrs Barch said to the hawk-nosed man.

"I told you Ed Coffin was coming with the tree today," Carmen said.

"I can't be bothered with it now," Mrs Barch said to the Coffins. "Put it anywhere. Put it in the lobby."

The Coffins carried the big tree in and placed it upright against a piece of furniture.

"You pay them, Carmen," Mrs Barch said. She took her coat off, gazing down at her short black leather skirt as though making sure it was still there and fitting her properly. She smiled at Hugh, aware he had been watching her.

Hugh followed her, with her hips moving more than they needed to, through the hotel lobby. It was a curious room, filled with furniture. There was so much furniture he lost sight of her once. "Here I am, handsome," she shouted. "Sorry about the clutter. They're antiques. I can't help myself. I keep buying them. It's for when the extension is built, whenever that'll be. Fred Skypeck isn't exactly getting on with the job. I got to get the furniture for it while it's available, if I want antiques and not junk or modern stuff." She made one of those faces when she said modern, a face that people make to show what superior taste they have.

The furniture was stacked up like a warehouse, some of the piles looked as if they might easily topple. They seemed quite dangerous.

Then Hugh saw the crippled Mr Barch watching his wife from the banister at the top of the stairs. He looked sinister, like a dwarf in a Gothic castle. Hugh realized that Mr Barch was the audience Mrs Barch had been saying her lines for.

"This used to be Jack Pringle's house," Wanda Barch said, "Jack Pringle, the hunk with the field-glasses. He had all this place just to live in but then he had to sell it when he went broke."

On the wall by the reception desk there were several posters framed under glass. They were from the Twenties and Thirties and the people in them looked very rich and glamorous. Hugh saw himself reflected in the glass of the posters. He thought he looked a bit solemn for someone who was on holiday in a new and exciting place where crazy men shot up ice cream parlours.

After Hugh signed the book at the reception desk Wanda called her husband down to carry Hugh's bags to the room. "I saw you there," she said. "You didn't think I did, but I saw you spying. We don't have an elevator," she said to Hugh, "I suppose you'd call it a lift."

It was embarrassing, the cripple carrying his bags, but Hugh thought it might be even more embarrassing if he attempted to take them from the man. Wanda Barch went ahead of them, walking with the suggestive movements of a woman on stage warming up before the real show began.

She caught Hugh by the arm. "He's jealous as hell," she said, "watch what you say. In fact, don't look too much. Isn't that right, Gus," she said to her husband, "aren't you jealous as hell?" She burst out laughing, and then went on ahead, swaying her backside in a comic, sexy way. She paused and turned to Hugh with her impressive breasts on display in the tight blouse.

This is what I came to America for, Hugh said to himself, this is real life. He thought he had put off such excitement for too long.

He followed Mrs Barch's hips up the stairs. The black shiny skirt was so tight that it rode up in a mass of wrinkles. There was a slit up the side of the skirt. She was wearing black stockings. For a moment he saw one stocking top with the black against the exciting white of her heavy thigh, then it disappeared then reappeared as she took another step.

Hugh almost tripped as an elderly couple came out of a room. They looked classy and somewhat out of place in the Lake House. They stood aside to let the crippled Gus Barch pass with the heavy baggage.

"What are you doing over here, Mr Styling?" Wanda asked. Before he could answer she said, "I was married to a U.S. Air Force sergeant and we went to England to a base in Cambridgeshire. It was nice but I couldn't stand him. He was nothing but a bohunk. Petrolnik, that was his name, Pete Petrolnik. What kind of a name is that?"

They reached the top of the stairs.

"This is it," she said. "You," she said to her husband, "just put the bags down."

"I got to rest," Gus Barch said.

"You mean you got to spy on me."

"My leg is bad."

"You're worried I might try something up here," his wife said. "Maybe you're worried Mr Styling and me did know each other over there in England and he's come over to renew the acquaintance."

Gus Barch didn't say anything, but he didn't go away.

"Maybe I got a lot of old boyfriends sneaking in here to stay incognito. You'd never know." She turned to Hugh. "You all right here?" she asked. "You like it?"

She moved about the room talking of England. Her blouse was awfully tight and her hips rolled in the short, shiny black skirt. "You know Cambridgeshire?" she asked.

"I was at Cambridge University," Hugh said. His voice didn't sound like his own, it was heavy, like the voice of an actor in a <u>film noir</u> when he first meets the smouldering <u>femme fatale</u> who will be his undoing, perhaps getting him framed for a murder he didn't commit. Or, maybe, the actor had committed the murder, Hugh couldn't remember.

"Well, what do you know, we were both in Cambridgeshire," Wanda Barch said. "We could have met. Wouldn't that be something?" She turned to her husband as she said this.

Gus Barch left the room, but they could see him still watching them from the hallway.

"When were you in Cambridgeshire?" Wanda asked in her stage voice, knowing her husband was listening.

When he told her she said, "We could have met. That was about the time I was married to that Air Force guy, Pete Petrolnik."

She turned and glanced at her husband in the hall. She stood in the doorway and then she turned, closing the scene with a last view of her breasts and the tight, short skirt that was wrinkled where it rode up over her hips. Hugh heard her high heels on the stairs and then the dragging step of Gus Barch.

Chapter 2

Phyllis Skypeck moved slowly through the snow which was beginning to pile up. She saw the blood. She hoped Joe Prew would be found soon so she could treat him before he lost too much or some complication set in. Joe Prew was a hired man, doing odd jobs, also a part-time drunk, he wore dirty clothes and if the dirt from his clothes got into the wound he would have an infection when the wound stopped bleeding.

But she had come down from the hotel porch without her black bag. That was stupid, she said to herself. She went back to get it. On the porch she bent down to take it from the chair where she had left it and when she stood up she saw her face reflected in the darkening glass of the window. It gave her a shock. I look like a nun with a pale face like that, she thought, except for the debauchery in my shade of pale I only look like an actress playing a nun. I've got to stop going out on the tiles, and try to get healthy instead, also respectable. When you drink too much, she said to herself as though she was giving herself a lecture, you are liable to make a mistake, and that is something very serious for a doctor to do.

She was wearing the red plaid lumber jacket and it was uncomfortable in the heat that was coming from the big radiator on the porch, but she didn't like to take it off.

As the afternoon darkened the glass in the window reflected her pale face as clearly as a mirror. Oh shit, she said to herself. She had a love bite on her neck. She had been going on her rounds all day without having noticed it. She pulled the collar of the jacket up and buttoned it. A hickey, she said to herself, that's what the girls who always seemed to have love bites called them. She wondered where they got that name, if there had been a Mr Hickey who had been particularly good at giving them.

She saw the good-looking English boy come on to the porch from inside the hotel. He glanced at her as he passed by. He's really interesting looking, she said to herself, tall and dark and mysterious. I guess I'm just too lecherous for my own good, but with all that school, I never had time to break into it slow and easy like a normal girl.

"Are you leaving?" the deaf mute Milly Tencza asked her, using sign language.

Phyllis put down the black bag and tried to remember the signs.

"I'm going out to see if they find Joe Prew and if he needs help."

"You work too hard," Milly Tencza signed.

Phyllis smiled. If she only knew, she thought.

Wanda Barch was on the porch, looking very large and sexy, full of health like a prize cow. She was deep in conversation with the good-looking English boy and then she turned and stood watching Phyllis speaking sign language to Milly Tencza. Phyllis wondered if she should say something rude about Wanda Barch to Milly, it would be good to make Milly laugh, she was very ill.

I can't stay here leching over the English boy, she said to herself. Besides, Jack Pringle is out there and he's the one I really want.

What the hell have I turned into? she asked herself. And it isn't even night time with a few drinks in me making me horny.

She hurried off the porch and back into the snow, trying to catch up with Boomer Daniels and the rest of them tracking Joe Prew. She saw young Artie Barch, Gus's son from his first wife, the wife who'd run off on him and completely disappeared. Artie was skating on the ice on the lake. It wasn't safe, even if he kept close to the shore. Out in the middle she could see where the water was running dark where it hadn't frozen over. Otherwise one could skate straight across to the far shore only a quarter of a mile away.

"Artie," she called to him, "you shouldn't be doing that. You'll go through the ice and drown."

"I can swim," he said.

"Not in that cold water you couldn't. Besides, you might slip under the ice and not be able to come up."

The child, eight or nine years of age, turned and looked about at the ice which now possessed a grown-up threat.

"They won't let me chase after Joe Prew," he said.

He wanted something exciting to do. He must be bored living in a hotel, she thought, not being able to make a noise, or play the TV loud.

She stepped on to the ice. It didn't give, it seemed thick enough, but there was that great dark slash in the middle. She slid to him.

"It's fun," she said, "but it _is_ dangerous. You mustn't do it."

She took him by the mittened hand. He already had his father's defeated look. Phyllis could not remember the mother, who was not from round here. No one had a good word to say about her, any more than they had for Wanda. She'd run off with a man of course. It was unusual that she had left the children with the husband, and it was unusual that there were several men right here at the Lake House today whose wives had had enough of them and run off. Joe Prew was the most dramatic, or, at least, he had now made a melodrama or a farce out of it, shooting up the Emperor of Ice Cream.

But Parker Daniels' wife had also left him, and for seven years Parker had the children until his wife wanted them back. It was sad, a man like Parker Daniels being left with young children to take care of, but if you added up the number of wives left alone they would greatly outnumber the sad men. And the men had careers or at least jobs they could earn a living by and occupy themselves with, while the wives usually had no work or only some little job they could do. They had trouble making ends meet.

But I'm a doctor, she said to herself, I will never have to depend on anyone.

She pulled Artie Barch along on his skates, making a game out of removing him from the dangerous ice. He was a sickly child, nothing important wrong with him, but always ailing, he would probably go through life like that and never have the vigour to make a woman happy or himself any real money.

"Now don't go back on that ice," she said. She had a bar of chocolate and she was going to give it to him, but then she didn't. "Do you promise me?" she asked.

"Yes," the child said.

17

But why should he promise me anything? Phyllis thought. He'll be back skating as soon as my back's turned. It's a wonder any of them grow up, the dangerous games they play. And what about you? she asked herself. The games you're playing now? After all the hard work to become a doctor, you're putting it in jeopardy. A doctor who drinks, nobody wants that. And one who fucks more than she should? I suppose they only find that amusing.

"Here," she said, and gave Artie the chocolate bar.

She ran to catch up with the police.

Parker Daniels turned and looked at her. "You here?" he said. "You shouldn't be here."

"I'm a doctor, where else should I be except where a man is bleeding?"

"You're hard to shave, Doctor," Parker said. "A good-looking girl like you —"

"A girl?"

"A woman then, a woman like you should be married." He paused for a moment and then said: "Your hands are shaking."

She glanced down at her hands. She could see that her fingers were trembling. She had felt something wrong, but wasn't bothered to look. She'd had too much to drink the night before. She still felt hung over and it was almost evening and time for another one.

"It's the cold. I don't have any gloves."

"A good husband would make sure you had gloves. A doctor shouldn't have cold hands."

"Is that a proposal?"

"I would propose to you if I thought I had a chance."

He was forty-two, the same age as Jack Pringle, but tall and thin, not handsome like Jack. And with a reputation for being goofy. She could see he needed a woman. The collar of his shirt was frayed. His shirts were always wrinkled. No one ironed them, or he ironed them himself and didn't do a good job. He brought out some maternal feeling in her. She thought about him sometimes on cold nights sitting alone in a spartan room staring at a broken TV with only his little mongrel terrier for company. She imagined Parker didn't eat properly. But at least he doesn't drink, she said to herself, at least not the way I do. I guess I'm in no position to be maternal with anyone.

It was becoming dark and there was a stiff wind, it rattled the leafless branches of the trees, they were swaying and knocking together, making an eerie noise that made her think of skeletons attempting to dance. Christmas was a good time for ghost stories.

She turned and looked where far away the lights of the city of Holford were on, but that dirty, run-down milltown didn't look any better for being snowed on, it was still murky, a town that had lost its purpose as the mills closed.

"Do you think you'll find Joe Prew now?" she asked. "That fool Davy Shea, why did he have to shoot him?"

"Davy's always been like that, ever since he was a kid," Parker said. "He's a bully, or he'd like to be only he's afraid someone might punch him back."

Davy Shea was only ten years younger than Parker, but Parker spoke as if a whole generation separated them. He's a fatherly man, she thought, unlike Jack Pringle, who's still like a boy. Parker's left his youth far behind.

"Why did Joe Prew do all that shooting?" she asked. "Was it really because of his wife?"

"Oh yes."

"How can you be so sure?"

"Because he's done it twice before."

"You're kidding."

"No, I guess you were away at college and weren't paying much attention to the big goings on at home. It's a good thing Milt Schmidt is an easy-going guy, he didn't prefer any charges. I was Milt's lawyer. I told Milt if he changed the name from Milt's Ice Cream Heaven to something else maybe Joe Prew would stop being reminded of his wife meeting that salesman in there, but I guess it didn't work."

"Poor Joe Prew," Phyllis said, "what a way to be."

"Yes, I guess he's crushed."

"Crushed?" She thought it was an unusual word to use.

Up ahead she could see Jack Pringle, the main object of her desire these days, and then she heard someone running up behind them and turned to see Wanda Barch looking out of place in the outdoors. Wanda went to where Jack Pringle was standing scanning the woods with his field glasses.

"I suppose," Parker said, "that it's the natural state of man to be crushed, at least by the time he has reached a certain age."

He seemed to be speaking from experience. There had been something comic about the man Parker's wife had run off with, but Phyllis couldn't remember what it was, only that people had thought it comical, except that Parker had been left with two daughters, ages three and five, to take care of. She wondered if their clothes had been ironed. She supposed they hadn't been. Anyway, when the wife had come back seven years later and taken the children, now ages ten and twelve, away with her, that had obviously been enough of a crushing for Parker but that was five years ago and maybe Parker should be over it by now.

She walked on to be next to Jack Pringle. He was looking very handsome today in conversation with Wanda. Phyllis wondered how she could break into their talk. Parker caught up with her. She decided to go on without speaking to Jack, but he and Wanda blocked her way for her and Parker. Parker bowed to Wanda in a mock courtly manner and the big sexy woman scowled at him behind his back as he passed by. Wanda Barch will never be crushed, Phyllis said to herself. Then she wondered if Jack Pringle was maybe crushed by life the way Boomer Daniels said most people were by a certain age. He didn't look it, but his business had failed, and his wife had left him. She had forgotten about that wife of Jack Pringle's. Jack never mentioned her. It was as if she had never existed. He was said to have money again but it wasn't like the money he had when the Pringles owned the big paper mill. That wife must have been a mercenary bitch, Phyllis thought, she probably left when the money ran out.

Phyllis remembered that she had something to say to Wanda Barch.

"Artie was skating on the lake," she said to her.

The big vacant eyes looked back at Phyllis, then they became bad-tempered, the eyes of someone being interrupted by a matter that was far below her and of no real importance.

"It's dangerous," Phyllis said.

"Kids," Wanda said.

Phyllis passed by.

"What's it got to do with her?" she heard Wanda say.

"You must find Joe Prew," Phyllis said to Parker.

"Look at this snow," he said. "We'll be the ones who freeze to death if it goes on much longer."

"What about him?" she said. "He's been shot by that bastard Davy Shea."

"Davy probably didn't hit him real good, Davy's not good at anything except a little low key bluster. Joe Prew is like an old cat, he'll take care of himself until he gets bored being a fugitive and decides to come home."

She felt like going back and talking to Jack Pringle. He would say humorous things and be very handsome. But she didn't turn back.

"I want to find Joe Prew," she said and she walked on ahead of the policeman into the woods.

"Oh now, Doctor," Parker called, "you don't know where you're going."

"I know these woods," she said without turning round to look at him, still walking through the deep snow with the fluffy flakes beginning to build up on her clothes. She didn't stop to see if Parker was coming with her.

"Phyllis," he called, "come back, it's too dark to go on."

But she didn't stop or even turn around.

Chapter 3

Hugh Styling was in his room waiting to go down to dinner. The snow was still falling and he put down the book he was trying to read and went and stood by the window and watched it, wondering what sort of effect it might have on a <u>film noir</u>. These favourite films of his were usually set in sultry locales which allowed the <u>femme fatale</u> to perspire, and caused what little she wore to stick to her in a sexy way. The snowy landscape did not lend itself to such scenes. But the shooting at the Emperor of Ice Cream had been interesting, though he craved a more personal excitement, involving, of course, a woman. There were girls in London whom he enjoyed thinking about. Unfortunately none took him seriously. They saw him as something of a joke because he still lived with his mother. He had to live with her. That, at least, was what he told himself. He was trying to write a novel, to write, in fact, another novel, for he had written several since coming down from Cambridge, but they'd failed to find a publisher. From time to time he dabbled in freelance journalism but that didn't bring in much money.

"You ought to be an actor," one girl had told him. "You're so good-looking girls would be mad about you. You'd get no end of fan mail."

But Hugh hadn't been in Footlights at Cambridge. He had no interest in drawing attention to himself on stage or in front of a camera. He saw his reflection now in the dark window. It was not a clear reflection. He was obscure. He seemed all eye-glasses and coat and tie, like a dummy in a shop window. His clothes were expensive. His mother bought them for him. She pretended they were special gifts, but actually they were a necessity, he could not afford to buy his own. He thought about telephoning his mother, but she wouldn't be home at their house in Islington. She was spending Christmas with an old BBC woman friend in Scotland. He could not reverse the charges.

"I'm a mess," he said aloud and turned away from the snow and the store dummy in the window.

He went downstairs for a drink before dinner. The search for Joe Prew had evidently been called off because of the dark. The tall thin police chief was in the bar, with the other policeman and the female doctor and the humorous man with the field glasses. The bar was noisy. With Life, Hugh thought.

"Hello," Phyllis Skypeck said to him.

She still had the red knitted hat pulled down on her head with the black curls showing round the edges. She wore jeans and a tailored grey suit-coat with aggressive shoulders, and a white blouse that fitted tightly at her throat, but he had seen the love bite on her neck.

"You've had some introduction to America," she said. "Milly Tencza, the deaf-mute woman, I'm treating her, she's ill, she told me you've just arrived from London. Poor Milly, I'm learning sign language so I can understand how she feels. Can you imagine how it is for a woman like her, desperately ill and no way to express it?"

The red hat and the black curls gave the young doctor a gypsy look.

Hugh tried to think of something to say to impress her. The talk in the bar was about the shooting at the Emperor of Ice Cream.

"How did it get that great name?" Hugh asked.

"Boomer gave them the idea," Phyllis Skypeck said. "Boomer is a reader of poetry." She said this as though it was a great eccentricity.

Hugh now turned to take in Parker "Boomer" Daniels, who was obviously a local character. The tall thin policeman's shirt was wrinkled, with the collar frayed. The trousers were old and billowed with wear on the exceptionally long legs, and his coat was even older. He looked like a scarecrow. He was nothing like the other exceptionally neat and well-pressed Americans around him. He might have been an Englishman, Hugh thought, but an out-of-date Englishman, a prep-school teacher who put on his oldest clothes for digging his garden or some other out of doors pursuit.

Parker Daniels was talking of the shooting at the Emperor of Ice Cream and his voice, Hugh noticed, did not have that heavy earnestness that he found in many American male voices. It was light and easy, as if Parker realized the comic figure he presented, and wished to make fun of himself, or at least not to take himself too seriously.

"I've notified the State Police," Parker Daniels said. "I've notified everybody. I put out an All Points Bulletin but I think poor old Joe is just shivering to death somewhere out there. Maybe shivering and bleeding to death, if Davy hit him in any serious way."

"What if he tries to get in here?" Gus Barch asked.

"I've thought about that, Gus," Parker said. "I'll have Davy stationed right here all night in case he does."

"What?" Davy Shea said.

"As a tribute to your marksmanship you get that honour," Parker said.

"What description did you give of Joe Prew?" Jack Pringle, the humorous man with the field glasses, asked. "Did you say he looked like a tramp? You better watch out, the State Troopers might start shooting at you."

"Yes," Parker said, glancing down at his own clothes, "yes, I guess that's true. I must do something about the attire some day."

Jack Pringle smiled at Parker and left the bar. Hugh could see him talking to Wanda Barch in the dining-room.

"If you find Joe Prew," Phyllis said to Parker, "you must get him to the hospital right away. Or call me, it doesn't matter what time it is."

"You're new at doctoring," Parker said, "you've still got enthusiasm."

"I can't bear thinking of him alone and ill out in this snow."

The snow was falling heavily. They could see it through the window.

"I can't understand why Joe Prew keeps going in shooting up that place," Davy Shea said, "unless he's just plain crazy. After all, his wife only worked there. What did the ice cream parlour have to do with her running off and leaving him?"

"It's symbolic," Parker said. "It represents something to Joe."

"I suppose you'd know," Davy said.

"What the hell do you mean by that?" Parker asked.

"You know."

"Sure, I know. But there's no call for you mentioning it." He turned to Hugh. "Little Davy Shea here is alluding to my past. The first Mrs Parker Daniels ran off with the man who came to install the new heating system in the matrimonial home. So far I have not shot up any radiators, but I might." He spoke with the voice of a man telling a humorous story, there was no tragedy left in it.

"When Boomer says the first Mrs Parker Daniels, it's a joke," Phyllis explained to Hugh. "He's only been married the once."

"I've been waiting for someone like you, Doc," the police chief said. "If Jack Pringle hasn't already got there first."

"I wouldn't worry about that," Phyllis said.

"Jack's a sad case," Parker said to Hugh, "the same as me. The good-looking young Doc here takes pity on sad cases. She has a soft heart. Jack's wife ran off too. But Jack doesn't know who with. He hasn't got ice cream parlours to shoot up or radiators to kick."

Jack Pringle wasn't there to comment. He was still in the dining-room. Hugh could see him still talking to Wanda Barch. But then Jack Pringle came back and stood by the pretty doctor. She didn't seem to Hugh to be interested in Pringle.

A few people started to come in, but the bar wasn't crowded, the snow was keeping them away, or the shooting. Wanda Barch had changed into a red dress. It was no more substantial than a slip. She wore large gold hooped earrings. Phyllis Skypeck was pretty, but Hugh found himself looking into the dining-room for a sight of Wanda Barch in the red dress and flashing gold earrings. She moved about, showing her remarkable breasts as she bent forward to say something to people seated at the tables. Carmen Barch came into the bar with a tray for an order of drinks and saw Hugh watching her stepmother. She stuck her tongue out at him.

Jack Pringle left the bar and Parker Daniels started talking about him again.

"Jack wants to buy this place," Parker said. "You going to sell it to him, Gus?" Gus Barch was behind the bar serving drinks. "He wants it pretty bad," Parker added.

"He shouldn't have sold it in the first place," Gus Barch said.

"He didn't exactly sell it," Parker said. "The bank took it off him."

"The big money the Pringles had," Davy Shea said, "and he went through it all."

"He couldn't help the mill closing," Parker said.

"Couldn't he?" Davy Shea said. "He didn't pay any attention to business."

"Jack wasn't to know," Parker said, "when old man Pringle said things were all right, Jack thought they were all right."

"What's he want this place for?" Gus Barch said. "He doesn't know how to run a hotel. Jeez, I'm having enough trouble running it myself. In the winter the heating bills are huge and I haven't got the rooms to take advantage of the good times in the summer season."

"He doesn't want it as a hotel, he wants it as a home again," Parker said.

"That's crazy," Gus Barch said. "It's a good business. Or it will be when I've got the extension built and I can pack the summer customers in."

"He's sentimental about it," Parker said. "He was happy here when he was a kid. It was the last thing he let go of when he went broke."

"Well, he can stay being sentimental," Gus Barch said, "I ain't going to sell it."

"It's sad," Phyllis said. "It's a sad story. Poor Jack."

"Now don't get too soft-hearted about old Jack," Parker said, "it's me, a blue-collar guy with a night school law degree, you should be soft-hearted about."

Jack Pringle came back into the bar and the conversation suddenly stopped.

"You've been talking about me," he said.

"Now why should we do that, Jack?" Parker said.

"I suppose because I'm very interesting," Jack Pringle said.

Hugh went in to eat. There was a big sandy-haired man sitting alone. He was like a giant. He made the table and chair seem as though they were made for children. His hands were exceptionally large and white, so big that the man seemed uncomfortable with them. The giant spoke to Wanda. He had an odd accent. He was from the South. This pleasant voice seemed out of place coming from such a large and clumsy man. At another table was a party of teenage skiers making much noise. And then two other teenagers came in. And then an elderly couple came to the entrance of the restaurant. They looked very rich and out of place in this noisy atmosphere. They gazed about the room, then backed away, as if they had seen something frightening.

The pretty Phyllis Skypeck came into the dining-room in her mannishly-cut grey suit coat with the collar of the white blouse buttoned tightly high up on her neck. She wasn't wearing the red hat and the dark curls fell about her face. She was with Parker Daniels and Davy Shea. They sat down at Jack Pringle's table and Wanda Barch, who was talking to him, moved away with swinging hips. Phyllis Skypeck glanced at Hugh. He thought she was going to invite him to join them, but she turned away, laughing at something Jack Pringle was saying.

The teenage brother and sister were seated near Hugh. He could hear their conversation.

"I'm worried about them," the boy said. He got up and left the room. When he returned he said, "They've gone to the College Inn, they've decided to have dinner there. I guess it's a better place for them than this. Maybe they should be staying there instead of here."

Hugh watched the snow falling. It was pretty, but he supposed he should be feeling sorry for the madman who shot up the ice cream parlour. It was dramatic. Hugh already had an American story to tell when he returned to England. He wondered who he could tell it to aside from his mother. It would have to be someone who could appreciate the name, the Emperor of Ice Cream, without having to be told it was a poem by Wallace Stevens.

When he finished eating he went into the bar. He wasn't there very long when Wanda Barch came in, marvellously sexy in the red dress, her wonderful shoulders and neck looking particularly naked. She called the people in the bar to order, like a schoolteacher, Hugh thought, a schoolteacher in a dream, people in dreams often failed to be dressed properly.

"Well," she said, "it's obvious no one's coming here tonight."

She spoke like someone making an official announcement.

"The snow and the idea that there's a maniac at large firing guns has put them off. Besides, there's something wrong with the heating and we're afraid the lights might go at any minute, so we're going to close early."

Hugh tried to catch her eye, but Wanda Barch was being very businesslike. Then, finally, she saw him looking at her and she smiled and came over to him.

"Here's something for you," she said. She gave him a glass. "A free drink on the house," she said, "to make up for the wonderful night we could have had together in the bar remembering Cambridgeshire."

Hugh went up the long flight of stairs to his room on the top floor. The room was not cold. If there was something wrong with the heating, as Wanda Barch had said, it was that it was too hot. He thought he might open the window it was so stifling.

He got into bed with the novel he had been trying to read. It was about a middle-aged Englishman, a scholar, who goes to California to work on the library of a multi-millionaire. The millionaire was a madman who was trying to find the secret of eternal youth. The Englishman apparently lived at home in England with his mother. A girl had given Hugh the novel. She had said the Englishman in it reminded her of him. Tomorrow, Hugh thought, he must call his mother in Scotland. And perhaps tomorrow too there might be a pathetic scene when the body of Joe Prew was brought out of the woods.

Hugh found he could not hold the book. Aldous Huxley's version of 1930s California dropped on his chest as he fell asleep.

Chapter 4

Joe Prew, behind a tree, watched the lights in the Lake House going out. He had stopped bleeding. It was a good thing having the snow because he kept getting thirsty; and hungry too, but the snow didn't help his hunger.

He could see into the ground floor rooms of the hotel. Wanda Barch in a red dress was walking back and forth, her head turning and her mouth opening, shouting at Gus Barch. Gus had a hell of a life with her. Gus should have known better, just looking at her, but then he probably couldn't help himself, she was such a looker. Gus was in the kitchen with Milly the deaf mute. Joe Prew knew Milly Tencza from long ago. He had protected her. Once a gang of boys were tossing stones at her, trying to make her scream with no sound coming out. Joe Prew had stepped in front of her. "Try to make me scream, you bastards," he said.

"Look at him," Davy Shea, only a kid then and not a policeman, had said, "one dummy protecting another." Old Milly must have been fourteen then, and Davy Shea and the rest of the little bastards were eight or nine. Milly had made a sign to Joe but he didn't understand. She'd taken a stick and written in the dirt, "Thanks". Davy Shea had thrown another stone and run away before Joe could catch him.

Dr Phyllis Skypeck, a tall girl with dark hair and a face like someone suffering, was coming out of the Lake House with Jack Pringle. He's a big shot, Joe said to himself, only not so much anymore.

Joe kept well down in the snow behind the tree. Jack Pringle had his arms round Dr Phyllis Skypeck. She was tall but Jack Pringle was taller. He bent his head down and kissed her and she kissed him back. She walked funny in the snow. She was dancing, or pretending to be dancing, her arms out, catching snowflakes. The world had receded with the snow. There seemed nothing but darkness out beyond the white flakes falling. Tomorrow, he thought, if I haven't frozen to death, I'll give myself up. He wondered if his wife Priscilla would read about him in the paper or see it about him on the TV where she lived. Would she think how he still loved her, or that he was still only a crazy son of a bitch? But it might put it in her head that he could come and shoot her, that way he would occupy her thoughts, make her think of him and be afraid.

He stayed where he was and watched as Boomer Daniels came out of the Lake House, a tall thin figure in the dark. Boomer stood watching Dr Phyllis Skypeck and Jack Pringle still gripping each other in the snow. Joe watched Boomer step back into the shadows so he couldn't be seen as he watched Dr Phyllis Skypeck and Jack Pringle. Then Jack Pringle got into his car and it wouldn't start. All that money for a hot foreign car and it don't start, Joe said to himself. Dr Phyllis Skypeck stood by her car, then she got in and started it right away – with a good Detroit-built sound, Joe told himself.

She kept her car running and got out and went over to Jack Pringle, but they didn't kiss again. They went instead to her car and drove off with the lights showing how heavy the snow was falling and then darkness beyond the lights. Boomer Daniels came out from the shadows. Joe felt like running out to him and saying, "I give up, get me something to eat, then maybe a hot cup of coffee and a nice piece of apple pie." But he stayed where he was and Boomer got into his car and drove off. Inside the hotel Joe could see Wanda Barch talking to Davy Shea, and in the back, in the kitchen, Milly Tencza and Gus washing the dishes and Carmen Barch shouting something at her father.

He could see Davy Shea in the lobby with all the furniture stacked up in it. That's no way to run a business, he said to himself, the first room anyone comes into looking like a junk shop or furniture warehouse.

Then he saw Wanda coming into the lobby. She was carrying a pot of coffee. The room was so full of furniture that she disappeared behind it and then she appeared again talking to Davy Shea, who made a feel for her ass. She backed away but not too quick. They're always glad when you make a play for them, he thought, even if they back away.

Carmen Barch was still shouting at her father in the kitchen. Then the kitchen door slammed and Carmen came out, walking quickly in a bad temper. In the dark of the parking lot Joe saw a boy come out of a car and stand waiting for Carmen. He was Duane Smek, a grease monkey at Oscar's Auto Body. He said something to Carmen which Joe could not hear and the girl got mad, but then they went off together in Duane's car.

Lights started going off in the hotel, but in an upstairs window Joe could see the heads of some ski kids. There was music playing from their room. More lights went off. The kitchen door opened and Milly Tencza was there, putting something out with the trash. It was the cat. It moved around but didn't like the snow. Then it came scurrying to where he was behind the tree. It made a sound like it was calling his name.

"Go away," Joe said, but the cat remained, its yellow eyes gleaming in the dark, calling his name, Prew. Then Milly Tencza came to where it was and she saw him. He didn't have to worry about her crying out.

Chapter 5

Hugh was dreaming. In his dream Wanda Barch was in his room in her sexy red dress, but there were a number of other people in the room as well, including his mother, seated at tables as if the bedroom were also a restaurant. Someone started to scream but neither his mother nor any of the others seemed to notice.

There was the sound of running footsteps. The door opened and a woman was there outlined in the light from the hall. She was shouting and she had a gun in her hand. Hugh didn't recognize her at first, but then he saw that it was Carmen Barch and it wasn't a dream.

"Wake up," she said. "My father's been shot. That cop, Davy Shea, is asleep and I can't wake him and my father I think he's dead. He's lying there on the porch in his stockinged feet, that's something he never does, walking around in just his socks. He doesn't move and there's blood. Where's Wanda?"

"She's not here."

"I saw her, you bastard, the way she was looking at you and the way you were looking at her. Where is she?"

"I've no idea," Hugh said. He got out of bed. The gun was still pointing at him.

"Don't shoot," he said.

He could see blood on Carmen Barch's face and hands and on the big baggy sweater she wore. He could see the expression on her face. She looked as if she was about to scream. She was shivering and her hands were shaking. He was worried that the gun might go off by accident. It was a big revolver and although she was no longer pointing it directly at him continually, the way her hand was trembling it did sometimes point in his direction.

Hugh put on his dressing gown and followed her downstairs to the forest of furniture in the dark lobby. Davy Shea was still asleep, snoring in a chair. Hugh shook him but he didn't wake. Carmen stood alongside Hugh. There was still blood on her face but she didn't look as ugly as she had when she burst into his room screaming.

"I told you he wouldn't wake up," she said. "My father's on the porch."

Gus Barch was stretched out on the floor by the radiator. There was blood all over his face and for some reason, as Carmen had pointed out, he was without shoes and his stockinged feet did look odd. It was, Hugh supposed, one of those observations a person would make seeing a father dead on the floor.

Carmen began to tremble and look ugly again."I'm frightened," she said, "what if he's still here?"

"Who?"

"The one who shot him. Joe Prew. Here, you take it, in case he comes."

She shoved the revolver into Hugh's hand. It was very heavy, with a long barrel.

"Is this the gun?" he asked. He meant, was it the one that shot her father, had she picked it up off the floor?

"No, it's Pop's. I got it from his room. Jesus, I've never been so scared."

"Have you called the police?"

"No, I couldn't think. When I couldn't wake Davy Shea I went looking for Wanda."

"Call them now."

"I can't. Look at my hands." They were trembling.

Hugh went to the phone at the reception desk. He looked at the clock. It was gone five.

Chapter 6

Phyllis Skypeck woke after a good night's sleep, but the old amnesia had returned. It wasn't the usual feeling of being hung over, though. She couldn't remember a thing and she felt as though she'd been drugged

"I'm here," she said. "What am I doing here?"

"Sleeping mostly, but not entirely," Jack Pringle said.

She was in his bed. The sun was up. It had stopped snowing. She should have been in a hurry, but she didn't feel like hurrying.

He's good-looking, she said to herself, even first thing in the morning and seen through hung over eyes. The feeling she was having now was different from the horror of yesterday morning in Springfield, or the many other such mornings when she had told herself she was learning about Life, as opposed to illness and dying which engrossed her during most of her waking hours. But even if it's different this time, she thought, the trouble is it still seems to be mixed up with drink. But he's being nice. It's surprising how nice he is. She imagined herself in a similar situation saying, "OK, now get the hell out of here."

Jack lived in Brown's Ferry, a good twenty miles by road from the Lake House on the other side of the lake. It had been difficult driving him home through the snow and it would have been even more difficult driving herself home through it last night — if, that is, she'd wanted to leave.

I must look like hell, she said to herself, but he isn't looking. He was lecturing her instead, like tall, thin, crazy Boomer Daniels had suddenly done in the snow — older men acting like fathers, but Jack had other ideas also.

"You shouldn't drink so much," he said. "It isn't good for a person your age."

"And also a doctor should know better?"

"I didn't say that."

"But you thought it."

"Of course I did."

Despite his earnest lecturing he became amorous again. She wondered how rude it would be to tell him that she was a busy woman and what was perfectly wonderful last night was a terrible inconvenience in the morning. She didn't think she could tell him that, she didn't feel exactly inconvenienced. But outside, through the window, the sun was very bright. She could see the incredibly blue sky and then nothing but snow, shiny and cold with the branches of the trees coated white and only their trunks stark black, glistening. The snowploughs were out, she could hear them, but even if the roads were cleared it didn't mean she wouldn't have trouble starting her car and getting it out of Jack's drive which would be deep in snow.

"We ought to do this more, Dr Skypeck," he said. "We ought to do this all the time, I recommend the treatment."

She stopped thinking about her car possibly not starting.

Jack's nice, she thought, but in the morning you can't hope for too much romance.

He got up and dressed.

"I'll go see if your car will start," he said.

He took her keys and she watched him from the window walk out into the bright sunshine. The car started and he left it running, with great clouds of white smoke coming from the exhaust. The snowplough had blocked the end of the driveway. There was a huge drift there. He was busy shovelling it away, being as energetic as he had been only a few minutes ago in bed. He's not really old, she thought, and he's not so formidable now that he's lost his great big Pringle money.

Her shoes were ruined from being out in the snow last night. They weren't that substantial anyway. They were still soaking wet. She looked in Jack's closet for some boots or overshoes to borrow. He had quite a collection. She took a pair that looked old and worn and probably wouldn't be missed. They were masses too big. She opened his chest of drawers and found two pairs of thick socks that made them fit better. She had an extra pair of good shoes at the hospital and a pair of tennis shoes in the trunk of the car that would do if she did not wish to go clumping into the hospital in those boots so obviously the property of a man.

She put on the red plaid lumber jacket, still trying to remember the name of her lover of the night of too much drink the day before yesterday, then she pulled on the red knitted hat and thought that with it and the lumber jacket and boots she looked like a girl who was used to blizzards, except the pale and pinched face in the mirror looked at her full of too much sex and drink. I look ill, she thought, or incredibly dissipated. The love bite was still on her neck, she buttoned up her collar to hide it.

She went downstairs. There was a broken window. She remembered, sometime early in the morning, she had woken, at least partially, feeling him getting back into bed. "Where have you been?" she'd asked.

"There was a shutter banging against a window," he had said, "it broke the glass, the floor's covered with snow and glass."

"You're freezing," she'd said. His hair was wet.

"Well, it's cold," he'd said, "standing about naked by an open window." It was four o'clock then by the clock on the bedside table. She went back to sleep. She didn't need drink or sex to sleep. She was always so tired at the end of the day that it was like turning off a light and tonight she felt this especially so.

The shutter was now tied with a piece of rope, but the wind still blew through, carrying some snow on to the floor.

She ran her message service from Jack's phone. A man had been shot at the Lake House. Stanley Howse, the county coroner, was apparently stuck somewhere in a snow drift — or drunk, she thought, Stanley Howse drank.

"I'll go," Phyllis said.

It's Joe Prew, she said to herself, they've shot Joe Prew and he was only a dimwit who couldn't cope with life.

She waded through the snow to her car. Jack was still clearing the end of the drive where a plough had just gone by heaping up another big pile of snow. The man in the snowplough waved to them. She knew him. It'll be all over town where I spent last night, she thought. I'm getting a nice little reputation as a whore.

"Can't you stay for breakfast?" Jack asked.

"There's been some trouble at the Lake House," she said, "I think the fuckers have shot Joe Prew."

42

"Joe Prew?"

"Of course," she said. "The bastards, that'll make their Christmas for them, shooting down a poor loony who never meant any harm. That'll make them feel like real policemen."

"Boomer wouldn't do that," Jack said.

Parker Daniels was a friend of Jack's. Phyllis could see he felt bad about the possibility of Parker having shot Joe Prew.

She got into the car and rolled down the window but he didn't lean in to kiss her. Then she said, "Come here," and he bent his head down and she kissed him. "That's better," she said.

He stood back, trying to look humorous, pretending to be an old hired man with his shovel over his shoulder. Joe Prew was a hired man who did odd jobs. If what had happened hadn't happened, he'd have been out shovelling snow from people's drives. She thought she might cry, but she only swore.

"Those cops," she said aloud, "they're all bastards, even Boomer Daniels once he got a badge and a gun."

Chapter 7

Parker Daniels got through to the Lake House and came up the still snow-covered steps of the hotel into the overpowering heat of the glassed-in porch. Davy Shea watched him coming in and he thought Parker looked like he'd slept in his clothes. Davy thought how he also had slept in his uniform, but Parker looked like he'd spent a month sleeping in his and that wasn't Davy's idea of a chief of police to work for.

Davy was standing in the porch with Carmen Barch.

"Now what the hell's going on here?" Parker asked, although it was obvious what was going on with Gus Barch lying there shot through the head.

"I just found him, or rather his daughter did," Davy said.

"That's right," Carmen said, "I was up at Oscar's Auto Body with Duane Smek. We had a date only we couldn't go out on account of the snow and so I just hung around there with him until I came home and found Pop."

"What time was that?" Parker asked.

"Just about five. I had to hurry because I was late, but the snow was so deep."

Oscar's Auto Body was only some four hundred yards away, up the small road that led from the lake to the main road between North Holford and Holford.

"Didn't Duane give you a lift?"

"No, old Oscar Picard was shouting at him to get to work. They got called out, as soon as it stopped snowing. There were accidents. There were plenty of accidents on account of the roads being bad."

"Yes," Davy Shea said," Oscar Picard will be pulling in the money after this blizzard."

"Let her tell her story," Parker told him.

Carmen said, "I came down the road in the snow, some of it drifted more than six feet and then I came in thinking Pop would be shouting at me for being late again and the breakfasts having to be made and Wanda sneering at me for having stayed out messing around with Duane until five o'clock in the morning, and there he was dead on the floor."

"What did you do then?" Parker asked.

"I didn't know what to do. I was scared Joe Prew was still in the place."

"Joe Prew's gone mad," Davy said. "I told you, Boomer, we should have shot him down yesterday when we had the chance."

"I went shouting for Wanda," Carmen said, "but she wasn't nowhere. I went shouting up the stairs. I went into the English boy's room. I thought she might be there, but she wasn't."

"Why'd you think she might be there?" Parker asked.

"On account of I'd seen her drooling all over him ever since he got here."

"She was?" Parker said. "I hadn't noticed."

"Well, he's so good-looking, and different."

Carmen seemed to be drooling over the young Englishman too, but then she remembered her dead father and her face got sad again.

"Where's Wanda now?" Parker asked her.

"I don't know."

"And where's the English kid, Styling?"

"In the bar having a drink. When he saw Pop he said he needed a drink."

Parker looked at Gus Barch on the floor. He could see why the English kid might need a drink. I could do with one myself, he thought.

"And Wanda is nowhere to be found?" he asked .

"I haven't seen her," Carmen said.

"And where the hell were you, Davy?" Parker asked.

"That's just it, Boomer, I was right in there."

He pointed to the hotel lounge where all the furniture was piled up. Parker thought it was pretty crazy, filling a room with all that furniture.

"It looks like a warehouse," he said.

"It's Wanda's antiques, or at least her idea of antiques," Carmen said, and for a moment her hatred of Wanda jolted her out of the shock of finding her father shot dead.

"But I didn't hear a thing," Davy said. "Do you think maybe he was shot outside and then brought back in here?"

"He doesn't seem to be wearing very many clothes for a man who was outside."

"His shoes are gone," Carmen said. "It was one of the first things I noticed, on account of he never walked around barefoot."

"He certainly wouldn't have gone outside in a blizzard in his stockinged feet," Parker said, "but who'd want to steal his shoes?"

"Joe Prew would," Davy said, "after running round in the snow all day his own shoes would be sopping wet."

"Maybe you're right," Parker said, "but why didn't you hear the shot? Were you drunk?"

"My hand to God, Boomer, I only had those few in the bar with you. In fact, Wanda gave me a pot of coffee to keep me awake in case Joe Prew burst in firing."

"But where is Wanda?" Parker asked again.

There was the sound of a vehicle pulling up outside and Phyllis Skypeck came in, wrapped up against the cold with her red knitted hat pulled down so the dark curls burst out round her pale face. Like a child, Parker thought, wearing a lumber jacket several sizes too big, and her feet in big boots that weren't her size either clumping on the floor leaving quick-melting lumps of snow.

She bent down and removed the boots and then took a pair of tennis shoes from her handbag and put them on, leaving the snow-covered boots on the porch.

"What's this?" Phyllis asked. "What's going on? Have you actually shot poor Joe Prew?"

Then she saw it was Gus Barch, looking very dead but still full of the pain of the crippled. She got down on the floor to examine him. Poor and under-nourished, she thought, the success of being the owner of a hotel hadn't touched him. The food and drink he served didn't make up for the illness and poverty of his youth. There should be some semblance of peace about him now, she said to herself, but the bullet in his head robbed him of that final dubious blessing.

"I thought it was Joe Prew," Phyllis said. "When I first saw him lying there I thought it was Joe Prew."

"Yes," Parker said, "he does look like Joe. Say, Davy, you sure you didn't mistake him for Joe Prew and finish off the job you started yesterday?"

"What the hell do you mean, Boomer?"

"I guess it's clear what I mean."

"I was asleep."

"That's a pretty convenient excuse. If I had shot Gus Barch by mistake I might make up a story like that, if I were you."

"Well you ain't me."

"No, I'm not. Being me, I would have thought up something better."

"I didn't shoot no one."

"Only Joe Prew a little yesterday," Parker said.

"He doesn't look long dead to me," Phyllis said.

"Where's Stanley Howse?" Davy asked. "We ought to have the real coroner here."

"He's stuck in a snow drift," Phyllis said.

"When do you think he was killed, Doc?" Parker said.

"Only about four or five hours ago," she said.

"That's three or four o'clock this morning," Parker said, "and Carmen discovered the body at five o'clock.".

There was the sound of a car and Stanley Howse came in. "I'm sorry," he said, "I went off the road into a snowbank." He got down beside the body.

"When was he killed? About three or four this morning?" Parker asked.

"No," Stanley said, "much earlier. About midnight."

"There's no rigor," Phyllis said.

"It's been and gone," Stanley said.

Davy looked at Parker as though he was going to say something about young female doctors, but he kept quiet.

"Davy," Parker said, "take a look around for Wanda. Start down the cellar and work your way up. She's bound to be here somewhere."

"She killed him," Carmen said, "you can bet your last buck that that bitch shot him down. In cold blood," she added.

There was the sound of footsteps on the porch and they turned and saw Jack Pringle.

"What's going on?" he said. "I was told someone shot and killed Joe Prew."

"Who told you that?" Parker said.

"Well," Jack said, realizing his mistake, "Phyllis did."

Davy looked at Phyllis and smirked.

"That's right," Phyllis said, "Jack and I were up screwing all night at his place and this morning I thought the message I got meant Joe Prew had been shot."

"Holy Christ," Davy said, "what a girl."

"Get going," Parker said to him, "start looking for Wanda." Then he turned to Jack Pringle. "It was Gus Barch who was shot and killed and now Wanda is missing."

Chapter 8

A little while later Carmen Barch came into the bar where Hugh Styling was sitting, still in his dressing gown and pajamas talking to Jack Pringle.

Carmen appeared composed now, very different from the girl who had burst into his room screaming that her father was shot dead. She had changed her clothes and was no longer covered in blood but she was still carrying the revolver.

"Say," she said, looking round the bar, "where the hell <u>is</u> Wanda? Is she on the run or do you suppose Joe Prew killed her too?"

"I can't see Joe Prew killing anyone but himself," Jack said. "And when you find Wanda tell her I want to see her."

He left the bar and they saw him go out to the porch and then the front door slammed behind him.

A few moments later Parker came into the bar.

"What the hell is that?" he asked, seeing the big revolver on the bar.

"Pop's gun," Carmen said.

Parker picked it up. "It's a good thing you didn't have to use this," he said. "It's an antique, it's got no firing pin." He put it back on the bar.

Davy Shea came in looking full of himself.

"Have you found Wanda?" Parker asked.

"No," Davy said. He turned and looked at Hugh. "But I found something else."

Then Phyllis came in and said, "What's going on?"

"I don't see what it's got to do with you, Doctor," Davy said. "I'm standing here after having made an investigation, reporting the findings of that investigation to my chief and I can't see what any of that has to do with you."

Phyllis laughed. Davy didn't like that.

"You're smiling," he said, "I don't see what you've got to smile about, unless you're laughing at yourself for getting the time of Gus's death so wrong."

Phyllis stopped smiling.

"That's better," Davy said. "That's more like you should be, with your mouth shut and remembering who you are and not barging in where you don't belong."

"Well, now, Davy," Parker said, "are you finished insulting the Doctor? What's this discovery of yours?"

"Wait until you see," Davy said.

"Well," Parker said, "I'm standing here and I'm waiting."

"It's upstairs," Davy said. "I found it upstairs."

"Jesus," Phyllis said, "what a mystery!"

Davy looked at her, but he didn't say anything this time.

"Let's go," Parker said and he started for the stairs.

"He better come," Davy said about Hugh.

"OK," Parker said, "he's coming."

They went up the stairs with Hugh. Phyllis followed.

"What's she doing here?" Davy said. "Who asked her?"

Parker didn't say anything and Phyllis continued following them up the stairs to the top floor to Hugh's room.

Davy turned on the light.

"There it is," he said.

Hugh saw it. He hadn't noticed when he got up in the dark. Carmen hadn't turned on the light when she came into his room and he hadn't turned it on when he got out of bed to go downstairs with her to see her father's body, but the light was on now and he saw what Davy Shea was talking about.

Wanda Barch's red dress was on the floor.

"And these," Davy said. He turned over an edge of the red dress. "Her underwear," he said, sounding as if it was something dangerous that might explode.

"You recognize them?" Parker said. It was hard to tell if he was being humorous.

"They're hers," Carmen said. She was standing in the doorway. They hadn't seen her following them up the stairs. "Lots of guys know her panties. She wasn't shy about showing them. At least when she was going formal and had any on."

"There's no love lost between you and her?" Davy said.

"You bet there isn't," Carmen said. Once again she wasn't looking so subdued now that she could be angry about Wanda.

Phyllis was in the doorway beside Carmen. She didn't say anything but she was looking at Hugh.

"What the hell are these clothes supposed to mean, Davy?" Parker asked.

"They belong to the murdered man's wife," Davy said. "She was wearing that red dress last night. Everyone saw her in it."

"Falling out of it," Carmen said.

Davy ignored her. "And now they show up in this guy's room with the woman's husband downstairs shot in the head."

"You think there's a connection?" Parker asked.

"Of course there's a connection. What else could there be, with the husband murdered?"

"She wasn't in here," Hugh said.

"What do you mean?" Davy said. "Do you mean you stole them from her? You some kind of a goddam panty sniffer?"

"No, of course not. I meant I never saw her in this room."

"She comes in," Davy said, "and takes off her clothes? A woman like Wanda? And you never noticed?"

"Where the hell is Wanda?" Parker said.

"This is the only trace of her I found," Davy said.

"You think she's vanished?"

"I think she ain't here," Davy said.

"She's gone," Carmen said. "She shot my father and she's gone." She was pale again. She looked like she was going to be sick. Then she started to cry. Phyllis put her arms around her.

"It could be Wanda," Davy said. "When I winged Joe Prew he dropped one of his guns. I'm sure I saw him drop one. Maybe Wanda picked it up. When Gus was found dead everyone would assume Joe Prew did it. It'd be a handy way to get rid of a husband."

"Except Wanda is missing," Parker said. "That's not much of an alibi, going on the run after your husband has been found shot dead."

"I looked all over the place, Boomer. She ain't here," Davy said.

"You better look again."

"Come on, Boomer, I've been up all night."

"Up all night? You were sleeping."

"It's not the same. It's not like in your own bed."

"I think we all ought to try to find Wanda," Parker said.

"Are you worried about her?" Phyllis asked. She was still holding Carmen.

"I'm unsettled about it," Parker said.

"What about him?" Davy said, looking at Hugh.

"What about him?" Parker said. "Getting entertained by a woman in your hotel room isn't against the law. At least it isn't any more."

"Not if no money doesn't change hands," Davy said.

"Boy," Carmen said, "if Wanda asked for money, she'd be rich by now." She moved away from Phyllis. She'd stopped crying.

Davy went out to look for Wanda Barch again.

"Don't get too worried," Parker said to Hugh.

"What do you mean?" Carmen said. "Why shouldn't he get worried? My father's shot dead downstairs and he's upstairs with my father's whore of a wife? What's that except something for him to worry about?"

Phyllis was still in the doorway, looking at Hugh. She was smiling, but when Hugh looked at her she stopped smiling.

"That Wanda, what a bitch she is," Carmen said. "I want it to come out. I want everyone to know that when my father was getting himself shot dead by Joe Prew, she was upstairs with a man. With a man who was a perfect stranger."

"She was, wasn't she," Parker said to Hugh, "a perfect stranger?"

"Say, that's right," Carmen said. "She was in England, with that Air Force first husband of hers, she lived over there."

"Did you know her in England?" Parker asked.

"Of course he's going to say no," Carmen said. "But my father heard them talking. They were in the same place in England at the same time."

"Is that right?" Parker asked.

"I suppose it is," Hugh said. "She was in Cambridgeshire and I was at Cambridge University."

"The same time that Wanda was there," Carmen said. "Ask him."

"Why did you come here?" Parker asked.

"I was supposed to stay with a girl in Boston," Hugh said, "but when I got there her father had been taken ill in Florida and she'd gone to be with him. Someone recommended I should come here."

"You've got the address of the woman in Boston?"

"Sure, but she's not there. She's in Florida."

"I'll bet," Carmen said. "He came to see Wanda. You wait, you'll find out he knew her. I don't know what she's got, but that ex-husband of hers, Petrolnik, he calls up on the phone to speak to her. She won't talk to him, I have to do it for her. He's stationed near Springfield at the base at Westover. Find him, ask him if Wanda didn't know this guy over in England."

Davy was at the door. He was excited. "Boomer," he said, "wait till you see what I've found now."

"Don't make it a mystery," Parker said. "What have you found? Just tell us."

"I'm trying to tell you," Davy said. "I've found Milly Tencza. You better come too, Doc."

Chapter 9

Milly was in her room, stretched out on the bed with a revolver lying beside her.

"Is she dead?" Carmen asked. "What the hell's going on? Is there a maniac loose?" She looked at Hugh.

"It must be Joe Prew," Parker said, "he must be crazier than I thought. Where's she shot? I don't see any blood."

"She's not dead," Phyllis said. "She's asleep."

"What do you mean, not dead?" Davy said. He seemed very annoyed.

The room was small and there was, Phyllis thought, the air of a coffin about the narrow bed. It's no wonder he thought her dead, she said to herself.

"She's sleeping all right," Parker said, "but what's that gun doing here?"

The gun seemed out of place in the room which was full of religious pictures and looked something like a chapel.

"She shot Gus with it," Davy said, "that's what it's doing here."

He had been disappointed when he learned Milly Tencza wasn't dead, but now he had a new theory about her being a killer and seemed happy again.

Phyllis went over the room, inspecting the shelves, the cupboard, the dressing-table and the chest of drawers.

"What are you looking for?" Parker whispered to her.

"Her medicine," Phyllis whispered back, "I gave her something to sleep, but it's not here."

Milly was deaf. It was quite ridiculous speaking in whispers. Parker and Phyllis realized this and smiled at each other, but they continued to move quietly about the room.

"Do you think she shot my father?" Carmen asked Parker.

"Sure she did," Davy said, "why else does she have the gun?" He had forgotten the mystery of the red dress in Hugh's room.

"Why'd she do that?" Carmen said.

"Because she hated him," Davy said. "The way he shouted at her."

"But she was deaf," Carmen said, "he had to shout."

"She wants to die," Phyllis said, "I suspected she was storing up the pills I was giving her."

"She's coming to," Carmen said.

"Ask her why she did it," Davy said to Phyllis, "ask her real quick, right off, before she has time to think up some story."

Phyllis made signs, going very slowly because she was unsure. Milly smiled. I must have said something wrong, Phyllis said to herself.

"What's she say?" Davy asked. "Has she confessed?"

"Quiet," Parker said.

"What for?" Davy said. "She can't hear me."

"I can," Parker said.

Phyllis was bent over Milly, asking her what pills she had taken.

"The pills," Phyllis said, turning her head to Parker, "she hasn't taken any, they've been stolen."

"Ask her why she killed Gus," Davy said.

Phyllis didn't know the sign for a gun. She made a childish sign with her index finger extended like a barrel and then squeezing it like a finger on a trigger.

Milly made a sign. Phyllis knew it. It was one of the first signs she had learned, the sign for pain.

"Has she said?" Davy asked. "Has she told you she done it?"

Phyllis didn't answer. Milly's fingers moved, as slowly as Phyllis's own, not because she was inept, but because she was exhausted, it was like someone panting for breath.

"Is she saying it now?" Davy asked. "Is that her confession?"

"Where is the pain?" Phyllis asked Milly.

Milly made a sign. Phyllis didn't know it. Milly made it again, still Phyllis didn't recognize it.

"What's the matter?" Davy said. "She saying something you don't understand? Maybe it's the confession."

"Leave her alone," Parker told him.

Phyllis understood the sign now. It was "everywhere", the pain was everywhere.

"Where'd she get the gun?" Parker said.

Phyllis asked.

"She found it in the snow."

"Where Joe Prew dropped it when he was shot?" Parker asked.

"No," Phyllis said, "later on, early in the morning when it was still dark and she couldn't sleep. She went out and she found it."

"Why'd she go out? It was snowing like hell?" Davy said.

"To see the snow," Phyllis said, "she wanted to stand in the snow."

Davy made a disbelieving sound.

"And she was going to shoot herself?" Parker asked. "Why was she going to do that?"

"Because she didn't have any more sleeping pills. She'd been storing them up, like I said, but they were stolen."

Milly was weeping.

"What's wrong?" Parker asked.

"I've just told her Gus Barch is dead," Phyllis said.

"You mean you've only just told her now?" Davy said. "What were you doing all the finger-yapping about?"

"I was asking her how she was."

Parker looked at Milly. She looked even more crushed now that she was weeping.

Davy started to say something but Parker interrupted him.

"Take the gun, he said, "we'll have it examined."

"And what about her?" Davy said. "Aren't we going to take her in?"

"She won't be going anywhere," Parker said.

"All this liberal shit of yours, Boomer," Davy said, "it's not police procedure."

They went downstairs to the lobby. It looked strange with Wanda Barch's furniture piled up and now the big, undecorated Christmas tree there too. The sun was coming through the windows and it reflected off the glass of the framed posters of Twenties and Thirties skiers on the wall by the reception desk. Outside they could see the unreal blue of the sky after the snow storm. In the middle of the lake was a long, dark and wide break the whole length of the lake where it wasn't frozen and the water showed through.

"If Milly's pain-killers and sleeping pills are missing, where have they gone?" Phyllis asked.

"I don't think we have to look too far for an answer to that," Parker said.

He was standing by the chair where Davy had slept through the shooting of Gus Barch. There, on the table beside it, was the pot of coffee and the cup that Wanda had brought Shea the night before.

Parker picked up the coffee pot, smelled it and then put his finger in and tasted it.

"There wouldn't be any taste," Phyllis said.

She took the pot and poured the dregs of coffee into the cup.

"There's a residue of something here," she said.

"We'll have to have it tested," Parker said.

"Was somebody trying to kill me?" Davy asked.

"Not kill," Parker said, "just make sure you wouldn't wake up."

"That couldn't have been Joe Prew," Davy said. "Boomer, this is something serious, this is more than Joe Prew going off his head with a couple of guns. Wanda gave me that coffee. Where's Wanda?"

"Yes," Parker said, "where is Wanda? She's got a lot of questions to answer."

Chapter 10

Phyllis Skypeck was leaving the Lake House. Parker saw her on the porch, showing a good-looking leg as she walked about hunting for something. Parker knew she had spent the night with Jack Pringle. She's in love, Parker said to himself. He tried not to think of love, except for when he associated it with his daughters, which was sentimental and almost safe, which was something he thought sexual love never was, even at a distance there was something grisly about it.

"My boots," Phyllis said to Parker, "I think someone's taken them." Then she went out wearing only tennis shoes into the deep snow.

Davy Shea came downstairs and said he couldn't find Wanda Barch.

"It's time to see the other guests," Parker said. "Maybe there's an obvious homicidal maniac among them."

"Who's staying here?" Davy asked Beverly Choquette, an exceptionally good-looking young woman who worked part-time at the Lake House.

"I don't know," she said, looking at the register. "I've been off for two days. I haven't been here." She didn't look at Davy when she spoke. She made a point of not looking at him.

Carmen came down the stairs to the reception desk.

"You don't have to be here," Beverly Choquette said to her, "I can take care of things."

"I must do something," Carmen said, "or I'll go insane."

She took the register from Beverly, who went off to whatever other duties she had. Parker watched Beverly go. She had an athletic figure, Parker remembered that she had been a high school drum majorette. In the reflecting glass of the old-fashioned skiing posters Davy was watching her and the way she walked.

"To business," Parker said to Davy.

"What?" Davy said, only now taking his eyes from Beverly Choquette. "What's she doing here?" he asked. "Her brother, Armand Choquette, I got him for an armed robbery, he's doing time."

"I suppose she's got to work," Parker said.

"No," Davy said, "I mean the store Armand robbed, it belonged to Gus. That was before Gus bought this place and turned it into a hotel."

"You think she's a suspect?"

"Gus identified Armand as the gunman."

"Is that a motive?"

"I don't know," Davy said. "I'm just surprised seeing her here."

"She doesn't like you."

"No, can you imagine that? A good-looking girl like her, giving me those filthy looks?"

There were only a few guests at the Lake House, it was too near Christmas for people to be staying away from home, and the snow was unexpected, serious skiers wouldn't arrive until well into the new year when the big snows came.

There was an elderly couple, the Masons, but they weren't in the hotel. Carmen said their beds hadn't been slept in.

"Maybe Joe Prew got them," Davy said. "Maybe he went through the whole place shooting."

"They didn't eat in the restaurant last night," Carmen said. "They said they would, but then they didn't."

"We'll go into that later," Parker said. "Who the hell are these names?" He was looking at the hotel register. They were a party of young skiers. Parker went and questioned them. Now that the initial excitement of Gus Barch's murder was over, they were keen to get out on the slopes and resented Parker stopping them.

"Did you hear anything?" Parker asked.

"I don't think so," a boy said, "we were listening to music."

"I heard something," another boy said. "It sounded like a gunshot or it could have been the sound of ice cracking on the lake." He seemed proud of knowing about the sound of ice on a lake. "Sometimes it makes that noise," he said.

"Did any of the rest of you hear it?" Parker asked.

"They were in the room with the music," the boy said. "I was in the hallway when I heard it."

"What time was that?"

"About midnight."

Davy glanced at Parker. "The wonderful Dr Skypeck was wrong about the time of death," Davy said, "midnight was the time Stanley Howse gave us. What were you doing wandering about at midnight?" he asked the boy whose name was Carl Greene. He was nineteen and a good-looking guy who would have no trouble getting girls, that and his educated accent put Davy off him.

"I was looking for an empty room," the boy said.

"Didn't you have a room?" Davy asked.

"It was full of people. I was with a girl."

"What about the girl," Davy said, "didn't she have a room?"

"Her grandmother was in it."

Parker laughed."That would get in the way of romance," he said.

"So you went round looking for an empty room?" Davy said. "You should watch out, people might take you for a sneak thief."

Parker let the boy go. He had the time of the murder now, unless it was the sound of ice cracking on the lake that the boy had heard.

He questioned two other skiers, a teenage brother and sister who weren't with the big party. The boy was fifteen and awkward, but his seventeen year old sister was already a woman or well on her way to it. Parker thought of his daughters, one of them was seventeen now the same as this grown-up seeming girl.

The boy was chatty enough, but his sister was more reserved. She became embarrassed when he asked if she had heard a gunshot.

"I suppose this is important?" she said.

Parker said it was.

"I heard a loud crack about that time," she said.

"Did it sound like ice on the lake?" Parker asked.

The girl blushed. "Did Carl tell you I was with him?" she said.

"You were?" her brother said. "What were you doing with him?"

The girl got angry with her brother for questioning her.

"Looking for an empty room we could use," she said.

"Use?" her brother said. "Use for what?"

"What do you think?" She turned to Parker. "I was staying in a room with my grandmother. We couldn't very well go there. But as it was she wasn't there."

The brother and sister were the grandchildren of the missing Masons. They cleared up that mystery. Their grandparents had gone to the College Inn for dinner.

"They obviously stayed over," the sister said, "because of the blizzard. They're on a nostalgia trip. Grandma was at college here. That's where they met. Tim and I came along to keep them company."

Parker let them go off to the ski slopes. "But watch out," he said, "there's a crazy man with a gun somewhere out there."

He went back to the hotel register.

"What about this one?" he said. "He's missing too."

There was a Mr Johnson registered, but no Mr Johnson in the hotel. Carmen said his bed also had not been slept in.

"Jesus," Davy said, "all these people paying for rooms and then not sleeping in them. Maybe Joe Prew got this guy too?"

"You're awful keen on this being a bloodbath," Parker said. "Mr Johnson is from Springfield," he said, looking at the register. "Maybe he heard all that gunfire yesterday and decided to go home."

"He was here last night," Carmen said, "I saw him in the restaurant, a big guy with blond hair but going bald. It must be awful being a man and going bald." Then she stopped. There was something more awful that a man could be. She started to cry.

"Maybe you shouldn't do this," Parker said. "Maybe you should go somewhere and lie down."

"No," she said, "it'll be all right. Go on."

"What is he?" Parker asked, still looking at Mr Johnson's name in the register, ashamed of himself for bothering her.

"I don't know. Just ordinary, except he's so big. A really big guy. Not so tall, not like you, but big." She extended her arms to show how wide Mr Johnson was.

"Did someone mention me?" a man said.

Parker turned and saw the giant standing in the lobby by the Christmas tree. Like Carmen said he wasn't as tall as Parker. He was under six feet, but he had wide shoulders and arms like a wrestler with big hands dangling at the end of them.

"I'm Johnson," he said. "Samuel Johnson."

He spoke with a Southern accent. He was about thirty-five or so, it was hard to tell his age because he was going seriously bald.

"Did you hear anything last night?" Parker asked.

"I wasn't here last night. Why? What happened?"

"Gus got shot," Parker said.

"Shot dead," Davy added.

Mr Johnson had a big ruddy face, but Parker saw him go rather pale.

"Who is Gus?" he asked.

"Gus Barch, the owner of the Lake House," Parker said.

"Yes," Davy said, "he was shot in the head. Sometime last night."

"If you weren't here, Mr Johnson, where were you?" Parker asked, but he was interrupted. Carmen was crying again. "You'd better go," he said to her. She left.

"His daughter," Davy said to Mr Johnson, "that's the dead man's kid."

"About last night, Mr Johnson," Parker said, "where did you go?"

"After dinner I went out. I went to North Holford."

"This is North Holford," Davy said.

"I mean the town centre."

"In all this snow?" Parker asked.

"I didn't know it would keep snowing. I went to the College Inn. By the time I was going to leave it was so bad I had to stay over. I wasn't the only one. There were plenty of people who got caught the same as me. An old couple, the Masons, who are staying here too, they got caught and didn't think it safe to try and get back."

"You registered at the College Inn? You signed the book?"

"No, they just let me stay. I see what you mean. No, I didn't have a room. There were a lot of people at the College Inn who were caught by the storm. The people in the bar and in the restaurant, they couldn't get home. I was a bit slow seeing it coming. By the time I thought I'd better stay over there was only the one spare room and I thought the Masons should have it. I slept on a couch in the hotel lounge. I didn't have to sign the book."

"You're not a skier, Mr Johnson?" Parker asked.

"Me? No, I'm from the South. You probably guessed that already from my accent. We don't go in for much snow."

"You ought to come here in the summer," Davy said. "There's good swimming here then. Boomer's a swimmer. He once won a race swimming the whole length of the lake."

"Mr Johnson doesn't want to hear about that," Parker said. "From the South?" he said to Mr Johnson. "It says Springfield in the hotel book."

"That's where I'm staying now. I'm in the Air Force, at Westover, but I'm getting out next month."

Parker asked him, "Do you happen to know Staff Sergeant Pete Petrolnik?"

"No, I don't think I do. I might know him by sight. I know a couple of Petes."

"Don't you Air Force guys have your names printed on your uniform?"

"Well, yes," Johnson said, "but you don't always look. I suppose I might have noticed the name Petrolnik. It's kind of unusual, like it was made up, but there are a lot of unusual names."

"Some people might think Samuel Johnson sounded like a made-up name," Parker said. "You've heard of Dr Johnson, I suppose?"

"Oh yeah sure, at school they kidded me, called me Doctor."

"You've got some proof of your identity?"

"Sure do," Johnson said suddenly sounding very Southern.

He reached into his back pocket and pulled an ID card out his wallet.

"Well," Parker said, "this says you're Sergeant Johnson all right. Would you mind giving me your phone number in Springfield, and at the base?"

Johnson told Parker the numbers and he wrote them down.

"By the way," Parker said, "you didn't happen to know Wanda before you came here?"

"Wanda?"

"Wanda Barch."

"Who's she?"

"Gus Barch's wife. A big, good-looking woman."

"I've never met her."

"But you've seen her?"

"I suppose I have, if she's here, but I don't remember."

"You said you didn't ski," Parker said, "but you didn't say why you came here."

"For a change. That's all. I wanted somewhere quiet."

"And instead you got Joe Prew shooting up the ice cream parlour and a dead body on the hotel floor."

Parker let him go.

"I wouldn't want to tangle with him," Davy said. "You see those shoulders on him? And those mitts?"

"He's a big guy," Parker said, watching the giant Sgt Johnson going up the stairs.

"Why'd you give him such a hard time?" Davy asked.

"There's something funny about him."

"Is there?"

"Sure, he pretended he hadn't seen Wanda Barch."

"Maybe she isn't his type."

"She's everybody's type," Parker said.

"You're some detective, Boomer, ready to pin a murder rap on a guy because he forgot to look at Wanda's tits."

"You take them in don't you, Davy?"

"I sure do. Anyone would."

"Well, there you are," Parker said. "I just think I might telephone this number in Springfield and see who answers."

"You're wasting your time. It was Joe Prew. It stands to reason it was Prew."

"Everyone's too ready to pin it on Joe Prew."

"Carmen Barch ain't," Davy said.

"No, she wants her stepmother to have done it."

"But everything points to Joe Prew having gone even more crazy than usual."

"I know Joe Prew. You know Joe Prew. Do you think he'd ever stop thinking of his own troubles long enough to bother to kill someone?"

"He shot up the Emperor of Ice Cream."

"He did, but even with all that shooting he was doing he never hit anyone."

"You're not a defense lawyer any more, Boomer. You're on our side now."

"You mean it'd be OK to forget the whole thing and lay it on Joe because we'd be sure to get a conviction?"

"I wouldn't put it that way, Boomer. But who else has been running round here firing off guns?"

"You're forgetting about your drugged coffee."

"No I'm not. Maybe Wanda drugged me because she didn't want me seeing her sneaking up to the English kid's room."

"You think Wanda was worried about her reputation? When did she ever worry about a little thing like that?"

"Maybe she didn't want to get me jealous. I had a sort of thing with Wanda."

"You did?"

"Oh, sure. I called it off, but you know how women are, they like thinking you're still crazy for them."

"I guess I got you for another suspect," Parker said.

"Say, what the hell do you mean?"

"I've only got your word for it that you're the one who called it off. You could be a jealous lover mad with passion."

"Stop the kidding," Davy said. Then he said, "Why'd you ask Johnson about Petrolnik?"

"Petrolnik is Wanda's ex-husband and Carmen said Petrolnik has called Wanda several times. Maybe Joe Prew isn't the only crazy ex-husband with a gun."

"That's some theory, Boomer, especially when we've got a maniac running loose with a gun that he's not shy about firing."

Parker went to the phone, looking pleased with himself, Davy thought. But when Parker came back he wasn't looking so pleased.

"I got a friend of Johnson's," he said. "He told me Johnson could be reached at the Lake House."

"That takes care of that," Davy said. "He ain't no mystery man. We're left with Joe Prew."

"Are we?" Parker said. "What about Wanda? Where is she?"

"And there's the boy Styling," Davy said, "with the red dress in his room. A jury would love an Englishman with that red dress, and those incriminating lace panties in his room."

"I guess you're right there," Parker said, "a jury would go for an English kid mad about Wanda. One look at Wanda in the witness box would convince them that she was worth killing for."

There was a crowd outside the Lake House now, curious to see the scene of the murder. Parker saw Hugh Styling there, his eyes looking worried behind large, round, studious glasses. Jack Pringle was there too.

"I wish all those people would get out of here," he said to Davy.

"This is nothing," Davy said, "wait till the roads are clear and the media arrive. I remember when The Geep went missing. We had media then. Everyone thought for sure he'd been murdered, but we never found the body."

"The Geep?"

"Edgar LaMay, the bookie. You weren't here then. You were in Boston being a big shot lawyer."

They were standing on the porch. The place where Gus Barch's body had been was roped off. Davy went down the stairs to the police car. Parker saw Davy get in the cruiser, but he didn't drive off. Then the door of the police car opened and Davy came running back through the snow to the hotel. He rushed up the stairs all out of breath.

"It's gone," he said.

"What's gone?"

"The gun. The revolver. It's not there anymore. I put it in the car with the coffee pot and the cup. They're still there, but the gun is gone."

"Did you lock the car?"

"No. I forgot to. I didn't think it necessary. This means Joe Prew was here. Right here all the time."

"If it was Joe Prew," Parker said.

"Who else could it be? Who else is a crazy fuck who's been shooting guns off?" Davy glanced anxiously around as if Joe Prew might suddenly appear.

Chapter 11

When Phyllis came back to the Lake House, to check on Milly Tencza, and to see a skier who had had a bad fall, there were TV men there. She was going to slip by them, but then she saw Carmen.

"Carmen," she said, "how's Artie?"

"Who's Artie?" a reporter asked.

"My little brat brother," Carmen said, looking not at all pleased.

"He's very young," Phyllis said to her, "he'll not show his feelings, but he'll be very confused."

Carmen's belligerent expression vanished. She seemed about to cry again. Phyllis quickly changed the subject. "I may need some crutches," she said.

"You know where they are," Carmen said. The Lake House had crutches. They were always needed in the winter.

Phyllis went to see the injured skier. He was fifteen and kept giving her longing looks and then blushed when he was caught out.

"I'm sure it's broken," the boy said, as if he wanted the drama of broken bones.

Phyllis explained how serious a sprained ankle could be.

Out of the window in the fading winter afternoon light she could see men moving in the woods, searching for Joe Prew. The State Troopers had been called in to help Boomer Daniels. She could see the wide-brimmed hats of the Troopers moving beneath the trees.

"He'll be long gone by now," the boy said.

"Not if he's wounded," she said.

"Oh, yeah, I forgot about that." He gazed down at his injured ankle. "I feel ashamed hurting myself on a little slope like this," he said. "It's embarrassing after the runs I'm used to out West in Colorado. In Colorado they're got real skiing."

"Why didn't you go somewhere more worthy of your talents?" Phyllis asked. The boy kept looking at her. Now it's me who's starting to blush, she thought.

"We had to come," the boy said, "my sister and I, we came with our grandparents."

"Oh, yes, the Masons." Phyllis had seen the expensive-looking old couple in the hotel.

"They're on some sort of trip into the past," the boy said.

He stood up, attempting to use the crutches. He was treating them like a new piece of sporting equipment.

"Their daughter, my aunt Sue, Sue Pringle, used to live here."

"Pringle?" she said. "Mrs Jack Pringle? That is your aunt?"

"That's right. Her husband still lives somewhere around here, only Grandpa and Granny don't speak to him. Old people, they get funny ideas. What's wrong? Did you know her?"

"No, I was only about your age when she disappeared."

"Disappeared?"

"Yes. Didn't she disappear?"

The boy became flustered again. "Yes," he said, "I suppose she did. I guess you could call it that."

Phyllis was thinking of Jack Pringle. He had already had a life. He was grown up and living it while she was still a kid, younger even than this boy. She had been thinking about Jack Pringle all day. If he had made his wife unhappy that was fifteen years ago, and he must have been unhappy too, with his father dying and then finding that the business was failing and soon he'd be broke. His wife left him because of that, Phyllis said to herself, she'd married him because he was rich and charming and when he was broke the charm wasn't enough.

"Where is your aunt now?" she asked.

"I don't know," he said and he looked again as though he was bothered about something.

Where was Mrs Pringle? Phyllis thought. Who knows? This is America, people are always going off somewhere and never being heard from. She'll probably pop up, when Jack's rich again — he's bound to be, a man like Jack —or when he dies and there might be money in it. But that didn't fit in with her idea of this boy's aunt, who would be rich enough on her own not to trouble herself about a man's money.

"That Pringle guy," the boy said, "he was in here yesterday, but my grandparents avoided him. They stayed in their room. I said to them, 'Hey, what did you come here for, you must have known you'd see the guy? Don't let him spoil your vacation.' But they wouldn't listen to me. And last night they went somewhere else to eat because he was eating here, but you know that, you were sitting at the table with him, you and that goofy police chief."

Phyllis left the boy.

Downstairs there was still much excitement with the media. And the police were still outside searching for Joe Prew, but it would be dark soon.

"Where's Artie?" she asked Carmen.

"Outside with his sled sliding in the snow. They're looking for him."

"Who's looking for him?"

"The TV people," Carmen said. "They want him on TV, him and me."

"You've got to take care of Artie," Phyllis said.

"That's Wanda's job," the girl said. "She signed up for it when she hooked my father."

Phyllis went out to the porch. She looked around hoping she might discover the boots she'd mislaid in the morning.

The porch door opened and Hugh Styling came inside. He was carrying snowshoes.

"Hullo," he said, "I can't quite get the hang of these. I keep falling down."

He was better looking than ever, his face full of colour from the exercise of falling down in the snow. He's taking being a murder suspect very well, she thought.

"I love snowshoes," she said.

"I wish you'd show me how they work."

"You just step along. It's perfectly natural."

He's good-looking, and more my own age, she thought. He wouldn't have a disappeared ex-wife.

"Do you ski?" she asked.

"I'm afraid not."

"You certainly made a mistake coming here. Just a minute."

She went into the hotel and returned with another pair of snowshoes.

Outside she bent down and tried to strap his snowshoes properly.

"It would help if you had better boots," she said. The boots he was wearing were old and didn't really fit him.

"Carmen gave them to me," he said.

"That's as tight as I can get them," Phyllis said, standing up. It was like being with a child. I'm used to older men, she said to herself. Am I picking him up? First Jack and now this cute English boy who's actually a few years younger than me. Only I didn't pick Jack up, Jack Pringle picked me up.

He had, in fact, been rather insistent in the bar. And then his car wouldn't start, or, at least, he said it wouldn't, which meant she'd had to give him a ride home, and after that there was nothing to it because she'd done it all before.

"Come on," she said to Hugh. "Just step along. That's it."

He seemed perfectly able, but not very fit. He probably has a job that's all sitting down, she thought, and doesn't take much exercise. Under the healthy glow there were dark pouches beneath his eyes. That's probably being a murder suspect, she thought. But he had an amusing way of talking, the tone of voice mocking the emotions of a man who was a suspect in a murder case. Still, he wasn't the innocent he seemed behind his large, round, schoolboy glasses. Wanda's red dress in his room proved that, but of course he could have been an innocent target of Wanda's man-hunting. I must ask him about Wanda. I want to know about women like that and if they do anything that's special.

With the snowshoes, they were able to walk on top of the snow drifts.

"The police ought to have these," Hugh said.

Ahead of them they could see the local police and the State Troopers wading through the snow. Parker Daniels came up to Phyllis. He was smiling and then he saw who she was with and he looked puzzled.

"The revolver," Parker said, "the one in Milly Tencza's room, it's been stolen."

She didn't know what she was supposed to say about that.

"You shouldn't be here," he said. "Joe Prew might start shooting."

"Then maybe I could patch up anyone he hit."

"That's true, but I don't like the idea of civilians sight-seeing," he said, looking at Hugh.

"I'm not a sight-seer," Hugh said. "I'm a suspect."

The tall, thin policeman looked down at Hugh and smiled.

"It's always best to be cheerful," Parker said to him.

Phyllis and Hugh moved on. They went easily across a flat field and then the going was more difficult as they began to climb a hill that led, eventually, to the mountain. Phyllis looked up to see if there were any skiers still on the slopes.

He's up there somewhere, she said to herself, he's wounded and sick. He should turn himself in, but of course he's got no sense.

They went on climbing for about an hour and then she said, "We'd better turn back. It'll be dark soon."

"Will you have dinner with me tonight?"

"I think I might have a date."

"Can't you break it?"

"Maybe I can."

Or he'll break it for me, that's probably more likely, she thought, after all I'm only the daughter of Fred Skypeck, a real blue collar guy, and Jack's a man who's been very rich. He's only screwing me, it's nothing more than that.

It was difficult going downhill, the snowshoes slid like skis. Phyllis kept turning round to see how Hugh was doing, and to look to the mountain where Joe Prew was. Someone will have to get him soon, she said to herself.

Ahead of her was a small wood of fir trees. The evergreen branches sheltered the ground. There was only a thin coating of snow under the trees.

"Jesus," Phyllis said. "Oh, Jesus Christ!"

"What?" Hugh said behind her. "What is it?"

He couldn't see what she was looking at. She took off her snowshoes in order to move more easily under the low hanging branches of the dense firs.

Under the dark green foliage there was a body on the ground. "My God," Hugh said when he caught up with her.

"Don't you know who it is?" she asked.

He turned away. He looked ill now despite the colour in his cheeks.

"Yes," he said. "I know. It's Mrs Barch."

Chapter 12

While Phyllis and Hugh were making their discovery in the woods, the TV men at the Lake House had set up a studio in the lobby, pushing the piles of Wanda's antiques to one side. Carmen was seated at a table facing the cameras. Carmen was in a mood remembering Phyllis Skypeck barging in to tell her what to do about Artie, as if it were any of Dr Phyllis Skypeck's business.

"Have the brother sit next to her," one TV man said.

"Carmen," the other TV man said, "what do you think happened to your mother?"

"She's not my mother."

"Your stepmother, what do you think happened to her?"

"I think she shot him and then ran away."

The TV men were surprised.

"Can we use that?" one of them asked. "Accusing her step-mother of killing her father, is it legal to use that?"

"You're not upset about your stepmother being missing?" the other TV man asked.

"Upset?" Carmen said. "You've got to be kidding."

"We can't use this," the TV man said. "Nobody will want to see a hard-faced little bitch like that. Ask her how she felt when she found her father's body. Ask her how she felt <u>inside</u>."

"How'd you feel, Carmen," the other TV man asked, "when you saw your father lying there, how did you feel, inside yourself?"

Carmen's face began to lose control.

"That's it," the TV man said, "ask her again."

"I felt scared," Carmen said. "I screamed. He was there and I couldn't..."

She stopped. Tears were in her eyes. She couldn't speak.

"You couldn't what?" the TV man asked.

"I couldn't believe it," she finally said and then broke down in tears.

"That's it," the TV man said. "That's what they want to see."

There was some commotion on the hotel porch.

"Now what the hell's going on?" the TV man said. "We've got to have some quiet in here."

"It's the woman," a State Trooper said. "They've found her."

"The woman?" the TV man said. "What woman?"

"The wife," the State Trooper said. "They've found her dead out in the snow."

"Holy Christ," the TV man said. "Let's get out there and see. We've got to have this."

They collected their camera and started for the porch.

"Did you see her face?" the other TV man asked.

"Whose face?"

"Carmen Barch's face."

"What about it?"

"Her face, when she heard the stepmother was dead. Didn't you see the expression on it? Jesus, was she pleased. Evil it was, the way she smiled."

Chapter 13

Dr Stanley Howse said it was difficult telling how long Wanda had been dead.

"Yes," Parker said, "it's like she's been kept in a freezer."

They were under the fir trees looking at Wanda Barch dead on the ground. Phyllis and Hugh stood a little way off, and still further away the TV men were being kept back by the State Troopers.

Wanda was wearing a fake-fur leopard skin coat and under it they could see that she was naked. Her skin was white like something left in a freezer. She had been struck on the left temple. Her hair on that side was stuck to her head. She still wore the gold-hooped earrings.

"I'd say she was killed about the same time as her husband," Stanley Howse said.

Stanley in the cold looked like a man who needed a drink, but then, Parker thought, Stanley always looked like that, until he had one, and then he looked like one more would kill him.

Davy Shea was standing back, looking at Wanda, who was still beautiful if Davy didn't look at the place where her head was bashed in.

Under the protection of the fir trees the body had not been reached by the snow. An icicle hung from a bough like a Christmas tree decoration, and dripped drops of water onto a patch of blood-splattered ground. There were footprints under the firs. The thin layer of powdered snow showed them up quite clearly.

"We're in luck," Parker said. "Here's Wanda's footprints, and there are Phyllis Skypeck's snowshoe tracks, and then her boots and Hugh Styling's."

Davy managed to take his eyes from the frost-white body of Wanda Barch.

"And no other footprints?" he asked.

"None but yours and mine and Stanley's."

"Maybe it was a sex attack," Davy said. "In fact what else could it be with her without a stitch on?"

Parker looked at Stanley Howse. The doctor shrugged. He wouldn't be able to tell until he did a proper examination.

"How tall is Joe Prew?" Parker asked. "He seems kind of short to me."

"Everyone seems short to you," Davy said, "but Prew's short, shorter than me."

Stanley Howse knew what Parker was talking about. "The blow was struck from above," he said.

"One blow?"

"Just the one. The blow came down on the left temple."

"A right-handed man," Parker said, "who was standing looking directly at her. I wonder what she said to get him so angry?"

Parker called over to Hugh. "Are these your footprints?" He went over to where Hugh was standing with Phyllis and examined the soles of his boots.

"What's wrong?" Hugh asked.

"I don't know," Parker said. "There's been a lot of trampling around." He went back to where Stanley Howse and Davy were still standing by the corpse.

"His prints," Davy said, "the English kid's prints, they're right there, right in front of Wanda. He was standing there."

"Yes," Parker said, "and your footprints are there too. He came and looked at her the same as you."

"Her dress and underwear were in his room," Davy said. "What else do you need, Boomer? Wanda was in the Englishman's bed. He left it to shoot Gus. When he came back to bed he told her what he did and she was frightened. She leaped out of bed. She threw on the coat and ran fleeing from him. He followed her, chased her out of the hotel into the woods and attacked and killed her."

"With a hotel full of strong young men she could have gone to for protection, why run out into the woods?"

"She was panic-stricken, she wouldn't be thinking when this crazy kid had just told her he shot her husband."

Parker turned and looked at Hugh Styling. He was tall enough to have delivered the blow that killed Wanda, but at the same time he was a classy sort of young guy who might by mistake get himself involved with a low rent type like Wanda but would he get so involved he'd commit a double murder in a crime of passion?

The wind picked up as they were bringing Wanda's body out of the woods to where the vehicle was parked waiting to take her away. Phyllis was with Stanley Howse. They were walking against the flow of the crowd that was coming to see Wanda's body. The ambulance men had not covered her yet. The wind blew back her coat. They should cover her, Phyllis thought.

"You," she said to an ambulanceman, "get something to cover that goddamn body. Yes, you. Do it now."

She turned to Stanley Howse. "What could they have been thinking of?" she said. "They should have had her covered. Those bastard photographers, do you think they paid them to forget to cover her?

Stanley didn't answer. The ambulanceman hurried down with a blanket and covered Wanda, with the photographers working hard to get final shots of her.

When they came to the Lake House Phyllis saw Parker Daniels standing motionless, deep in thought, his head bent slightly down. She couldn't tell who he was looking at and then she saw that he was studying the hole in the frozen ground where her father had started digging out the foundations for the hotel's extension. Work had stopped when the ground froze. The hole was full of snow, only the edges of some mounds of newly-turned earth showed where the work had been done.

Parker saw her looking at him.

"I wonder if they'll complete this," he said, "now that both Gus and Wanda are dead. I can't see little Carmen being much of a hotel owner. Maybe she'll sell this place and buy Duane Smek an auto body shop of his own, if she ever forgives him for letting her walk home alone at five o'clock in the morning to find her father dead."

"Jesus, Boomer," Davy Shea said, "we've got other things to think about."

Phyllis went to Hugh Styling. He was walking like a ghost across the snow, dragging the snowshoes as if they were an implement of penance. He had gone pale again despite the fresh air and exercise.

"Are you all right?" she asked. "You'd better go inside and sit down."

She guided him up the steps on to the glassed-in porch and into the forest of Wanda's furniture. The big

Christmas tree stood looking very bare. It'll never be decorated now, Phyllis thought.

There was a waitress, Phyllis knew her from schooldays but could not remember her name.

"Please," Phyllis said to her, "could you get a glass of brandy. Two glasses."

The young woman didn't move. She was trying to see the media men and the ambulance, and of course Wanda's body. She stood on her toes trying to get a better view.

"Listen," Phyllis said, "this man is ill. Go get it."

"All right," the woman said, "you don't have to use that tone of voice to me, I've known you since high school."

"So you have," Phyllis said, recognizing Beverly Choquette. She had been a cheerleader. More than that, a drum majorette, with a furry white helmet and a baton, with flashing white boots stepping out with high steps while the marching band played behind her on the football field.

"Am I?" Hugh asked.

"Are you what?"

"Am I ill?"

"I don't know, but you're going to be when they come to arrest you."

Chapter 14

When they came into the Lake House to arrest Hugh, Parker saw Beverly Choquette behind the reception desk give Davy a filthy look. Then Davy gripped Parker by the sleeve and said, "What a girl. Isn't she some girl? But I don't like the way she looks at me."

"I don't think you should have arrested her brother."

"I had to. It was the only way I could get him for killing Edgar 'Geep' LaMay."

"Is Geep LaMay dead?"

"Sure, what else would he be? Only thing was, we couldn't find the body. I knew it was Armand Choquette who did it, he was a big horse player, he was into Geep for loads of money. But I couldn't prove it. So I got him on the armed robbery. He's doing ten."

"You're some cop, Davy, nobody has to worry when you're on the job."

"You bet they don't," Davy said, and then he stopped smiling and pulled Parker into the cover of the late Wanda Barch's piled-up furniture. "Justice, it's a funny thing," he said.

"I'll bet Armand Choquette isn't laughing," Parker said.

"Cut the kidding, Boomer, you know how it goes. Someone gets away with something big, he gets away with murder, for example, and you know he's done it but you can't prove nothing, so you got to serve society by making sure you lay something else on him. It's only fair and Armand Choquette was the last person who saw Edgar 'Geep' LaMay alive."

"Or at least before he went missing."

"What?" Davy said.

"I don't remember that case," Parker said.

"It was years ago when you were in Boston having your chance to be someone."

"My chance to be someone? I wouldn't call it that."

"What would you call it then?"

"During the time of my unfortunate marriage, that's what I'd call it."

"That wasn't an unfortunate marriage, Boomer, that was a lucky break, a blue collar guy like you marrying the daughter of well-off, wealthy people like that. Look what they did for getting you in that big law firm, a working stiff like you."

"Yes, a stiff like me. But I didn't like those three-piece suits."

"That's only more kidding," Davy said. "A tall, good-looking guy like you, with a rich high-class old Bostonian wife, you could have been something, except you took things too much to heart."

"You think I made too big a thing out of my wife running off with someone?"

"I certainly do. Especially if you let it interfere with business. You should have stayed in Boston. You were nuts coming back here."

"You forget that her father owned the firm," Parker said.

"So," Davy said, "there's a moment or two of embarrassment because his daughter is such a bitch, but you're still the father of his grandchildren. Anyway, she'd have come back. Running off with the guy who came to fix the central heating isn't a serious proposition. And it gives you the green light to start fooling around yourself. You missed your chance there, Boomer."

When they came out from the cover of Wanda's furniture Beverly Choquette gave Davy another long and filthy look.

"She looks real good when she's angry," Davy said.

"Yeah," Parker said, "don't they all."

"Can you imagine a guy being nuts about a girl and her giving him looks like that?"

"You're a guy nuts about a girl?"

"You bet."

"Why?" Parker was always interested in the mystery of love.

"Why?" Davy, who never saw much mystery about it, said. "Don't you see the ass on her? Don't you see those tits? And what about those legs?"

"I also see those looks."

"Yeah, that's bad. What do you think?"

"I think you shouldn't have framed her brother."

"I hadn't seen her then. I hadn't seen that ass or those tits."

"I guess next time you better have a line-up of the suspect's female relatives."

"It's no joke, Boomer."

"No, somehow I don't think it is."

Then Davy stopped and said, "There's another one, a looker with a filthy look at a guy."

Phyllis Skypeck was standing there as though she was going to block their way.

"What are you up to, Parker?" she asked.

"Your boyfriend," Davy said, "the English one, we're arresting him."

"On what charge?"

"On what charge do you think with Gus shot and Wanda bashed over the head?"

"Is this true?" she asked Parker.

"I don't see what else we can do," Parker said.

"We'll get a confession out of him," Davy said. "Then you can visit him as much as you like."

Parker watched Phyllis's dark head turn and look at Davy Shea.

She looks like a creature about to strike, Parker thought. But her long pale face under the dark curly hair gave nothing away.

"We'll have to see about that," she said.

She turned and the heels of her shoes sounded on the wooden floor where the carpet did not cover.

"The boy with the sprained ankle," Parker heard her say to Beverly Choquette, "what room is he in?"

"Well," Davy said, "at least we won't have her playing attorney-at-law for that Styling guy."

"I'm not so sure about that," Parker said.

He and Davy went up the stairs to Hugh Styling's room.

Hugh was lying on the bed reading the novel by Aldous Huxley. Parker took in the title, <u>After Many a Summer</u>, but it didn't mean anything to him.

"Here we are," Davy said to Hugh, "but I guess you must have known we were coming. You confess, and I guarantee you'll feel a lot better. A sensitive guy like you, he don't want to carry round a whole bunch of secret guilt shit."

Parker gave Davy a look, trying to tell him to stop being colourful, but Davy was beyond recall.

"So sensitive," Davy said, "it must have been a real shock for you seeing that bullet going into Gus Barch's suck. And then, my oh my, having to bash in Wanda's skull. I guess that must have been a shock for a sensitive boy like you."

"Is this abuse strictly necessary?" Hugh asked.

"He talks classy, don't he?" Davy said. "Listen, you're coming down to the station with us. You'll sign a nice confession, and then we'll stop being sarcastic, and maybe even let Dr Skypeck come in and feel sorry for you."

"I think you'll have to come," Parker said to Hugh.

Davy said, "What do you mean, think, Boomer?"

Hugh got off the bed. Parker watched him turn, with a tremendously sad, slow movement, to gaze out of the window. There was a fog rising off the snow cover, from the window they could see it floating up into the black branches of the trees. The lake was hidden under the mist.

"I didn't do it," Hugh said. "You've got to believe me."

"We don't have to believe nothing," Davy said. "Come on, get a move on."

"Give him time," Parker said.

"Time? We haven't got time," Davy said. "There's also Joe Prew out there. We also got to remember not to forget Joe Prew."

There was a knock on the door and when Parker opened it Phyllis Skypeck was standing there with a scarf round her neck now, hiding the love bite. She's having a big romance with Jack Pringle, Parker thought, but I wonder if she knows everything there is to know about Jack Pringle?

"I've got to talk to you, Parker," she said. She turned her head to someone in the hall. "Come here," she said to them, "don't go away."

Parker saw two ski kids standing behind her.

Phyllis came into the room.

"Now what?" Davy said. "What's she going to do now, Boomer? She shouldn't be allowed in here. And who the hell are they?"

Parker recognized Carl Greene and Constance Mason, the lovers who had gone in search of an empty room on the night Gus Barch was shot.

"Before you get yourself into a mess," Phyllis said to Parker, "you should hear what Carl and Constance have to say."

"Throw her the fuck out," Davy said. "This is serious police business, Boomer."

Parker saw Carl Greene smile. This was obviously the way he thought cops should talk, but Constance Mason didn't smile. She was nervous. "Tell him," Phyllis said to Carl. "Tell him what you saw."

"It's kind of embarrassing," Carl said, "that's why I didn't mention it before."

"Yes, yes," Phyllis said, "forget the embarrassment."

"We saw him," Carl said, nodding his head towards Hugh, "when we came up to this floor looking for a room. He was in bed, asleep."

"Tell him what time that was," Phyllis said.

"About midnight. Just exactly midnight."

"The same time that you heard the shot," Phyllis said, "tell them that."

"That's right," Carl said, "just before we heard the shot."

"You saw him too?" Parker asked Constance Mason.

"I saw him too," she said. She was still embarrassed. "Listen," she added, "this doesn't have to come out in public, does it?"

"How old are you?" Davy suddenly asked here. "Are you under age?"

Phyllis laughed.

"I'm of age," Constance said. "Certainly I'm of age. At least I am back home. How old do you have to be here? I'm seventeen. Seventeen is OK back home."

"Forget that," Phyllis said to her. She turned to the boy. "Tell them what else you saw."

"We went into the room next to this one," Carl said, "it was empty but I was worried that it might be someone's. Then I heard footsteps on the stairs. I thought someone might come bursting into the room. So I got up. I went to the door. That's when I saw someone."

"Who?" Davy said. "Him? The Englishman?"

"No, it was a woman. It was dark in the corridor. The light wasn't on."

"Tell them what she did," Phyllis said.

"She came to this door. She opened it. Then she did something odd."

"Odd?" Parker said.

"I didn't know what she was doing, it was so dark. I could only see her outline, from the window at the end of the hall. She bent forward and sort of moved around, like she was trying to do a dance. She was wearing a coat. A fur coat, I saw that."

"She was dancing?" Davy said. "While she was opening the door?"

"No, she had already opened the door. Then she went in."

"When she had finished dancing?" Davy asked.

"That's right, only she wasn't dancing, she was taking her clothes off. And then I was just about to close the door when she came out again."

"It was then," Constance Mason said, "when you were standing by the door, that we heard the shot."

"Yes," Carl said, "that's right. And the woman must have heard it too because that's when she came running out."

"How long was she inside the room?" Parker asked.

"Only a few seconds," Carl said.

"Did you recognize her?" Parker asked.

"Yes, I did."

"Was it Wanda Barch?"

"Yes, it was her."

"And she came out <u>after</u> there was the sound of the shot?" Parker asked. "You're sure about that?"

"Oh yes," the boy said.

"And you didn't see Mr Styling leave his room?"

"No. He didn't leave it."

"How can you be so sure?"

"I stood at the door watching. I was nervous. I didn't think it was such a good idea to be in a room that wasn't ours."

"How'd you get all this?" Davy asked Phyllis. "What made you stick your nose in this?"

"I was looking at her little brother's sprained ankle and Constance was in the room and we got talking. I was just doing what you should have done."

"Jesus Christ, pal," Davy said to Hugh, "you sure are one lucky Englishman."

Then he turned to Phyllis and gave her a filthy look, almost as dirty, Parker thought, as one of Beverly Choquette's.

"You see," Davy said to Parker, "we're no closer now than we were, and we've still got Joe Prew on the loose."

Chapter 15

Joe Prew looked out on the white and empty landscape, hoping that a skier might pass by so he would at least be reminded of human company. There was no skier. He put down the gun.

He was in Hendrick's old ski lodge. The roof was collapsed and one wall was missing. The floorboards were rotting. When he looked down he saw the earth showing through. A good hiding place, but he had not thought of it himself. Phyllis had come running breathless through the snow to tell him to hide here. He did not have to be told twice, not with Davy Shea shooting at him, hitting him in the arm. The bleeding had stopped, but the arm was sore.

He wondered what sort of fame his shooting up of the Emperor of Ice cream had achieved in a busy world.

If it's on TV or in the papers, he said to himself, she'll see it.

She was his wife Priscilla in Hartford, Connecticut. It was pleasant to think of her learning about him, having to think of him again, perhaps after long years of no thoughts. She might think that he would come for her with his last remaining gun. He had dropped the other. When Davy Shea's bullet struck him the gun had fallen from his hand and he had no time to retrieve it.

He was cold and there was a fireplace at Hendrick's, but he didn't light a fire, he feared that the smoke might be seen.

When they come for me, he thought, I wonder if I will shoot at them or only shoot myself?

His wife would learn about that all right, even way down in Hartford, Connecticut she'd hear about an ex-husband killed by others or by his own hand. Then she would feel safe, but also perhaps sorry for someone she had done wrong.

There was a breeze getting up. The wind carried the snow swirling off the ground twelve feet into the air making it difficult to see, but he thought he saw someone. He held the gun up ready to shoot if it was Boomer Daniels or Davy Shea. If it was Shea he wouldn't mind shooting. Maybe not killing, but wounding him in return.

In the swirling snow it was difficult to make out shapes, but he saw a flash of colour.

"I almost shot you," he said.

"I'm awfully glad you didn't," Phyllis said, bending down to step through the place where a window had been. She wore a red hat and a red plaid lumber jacket that was far too big for her.

"You look like a man in that coat," he said. "You ought to watch out, I might have shot a man."

"I had the same coat on when I came before," she said.

"I didn't notice," he said.

"I've brought you some food," she said. "But first let me take a look at your arm. God, it's cold in here, but take your coat off, and your sweater and shirt. It's something you'll have to put up with if you're going to be a fugitive."

Hendrick's old ski lodge was a good long tramp up to a remote side of the mountain. She was warm from the exertion of the climb. Joe Prew took his shirt off. He kept his red cap on, the ear-muffs hanging loose. He looked like a maniac.

How stupid am I being? she thought. What if the general opinion of the town is correct and Joe Prew is the actual murderer?

But this would not explain Wanda Barch sneaking into Hugh Styling's room to leave the alibi evidence of the red dress and sexy underwear. It was not in any way conceivable that Wanda would be in league with Joe Prew, with the somewhat dim-witted Joe Prew shooting her husband for her while she pretended to be in bed with her young English gentleman lover.

Whatever, Wanda had been in league with someone, Phyllis thought. The alibi of the red dress and underwear would have held true. Wanda was not to know that she would be a corpse who would be examined for semen and recent agitation of the vagina. Stanley Howse was doing that autopsy right now. Yes, Phyllis told herself, if she hadn't become a corpse Wanda would have returned to Hugh Styling's room and made sure sperm and agitation were in evidence. But there had been a rather drastic falling out with someone, so Wanda was unable to complete her plan.

When there's a murder, Phyllis thought, so many suppositions flash across the mind. A picture of Carmen Barch came into her head. What if she had come home early from her love-making in the repair shop office at Oscar's Auto Body to find her father dead with Wanda standing over him and the man who had killed him for her fled, no longer there to protect her against the daughter's anger? Wanda was in Hugh's room when the shot was heard, but she could have gone downstairs to make sure her accomplice had done the job. Carmen could have found Wanda gloating over Gus Barch's body. It was melodramatic but it was the sort of thing a wife might do. Hugh Styling had said Carmen woke him, coming screaming into his room. "She was not pretending," Hugh had said. His judgement, however, was not final. People put on acts and lie so much. I should know, Phyllis said to herself, I do it all the time. And why shouldn't Carmen scream for her dead father even if she had just chased Wanda into the woods and killed her?

"Has it been in the papers?" Joe Prew asked.

"Yes, as well as shooting up the Emperor of Ice Cream, they think you killed Gus and Wanda Barch. You're in the newspapers and on TV about that."

He puzzled over this information. After a time he said, "She'll see it."

Phyllis had no notion who this she could be. Then she remembered his wife.

"The longer you stay in hiding," she said, "the more guilty you'll look."

"What?" He had not been listening.

"They'll think you really did kill Gus and Wanda."

"Why would I want to do that?" he said, dismissing the idea as though it was of no importance.

"I can't keep doing this," she told him. "Sometime someone is bound to see me coming here."

"There's Milly, she could come."

It was annoying, the way he took it for granted that he would be helped. It's being simple-minded, she thought, he doesn't understand.

"Milly's ill," she said. "She can't climb up here."

"I'll go down. By the kitchen like before."

She felt like hitting him, but instead she smiled and attempted to explain about the danger.

He wasn't afraid.

"I can see them coming," he said, "like I saw you."

"But at night, in the dark?" she said.

"I can hear them."

"When you're asleep?"

"I don't sleep."

She looked at him. She didn't suppose he did sleep.

"I've got myself to think of," she said. "I'll get in trouble."

There was no comprehension.

If I didn't come he would let himself bleed to death, she thought. For some reason he really doesn't care, except he gets hungry and wants to eat.

She wondered how dangerous Joe Prew would be if a skier suddenly came upon him. If he shot someone, I'd be responsible, she said to herself.

Coming back down the mountain Phyllis thought she should tell Jack Pringle about Joe Prew. Jack was a man who had been friendly to Joe in the past. He might also come to the broken-down ski lodge, alternating visits with her, bringing food, possibly drink too, although that would be bad for Joe Prew. Anyway, he could generally help her to take care of the fugitive until the real killer of Gus and Wanda Barch was found and Joe Prew could come out of hiding free from the rough justice of Davy Shea. Jack Pringle might do that, he was an easygoing person, helping out the hired man was something he might do.

Chapter 16

When Phyllis came down from the mountain after seeing to Joe Prew, she went straight to the Lake House.

Jack Pringle was there, and Phyllis felt that the hand of fate or lovers' luck had put Jack where she could meet him again.

But there was also a blonde woman with carefully done hair and the look of the city, Boston or possibly even New York, standing talking to Jack by the reception desk with a confident air.

"Who's that?" Phyllis asked Carmen Barch, who was standing hidden, sulking behind the piled-up furniture in the lobby.

"I should have known, with my luck," Carmen said. She gripped Phyllis's arm and spoke with a conspiratorial whisper.

"My father, he left a will. I can't believe it."

Her voice was low. Phyllis was reminded of patients speaking of embarrassing symptoms. She had to incline her head to hear.

"My father left a will," Carmen said again, as if it were a dishonourable thing to do. She moved even closer to Phyllis, gripping her wrist. "He's left it all to her, my father did," Carmen whispered.

Phyllis stared again at the blonde woman. She could not imagine Gus Barch, a limping, pathetic creature, going behind the violent Wanda's back to have another woman, and especially a well turned-out female like this. She could see Jack Pringle, still in conversation, smiling at the woman, Jack standing a bit straighter than he usually did as he spoke, making sincere gestures with his hands, which was annoying.

"Who is she?" Phyllis could hear the tone of a jealous woman in her voice.

"She's my father's sister, my aunt Mary. She used to be here. She was here before Wanda came. She left me alone to cope with Wanda when Wanda came. She couldn't stand Wanda, I'll say that much for her. After my mother ran off Mary came and I thought I'd have her for life, which I wouldn't have minded, but then Wanda came. Mary works in a hotel in Boston but she won't any more now that this place has fallen into her lap."

"She's going to stay on?" Phyllis asked.

"You bet she is."

"I'm sure you'll be all right."

"Are you? I can't imagine why you should be sure of that. She never liked my mother. I get the idea when she's looking at me she sees my mother. I wish I knew where my mother is. I bet wherever it is she's at least having fun."

"Yes, well, there is always fun," Phyllis said.

"Is there?"

Carmen, at seventeen, was not sure about that.

"I suppose Wanda didn't know about the will," Phyllis said.

"She wouldn't have stuck round five minutes if she did."

Carmen seemed to be enjoying herself again with the chance to attack Wanda.

"I guess," she said, "that will must have been Dad's little secret. I suppose it made him feel better when Wanda was acting like a whore."

"And you, did you know about it?"

"No, I never knew anything about what he did."

She doesn't realize, Phyllis thought, that that statement makes her a suspect. Phyllis couldn't imagine Carmen killing her father. But her boyfriend Duane Smek might have done it for her. Carmen could have got him to commit the murders.

"Wanda didn't die in a sex attack," Carmen suddenly said. "It's a shame because it would make things easier. It would have to be a man, for a start."

Stanley Howse had only just completed his autopsy, but apparently Carmen knew about it. There had been no sex with Hugh Styling or anyone else.

But, Phyllis thought, Wanda had been the dancing woman. The boy, Carl Greene, in the dark of the corridor, had seen her hastily removing her dress and underwear. Wanda, with her fake-fur coat draped over her shoulders, would have looked at first in the dark like a woman dancing as she wriggled out of her clothes ready to greet Hugh naked when she tip-toed into his room and woke him, a stunning surprise for the young visiting Englishman. It was, Phyllis thought, the sort of trick a vulgar woman like Wanda would enjoy. Or perhaps she had no intention of waking him and simply wanted to make it look like she had spent the night in his room while Gus was being murdered. And then Wanda heard the shot and left the room. If it was a shot and not the sound of ice cracking on the lake. Phyllis was still convinced that Stanley Howse was wrong, and that Gus was only recently dead when the body was discovered.

Jack Pringle was no longer talking to Mary Barch. Phyllis left the cover of Wanda's furniture, but Jack, without seeing her, went into the dining-room. Phyllis was shy about following him, making her feelings, which were rather new, too obvious. And Mary Barch was blocking her way. Phyllis couldn't avoid talking to the grieving sister, who was in black, mourning for her brother.

Phyllis spoke to her of Artie Barch and she was understanding. Life might be better for Artie now, even with the tragedy of a father shot dead.

"I've been working in a hotel in Kenmore Square, in Boston," Mary told Phyllis. "It's quite different from this." She glanced at Wanda's crazy furniture in the lobby. "People are in and out quickly in a big city hotel. Here you have to look after them on a more personal level. I like this better. I was sorry to leave here, but ..."

She stopped. Phyllis knew she meant that she had to leave when Wanda arrived. Phyllis thought there must have been a tremendous clash of personality between the earthy Wanda and this almost prim creature with the done hair.

"So you're going to keep on here?" Phyllis asked, but her eyes were on the dining-room doorway, looking to see Jack Pringle.

"Oh yes." Mary Barch seemed surprised by the question. "It's what I've always dreamed of, and there's Artie to think about."

The beautiful Beverly Choquette, still with the splendid muscular energy she had when twirling a baton in front of a marching band, came out of the dining-room with a tray full of dirty dishes. Phyllis saw the professional eye of Mary Barch take her in and decide that here was a good worker.

Phyllis walked away, but Carmen caught her on the stairs.

"Jack Pringle is that pissed off," she said. "He wants to buy the place, but Aunt Mary won't sell."

Carmen had the eager face of someone first with the news. Then her expression darkened.

"Listen," she said, "I know what you meant when you asked if I knew about the will."

"I didn't mean anything."

"Sure you did. I know what you're up to, trying to make it look like I was in on it."

Carmen had been slow, but she wasn't slow any more.

"You better keep out of it," Carmen said. "You better mind your own damn business and leave me alone or else."

"I've got to go," Phyllis said, but she wanted to stay at the Lake House a while longer so she might see Jack Pringle again. Anyway, Carmen was holding her arm. She couldn't move.

"Some girls," Carmen said, "they might just burst into tears from what you said, but I'm not one of them."

"You misunderstood."

Phyllis tried to remove her arm but Carmen held on tight.

"I didn't misunderstand nothing. And you better understand me. I'll give it to you real good, implicating me with that mouth of yours."

"I've got patients to see." Carmen still held her. "I want to see Hugh Styling."

"Listen, how many boyfriends do you need?"

Carmen let go of her arm. The girl was stronger than she looked and Phyllis's arm hurt.

"You're getting yourself a reputation," Carmen said. "Chasing after Jack Pringle, an older man like that, and now the English guy. It beats me how anyone could stand Wanda's leftovers." Carmen shuddered over the idea of how disgusting it would be to go with a man who had been with Wanda.

Phyllis hadn't intended to see Hugh, but she went up to his room.

"I've come up to escape from Carmen," she said. "You ought to try skiing. If you want I could go out with you some day."

"When?" He put down the book he'd been reading and seemed eager.

"Oh, any time you're free and I am too."

She walked about the room. He must think me peculiar, she thought, wearing this lumber jacket several sizes too big.

"What do you do in England?" she asked.

"Nothing really. I thought I might write."

Looking at him she thought she had never seen someone his age so adrift without alcohol or drugs to blame. He seemed very young to her, and protected by privilege, able not to work at a job that didn't agree with him.

When Phyllis went downstairs Jack Pringle was back in conversation with Mary Barch, who was still looking glossy and neat in black.

Phyllis decided to be forward.

"Will I be seeing you tonight?" she asked.

Caught unawares he had an awkward moment.

"Oh yes, yes, certainly," he said.

Mary Barch smiled like a receptionist amused by the private lives of clients but unable to show any mockery.

She's like me, Phyllis thought, she knows she has to work and earn her living. She knows she can't make a game out of life, like Jack Pringle and Hugh Styling do. But now, of course, she's had a lucky break, she owns the hotel.

"'Bye, then," Phyllis said, and left them together.

At the hospital, as she was changing out of her ski pants and boots, hanging up the borrowed lumber jacket, she thought of how little interest she had shown in the man who had lent her the coat and had been her lover, at least for that one night.

"I didn't even want to know his name," she said aloud.

The name was written in the label of the coat.

She turned the coat inside out to learn it finally.

He was Samuel Johnson. His address was there too.

She recognized the street, it was the same address as the Samuel Johnson who was registered at the Lake House.

But he was not the same man.

Chapter 17

"So you're still playing detective," Davy Shea said.

"Someone has to," Phyllis said.

"And just how did you get this coat?" Davy asked, although she had made herself perfectly clear how she had acquired it.

They were in the police station in North Holford. She had come running to them as soon as she made her discovery.

Parker watched her, thinking that she wasn't at all embarrassed. He didn't know if this surprised him.

"And you didn't see right away that this Samuel Johnson wasn't the same man?" Davy asked.

"It was a one night stand," she said, "I couldn't remember his name." She turned to Parker. "Why is he so thick?" she asked.

"There's no reason to be insulting," Davy said.

"Isn't there?" she said. "It looks to me as if there's every reason to be."

"The point is," Parker said, "if Mr Johnson is not Mr Johnson, then who is he?"

"I've got to be going," Phyllis said.

"I think you should come with us to the Lake House," Parker said.

"Of course she should," Davy said. "She's the one who knows the real Johnson."

"It won't take long," Parker said, trying to be friendly, as if the reason why she knew the real Johnson had no special interest for him.

They left the station and drove through the slushy streets of North Holford. But out of town in the country the snow had not melted. It rose in high, glistening banks where it had been ploughed off the roads. These banks narrowed the road to the width of only one car.

Parker watched Phyllis in the rear-view mirror. Parker's long legs were uncomfortable with the seat pushed forward so Davy could reach the pedals. But that's not the only thing making me uncomfortable, he thought.

The lake was still frozen. Some hockey players were on the ice, and some daring skaters flew out towards the middle where the ice had not formed and the dark water signalled danger.

When they went up the steps to the glassed-in porch at the Lake House, Armand Choquette's young sister, Beverly, was behind the reception desk. She gave Davy Shea only a fleeting filthy look.

She said Mr Johnson was in the bar. Parker watched Davy ease his revolver up and down in its holster, to make sure he would be quick on the draw. Parker smiled, but then he wondered if Davy might be correct. If Johnson was a double slayer, he might resist them.

"You'd better stay out here," Parker said to Phyllis. "There might be trouble."

"Oh, for Christ's sake, Boomer," she said.

Parker and Davy went into the bar and Phyllis came with them and there was Mr Johnson looking very big at the bar talking to the glossy and still neat-in-black Mary Barch. He glanced over as though caught out in something when they came in.

Davy said out of the side of his mouth, "Watch him, Boomer. He's a big sonofabitch, you better watch him."

"Mr Johnson," Parker said, "we have reason to believe you are not who you say you are."

The big man smiled.

"That's right," he said.

Mary Barch moved closer to him. She put a hand on his big shoulder.

"I think you'd better explain," Parker said.

"What's there to explain?" Davy said. "It's obvious. Read him his rights. There's a strict procedure in these cases, Boomer."

"I came here under a different name," the man said, "because I didn't know how Gus would feel about it."

"And what's your real name?" Parker said.

"I thought you'd know that," the man said. "If you knew I wasn't Johnson I thought you'd know who I am."

"You tell me," Parker said.

"Petrolnik," the man said. "I'm Pete Petrolnik. I used another name because Mary and I were worried what Gus would think about an ex-husband of Wanda's hanging around."

He had lost Mr Johnson's Southern accent. Mary Barch stood next to him with her hand looking small on his big shoulder.

"It was one of those things," Petrolnik said. "Wanda knew, but Gus didn't. After my marriage to Wanda broke up, I just happened to meet Mary. You can imagine how we felt when we learned that her brother was married to my ex-wife. We didn't know what to do."

"Oh, yeah," Davy said. "It seems like you knew exactly what to do."

Petrolnik ignored Davy, he spoke to Parker.

"I came up here to ask Wanda how she felt about it. She thought it was funny. I had it in mind that she would break the news to Gus, but she refused to be helpful. Mary came up from Boston. She said she'd tell Gus."

"Here? When did she come here?" Davy said. "She wasn't here."

"Not here at the Lake House, she was at the College Inn," Petrolnik said.

"She was here on the night of the murder?" Parker asked.

"Yes," Petrolnik said.

Mary didn't say anything. She was letting the big man do all the explaining.

"Why were you so concerned about Gus's blessing?" Davy said.

"Mary didn't want him upset by the situation."

"The story you told about giving the one remaining room to the Masons, that was just a story?" Parker said.

"Not really," Petrolnik said, "I did tell them they should have it."

"And you didn't sleep in the lounge?"

"No, of course not."

"He's got no alibi," Davy said. "She's no alibi. They were in it together. They've got the motive. She owns the hotel now."

"I didn't know anything about that," Mary Barch said. "How should I know what was in Gus's will?"

"They had the opportunity," Davy said. "All he had to do was sneak out of the College Inn and drive down here. Who's going to see him at midnight in a blizzard? He knocked on the door. Gus saw it was Mr Johnson who was staying at the Lake House and so he unlocked the door. Then he got himself shot."

"Which you didn't hear," Parker said. "You didn't hear the shot and you didn't hear anyone knocking at the door."

"Of course not. I was drugged."

"So who drugged you," Parker said, "if it wasn't Wanda? It couldn't be Sgt Petrolnik, he wasn't here, and neither was Mary Barch."

"Maybe Wanda drugging me is unrelated," Davy said. "Maybe it was only like I said. She wanted to go to Styling's room without me seeing her. It's Petrolnik, who else would want Gus and Wanda dead?"

"I couldn't have got here," Sgt Petrolnik said. "That's why I had to stay over at the College Inn. My car was in the College Inn parking lot. It was snowed in. All the cars were."

"Who says?" Davy said.

"They'll tell you at the College Inn. My car was not only blocked by snow, there were other cars blocking it too. In the morning I had to get them to move the cars before I could get out. Ask Blanchard, the manager of the College Inn. Blanchard saw to it for me in the morning."

"But how do we know where you were at midnight? You've got nobody but Miss Barch to say where you were," Parker said.

"I've got people to say where I was," Sgt Petrolnik said. "It was like a party at the College Inn with everybody snowed in, the manager was very good, he kept the bar open, and the kitchen. There were a dozen or more people preparing to sleep in the lounge. We all got very friendly."

"Do you know their names?"

"I know some of them."

"And I know others," Mary Barch said.

STANLEY REYNOLDS

"But afterwards," Davy said, "you could have got to the Lake House some other way."

"He couldn't have walked it," Phyllis said, suddenly breaking into the conversation. "I was out driving in the storm at ten and it only got worse. He couldn't have walked there in time."

"At midnight," Mary Barch said, "I called room service."

"How you so sure of the time?" Davy asked.

"Because I thought it rather late to ask for room service. But I know Bob Blanchard. He brought the drinks up himself. He didn't mind."

"Sure," Davy said, "Bob Blanchard was making himself a fortune, all those people snowed in."

"What did you order?" Phyllis asked. Parker gave her a look, he wanted to tell her to keep out of it.

"Champagne," Mary Barch said. "I asked for a bottle of French champagne and two glasses."

"Convenient," Davy said, "Bob Blanchard would remember a good-looking blonde, while the boyfriend is off committing murder."

Parker saw Phyllis smile. He wondered what the smile was for, then he realized she was amused at the way Davy had referred to Mary Barch as a blonde. Mary Barch was a blonde, but not blonde the way Davy usually meant when he talked of blondes. Mary Barch was a natural blonde, not bleached.

Parker said, "We'll have to check with Bob Blanchard."

Parker and Davy dropped Phyllis at the hospital, then went on to the College Inn.

"It's a waste of time coming here," Davy said. "Mary Barch wouldn't have made up that room service story if it couldn't be confirmed."

112

"Well," Parker said, "you never can tell."

Bob Blanchard remembered Mary Barch and Pete Petrolnik on the night of the blizzard.

"He's so big, of course I noticed him," he said.

"Did you see him go up to Miss Barch's room?" Davy asked.

"No, but I saw them being friendly."

"Friendly?" Parker said.

"Kissing," Bob Blanchard said. "I noticed them in particular because I knew Mary and understood why she was staying here and not at the Lake House."

"Because she didn't get on with Wanda?" Davy said.

"That's right. But I didn't know the man, and her behaviour with him was unusual for her."

"Even when snowbound?" Parker said.

Bob Blanchard smiled. "Yes, that's right. But there were so many people in the lobby, I couldn't have watched one couple, even if I wanted to. But then Mary surprised me again when she ordered room service."

"At midnight?"

"That's right."

"And you saw the man with her in the room."

"Not exactly," Bob Blanchard said.

"Then what exactly did you see?"

"I saw his clothes on the floor. When Mary answered the door I handed her the champagne and the two glasses. Behind her, on the floor, I saw the man's clothes."

"How was she dressed?" Davy asked.

"She was wearing something."

"But not much?" Davy said.

"No," Bob Blanchard said, "not much."

That seemed to satisfy Davy.

"And then," Bob Blanchard said, "there was a complaint. The people in the next room complained about noise."

"What," Davy said, "were they playing music?"

"No, it was the other noise."

"Other noise?" Davy said. "What do you mean, screwing noise?"

Bob Blanchard was embarrassed.

"Yes," he said.

"What did you do?" Davy asked.

"I went to the room."

"What time was that?"

"Just after midnight."

"And you saw them?"

"I saw her. She came to the door."

"I'll bet she was embarrassed," Davy said.

"No, I was."

"What was she wearing?" Davy asked.

"No much. She was holding something."

"Holding something?"

"In front of her. I said there'd been a complaint and she said she was sorry."

"And that was it?"

"Yes, for then."

"For then?"

"A little while later there was another complaint, but this time when I went upstairs I stood by the door and I didn't hear anything. I didn't knock."

"And when was that?"

"About two o'clock."

"Who was this who made the complaint?" Parker asked.

"Mr and Mrs Richard Cleever."

"Well, maybe I ought to speak to them," Parker said.

"They checked out in the morning, they only stayed over because of the storm."

"Who is this Richard Cleever?" Parker asked. "That wouldn't be Dick Cleever, the Holford car dealer, would it?"

"That's right," Bob Blanchard said.

"I'll bet it was his wife who complained," Davy said. "Dick Cleever's got a real bitch of a wife. She had a good set of tits on her when they married twelve years ago, but not no more."

"Your local knowledge amazes me," Parker said.

"Yeah, well, I bought a used car from Dick a few years ago."

"And you checked the wife's tits while you were at it?"

"You bet I did, Boomer, she was still working as Dick's secretary then."

"We better stop this line of inquiry," Parker said, "we're embarrassing Mr Blanchard."

Driving back to the station Davy was in a good mood. He spoke at some length about how you could never tell when a woman would be a hot number. He had met many who looked hot but had turned out to be frigid, while others who looked incredibly respectable, like Mary Barch, had proved insatiable. Then he started going into details about these insatiable women.

"Tell me about the alleged slaying of Edgar 'Geep' LaMay," Parker said.

"There's no alleged about it, Boomer," Davy said. "He's missing and he ain't been seen. He's dead all right, and I know who killed him, Armand Choquette done it."

And then he carried on right through the afternoon on the case of the missing bookie Edgar 'Geep' LaMay, a good-looking guy apparently, and a great man for the ladies.

It was not particularly interesting, but it got Davy off insatiable women and kept the conversation almost clean.

Parker thought he'd better check out the story of the night of the storm with Dick Cleever, but when Davy telephoned the car dealer's the secretary told him Cleever was out giving a test drive to a potential buyer. Davy said he thought the secretary sounded like she had a good set of tits on her.

After that Davy might have called Dick Cleever again but he never mentioned it and Parker forgot about it.

Chapter 18

In the late afternoon Phyllis went again to see Joe Prew.

"You can't stay here forever," she said.

"But they want me for murder," he said. It had taken him all this time to work out the situation.

Maybe he did do it and simply forgot, Phyllis thought. After all, what do I know about him, except as an odd-job man doing good work for a day or two and then failing to show up for a week, even when there was pay waiting for him. He was a drunk. There was no telling what he would do, except shooting Gus and stoving-in Wanda's head was not like mending walls and repairing cellar doors.

"I didn't shoot nobody, but I thought maybe she'd think I might come for her when I shot up the ice cream parlour," Joe Prew said.

So that's it, Phyllis thought, it was love that made him cause that commotion at the Emperor of Ice Cream. There was something male and crazed about him wanting to make his ex-wife fear him.

"You got a pen and paper?" he asked. "I might want to leave a message."

What's he talking about now? she said to herself, but she looked in her bag for a pen and paper.

"Here," she said, "but who are you going to write to?"

"To everybody." He wasn't smiling.

"Oh, no," she said. She felt like taking the pen and paper back as if they were dangerous weapons. "You mustn't do anything silly."

"Why not?" He wasn't joking this time either.

"There's no reason for it, and it would be wrong."

"I'll have to leave a message," he said. He looked away, not paying any attention to her any more.

She took a look at his wound. He was silent, then he said, "You're a Polish girl."

"That's right," she said.

"Fred Skypeck," Joe Prew said, "he's your father. I've done a lot of work for him. He's a Polack."

"Too true," she said. "I admire your deductive reasoning." But she could see sarcasm was not much use for mending things. "You're a wonder," she said, looking at the wound. "Anyone else would be dead by now with a wound like that, but it's healing."

And anyone else would be dead from exposure by now, hiding out up here, she thought. But, of course, he doesn't have any alcohol to drink. If he had a couple of bottles here they'd probably find him dead out in the snow somewhere. He's a poor creature, she thought, that insane idea of making his gone-away wife fear him is pathetic.

"Maybe it was Shea who done it," Joe Prew said. "I've seen him grabbing her ass. More than once I've caught them, him and Wanda, when they didn't know I was looking."

Phyllis thought she'd like it to turn out to be Shea. There would be something in that to appeal to her sense of the Universe being somewhat like the movies, with God doing a good job of casting.

"He's been nuts about her since she came to North Holford," Joe Prew said. "I was putting in the new bar at the Lake House and Shea came in three days in a row to look at her walking, and bending over in shorts."

She said, "And Davy Shea showed his appreciation of the marvel of Wanda in shorts by bashing her over the head after he'd killed Gus?"

Joe Prew's face contorted with the effort of thought. Her father had told her Joe could measure up a new window frame practically sight unseen, but murderous human passions were something else.

"She didn't like the Lake House with Gus Barch in it," he said, "but then she didn't like the job of work Shea done removing him."

That's a handyman-carpenter speaking, she said to herself, the words of a man used to a woman ordering one thing and then deciding she didn't like it and wanting something else. And, of course, they only had Davy Shea's word for it that he was out cold, drugged by the coffee Wanda had given him. He could have put the drug in himself. It wasn't beyond human accomplishment for Davy Shea to get his hands on Milly Tencza's medicine. He was one of those cops who was always snooping around, turning up on a street corner to stare at you and then popping up on the other side of town to watch you again, as if he was not bound by the ordinary geography of street maps. There was a case against Davy.

If Wanda had rejected him, once he'd disposed of Gus, Davy might have flown into a rage and struck her down. His footprints were at the scene of the crime under the fir trees. He had been tramping all over the place alongside Boomer, who took no notice of his sidekick's prints any more than he did of his own or of Dr Stanley Howse's.

"Are you going to tell on me?" Joe Prew asked.

"I haven't told yet."

"Milly Tencza, she can't tell. She can't talk."

"She can talk to me."

He smiled as though she was making a joke.

"With her fingers," Phyllis said, "she can talk to me with them."

"I've heard about that," he said.

Phyllis wondered about this wife of Joe Prew's. What could she have been like to marry him, and if she was anything like Joe Prew, what had the salesman from Hartford been like to have fallen for her and taken her away? It was a mystery, the attraction some people had for one another while with other people you saw right off what had drawn them together. I must ask my father about Joe Prew's wife, she said to herself.

"I won't turn you in," she said. "It would look much better if you gave yourself up, before the winter does it for you."

She hoped she was doing the right thing.

Later that evening, in bed with Jack Pringle, she said to herself: What does a man like this see in me except the obvious? And even then I'm too skinny. And the wrong sort of person, Fred Skypeck's 's daughter, the Polack builder's girl.

They were in Jack Pringle's house. It was a fine house, but, she thought, not what he was used to, and from this house he could see across the water to the Lake House that once had been his, that must be galling, seeing every day, or at least in clear weather, only a quarter of a mile away what you'd formerly had. The extension which her father was to have built for Gus Barch would spoil the outline of the Lake House for

Jack Pringle gazing from the other side of the water and thinking of his childhood there.

She thought again about how ill-suited she and Jack were, but it was a wasteful process worrying about what attraction she might have for the rich Jack Pringle.

"I'm in trouble," she said.

"You're in trouble?" he said, in a tone meaning no one could possibly have trouble like he'd seen.

"It's Joe Prew. I've been taking care of him."

"Where?"

"He's hiding out."

"At your place?"

"No, not at my place. Up on the mountain."

"I thought he'd be long gone. Or dead somewhere."

"Well, he isn't. I've been treating him, and feeding him. No drink, I haven't been giving him alcohol. It would be bad for him."

"Where is he?"

"At Hendrick's old ski lodge."

"Is that old place still there?"

His face took on a faraway look as though he was imagining Joe Prew alone and injured, also sober, in the ruins of Hendrick's.

"His wife, what was she like?" Phyllis asked.

"How should I know? Why do you ask?"

"I was wondering what the man who took her away could've been like, if she was Joe Prew's lady."

"I see what you mean," he said.

But he was amorous once more.

"That love bite," he said, with his face in her neck, "did you think I hadn't noticed it?"

"It's old. My skin's so pale it takes a long time going away."

"Don't hand me that," he said, "I know what's what." And he was hot for her. She thought she should be more responsive, but she was thinking of Joe Prew and his wife. He wanted the pen and paper for a suicide note, and if he kills himself, she said to herself, it will be my fault.

Getting dressed, because with an early call at the hospital there was no chance of staying overnight, she said, "Those boots of yours I borrowed, I wanted to return them but I can't find them."

"Boots?" He was still confused after the rigours of making love, ready to fall asleep.

"I borrowed them the morning after the blizzard. I wore them to the Lake House, I took them off when I got inside, but when I went to put them on again they weren't there."

"They were old," he said, "very worn, I don't mind."

"I'll try to find them."

"Don't bother. It doesn't matter."

"Do you think Joe Prew might have killed Gus and Wanda?" she asked when she was dressed, preparing to leave.

He laughed. "Are you still thinking of that?"

He doesn't know I never stopped, she said to herself.

"Are you going to turn Joe Prew in?" he asked.

"I don't know. I don't think so."

Driving home she thought: So that was another evening of liberated sex. Then she imagined Joe Prew returning to the Lake House for something and Gus Barch surprising him.

Then she went back to thinking of sex, and all the money the Pringles once had and the pretty girls this had allowed Jack Pringle to screw.

Chapter 19

A skier found some clothes in the woods near where Wanda Barch's body was discovered. At least he came upon three socks which had gone unnoticed before and might have continued to be unremarked except for their closeness to the scene of the crime — the skier, like everyone else in North Holford this Christmas, was playing detective and he brought the socks to the police. Word quickly went round that the socks were "blood-soaked", but this was not true.

"How did we miss these?" Parker said.

"Three socks?" Davy said. "They'd be easily overlooked. I can't see how they have anything to do with it."

Davy considered himself a real policeman rather than a make-believe one which was the phrase Parker had used to describe himself, and he thought that Parker, who was after all only a political appointee, used too much imagination and should stick to routine. The fact that Davy's own imagination was often working time and a half didn't occur to him when he made this criticism of his boss.

Parker and Davy were standing under the fir trees. A few yards away, at the edge of the woods, Wanda had been murdered wearing nothing but her fake fur leopardskin coat, shoes, and gold hooped earrings.

The marks on the pine-needle floor were still visible where the scene-of-crime squad, actually only one policewoman, had made plaster casts of the footprints around Wanda's body.

"These sock," Davy said, "they don't match."

That was obvious. One was green, one blue and one grey.

"We're looking for three one-legged men," Davy said. "What's the point of this? Some people were out in the woods last summer and they took off their shoes and socks and forgot where they left them."

It was cold and Davy tried to look even colder than he was so Parker might take pity on him and tell him to go back to the Lake House and get warm. Davy thought he'd like to see Beverly Choquette walking about on her drum-majorette legs. But Parker was still obsessed by the three mis-matched socks. Davy shivered and watched the make-believe policeman, his boss, that tall, thin, goofy-looking figure, walking about bent double under the trees looking at the ground. Parker himself was cold. A tall, skinny guy like him, Davy thought, he feels the cold. Davy could see him shivering, but Parker was too engrossed to mind.

"How long is this going to go on?" Davy asked him.

Parker didn't answer. He kept circling around with his head bent studying the ground where there was nothing to see but snow.

After a while, when he didn't find anything, he came back to where Davy was standing, moving in a slow and deliberate manner which Davy thought was done to keep him out in the uncomfortable weather.

"I think," Parker said, "we ought to ask people if they're missing any clothes."

This seemed to Davy to be another instance of the make-believe policeman's overworked imagination, but it would at least bring them into the warmth of the Lake House and possibly within sight of Beverly Choquette, a gorgeous girl in spite of having a criminal for a brother.

The former drum-majorette, however, was not in view when they came into the Lake House. Mary Barch was not there either. Carmen was.

"Carmen," Parker said, "have any of your guests complained about clothes being stolen? "

"What's this now?" Carmen said. "Isn't my father shot dead enough for you, you've got to bring up petty thefts."

Parker attempted to explain. Carmen took little interest until she got the idea that the missing clothes might involve her late stepmother in her father's murder. Then she stopped sulking and became quite active arranging for the guests to look in their rooms to see if any clothes were missing. This took about an hour and ran rather smoothly except when Mary Barch came home and wondered, quite naturally, what was going on. She'd been in North Holford trying to buy something in black because she only had the one black outfit suitable for mourning and couldn't go on wearing it day after day. Sgt Petrolnik was with her, wearing a black tie, or at least a necktie that was almost all black — there was a pattern of tiny silver arrows in it.

Carmen wasn't pleased by her aunt's presence, and she kept giving Sgt Petrolnik curious glances, as if she were attempting to see what it was in the giant that had attracted him to the hated Wanda. Or perhaps she was trying to see what her aunt saw in him. Carmen no longer felt like playing the missing clothes game and once more she began to sulk.

None of the guests had found anything missing. They seemed rather amused, most of them, about the search for missing socks.

"We'll try Gus's room," Parker said. "That's the obvious place to look, after all the boots were stolen off his dead body."

Carmen was reluctant to lead a search through her father's possessions.

"How should I know what clothes my father had?" she said.

"You saw him every day," Parker said. "You must have noticed what he was wearing."

"He always looked the same to me," she said.

But when they opened Gus's bureau drawer she did find things were missing.

"He had a couple of old sweaters he was always wearing," she said. "I remember Wanda kept telling him to throw them out, so I told him I liked them. There are some of his shirts missing too. I know because I washed them the other day."

"Gus was certainly never no dude," Davy said.

Carmen remembered some trousers, another favourite item of wear that Wanda didn't like and which her father wore in spite of her. They were missing.

"And this sock," Davy said.

He picked it out of the drawer. It was a match for one of the socks found in the woods. He was keen now.

"What else is missing?" he asked.

"How would I know?" Carmen said, but she went to the closet. "I can't tell," she said.

She began to weep. Parker saw her tears falling on a shoe. It was for the right foot and it was worn away where Gus Barch had dragged it with his cripple's walk.

"All his shoes was like that," Davy said, "we find them missing boots of his they'll be the same."

"We'd better all go now," Parker said.

He couldn't bring himself to look at the weeping girl, but he felt somebody ought to do something. He put an arm round her to lead her out of the room. Her hands were moving in a curious way, like someone suffering from a nervous disorder. Then he realized she was looking for a handkerchief. He reached into his pocket and gave her his. It was perfectly clean, but wrinkled, he never bothered to iron them.

Carmen wiped her eyes. Then she stood still and looked down at the handkerchief as if she were wondering what it was doing in her hand. She threw it down on the floor as if it was something dirty and disgusting. Davy Shea laughed, but Parker pretended not to notice.

Coming down the stairs Davy said, "Maybe it wasn't such a crazy idea after all searching Gus's room. We know now someone stole his clothes, and who'd want to do that except Joe Prew, coming back here to get some warm things for hiding out in the woods? Gus caught him at it and Joe shot him and took the shoes right off his feet. Then he killed Wanda when she went after him for killing her husband."

"That'd be a pretty fearless thing for Wanda to do," Parker said.

"She was off her head after seeing her husband shot dead. She didn't think."

"That could all be true, Davy," Parker said, "but until we get ahold of Joe Prew we've no way of knowing."

"You'll see, Boomer," Davy said "when we find Joe Prew we'll find Gus's stolen boots, sweaters and shirts and socks and them missing trousers with him."

And when we find him, Parker thought, it may not be as simple as that. Joe Prew is out there somewhere, a desperate man with at least one gun and an unknown amount of ammunition.

"There might be a terrible gun battle when we find him," Parker said. "If he did kill Gus and Wanda Barch he's not going to come in easy."

He had a vision of Joe Prew shooting at them somewhere in the woods. In his vision Parker was standing up out in the open watching and he thought he'd better take cover.

Davy had a vision too. He saw himself bursting through a door, gun blazing, and Joe Prew falling down dead at his feet. Davy smiled. This daydream made him very happy.

Chapter 20

Hugh was on the telephone talking to his mother in Scotland.

"Do you find it rather heavy going?" she asked. At first he thought she was referring to the snow but then she said, "I always find Americans rather overly earnest myself."

Hugh attempted to amuse her with the story of the police chief searching the hotel for missing socks.

Hugh described the tall, thin Boomer Daniels, trailed by Davy Shea, going in search of lost socks, with Boomer bent over, not actually with a magnifying glass but with the manner of a detective with a magnifying glass.

"Priceless," his mother said.

When Hugh had finished talking to her he went downstairs to the lobby where Wanda's piled up furniture seemed to absorb all the light. The big still undecorated Christmas tree gave a touch of the surreal to the heaped up furniture.

On the porch there was bright sunlight. It struck the windows and created a white dazzle that hurt his eyes. There were others on the porch but he could not tell who they were. Outside he could see men repairing the sign of the ice cream parlour.

"Maybe they're attempting to lure Joe Prew into having another shot at it," a man said.

It was Jack Pringle. Hugh felt momentary discomfort standing alongside him. He knew this still-rugged former athlete was one of Phyllis Skypeck's lovers. She had told him so. Hugh seemed to be having yet another friendship with a girl who spoke freely of a more serious relationship with someone else.

"Sure," Jack Pringle said, "Joe Prew'll come down and start shooting at it again and at last Boomer Daniels will make an arrest."

Mary Barch was standing close to them. "Oh my God," she suddenly said. She was peering out at the lake where Artie Barch was skating. "I told him not to and there he is."

"He'll be all right," Jack Pringle said, "it's perfectly solid, except for that bit in the middle."

"No it isn't," Mary Barch said, "it's not safe at all."

"Maybe you're right," Jack Pringle said, "I'll get him."

He went quickly from the porch and ran down to the lake and went across the ice, moving very quickly almost as if he were wearing skates.

"He's a good man," Mary Barch said.

Phyllis Skypeck came on to the porch looking very pretty, dressed almost like a boy except for the way the dark curls fell down over her forehead and one side of her face where the red-knitted hat pushed them out in a very girlish way.

"Oh, it's you," she said to Hugh. "I'm here seeing Milly Tencza and I thought I might see you. We must arrange about going skiing, if you're still on for it." She turned away from him, looking to the lake. "Is that Jack Pringle on the ice?" she asked.

"He's bringing Artie in for me," Mary Barch said.

"I thought he was skating," Phyllis said. "The way he's moving, he looks like he's wearing skates. By the way, have an extra pair of boots shown up? I left them here and they're not mine. I borrowed them."

"Yes, I know," Mary Barch said. "Jack told me. He was asking me about them just now."

Jack Pringle came back with Artie. He came up the steps to the porch, looking very handsome, and passed by Phyllis as if she weren't there.

What's he doing? Phyllis thought, why's he doing this? Is he embarrassed about this thing we're having.

She could feel herself going hot with anger. The son of a bitch, she said to herself, as if everybody doesn't already know he's screwing me.

She turned to Hugh.

"Listen," she said, "would you like to go to a dance with me? My father's got a Polish polka band. He's playing at a Christmas charity dance at the College Inn. It's a big thing for him. I'll have to go. I thought it might be interesting for you to see blue collar ethnic America at play."

She spoke in a loud voice. Jack Pringle was standing not far away talking to Mary Barch, he couldn't help but hear. Still, he didn't look at her. That's it, she thought, I'm not going to bother myself about it anymore.

She had a little time yet before she had to return to the hospital. Hugh walked down the porch steps with her towards her car. She had missed Parker Daniels' search for the socks. Hugh now told her about it, attempting to look tall and stooped like the great detective bending over a clue. Phyllis laughed.

"That's just exactly like him," she said.

She couldn't see Hugh with Wanda. That was really impossible. And yet Wanda had gone to his room.

Phyllis opened the door of her car.

"Tell me," she said, "what would you have done if Wanda had stayed in your room.?"

It was a silly question. She hadn't meant to ask it. She thought he'd laugh, but instead he frowned behind his large round glasses, as if in deep thought.

"I'm sure I can't imagine," he said.

Chapter 21

Despite the evidence of the stolen clothes which pointed to Joe Prew, Parker went to Springfield to see the real Sgt Johnson.

The house was a wooden clapboard, the snow in the street outside was dirty and slushy underfoot and inside there was old lino that once had been too bright, it had faded but not enough. The furniture was cheap and old and broken-down. Parker guessed the place came furnished. When he heard Sgt Johnson's deep Southern accent he got an impression of him as a man who was simply camping out.

Parker stood talking to Johnson and all the time he was thinking of Phyllis Skypeck getting herself drunk and being picked up by the man, or picking the man up, and then coming back to this place to spend the night. These thoughts of Phyllis made Parker uncomfortable while he was questioning Johnson about Pete Petrolnik confusing the investigation by coming to North Holford under Sgt Johnson's name.

"Pete was in a tricky situation," Johnson said in his pleasant Southern accent. "I was just helping him out."

"Yes," Parker said, "I can see that. But something that was more or less humorous becomes quite suspicious once murder has been committed."

When Parker was handing the lumber jacket Phyllis had asked him to return over to Sgt Johnson a redheaded woman came into the room.

"I knew that Doctor Skypeck girl was trouble," she said. The redhead had a Southern accent too, but it wasn't very pleasant.

"There's nothing illegal about letting someone pretend they're you," Parker said.

"Isn't there?" the woman said. "It sounds pretty illegal to me."

"Not unless a crime has been committed," Parker said.

"Murder?" the woman said. "Isn't that a crime? I'd call that a pretty damned big crime."

"I was just helping out a friend," Sgt Johnson said. "It was an unusual situation he was in."

"And you got yourself in trouble," the woman said.

"He's in no trouble," Parker said.

"Isn't he?" the woman said. "Don't tell me you've come all the way down here to return that coat out of the goodness of your heart. You're looking for something. You're trying to figure out if one of us could have snuck up to that hick hotel and killed those people. Did that lady doctor tell you we all looked like the criminal type? I suppose you know all about that doctor, up in a hick town like that, I'll just bet she's known as bad news."

"She didn't do anything wrong," Sgt Johnson said.

"Didn't she?" the woman said. "She got between you and Evie. She broke that romance of yours up not doing anything wrong."

"Yes, well, that's true," Sgt Johnson said.

"You bet it is," the woman said. "And Pete Petrolnik hasn't done you any favours either pretending he was you. He's all right. He's getting out of the Air Force.

But you've got to stay in. He'll be up there running a hotel while you're still in the Air Force with a mark against you because you were involved in a murder."

"He wasn't involved," Parker said.

"Wasn't he?" the woman said. "You don't know the Air Force. You don't know how suspicious they can be. Letting someone pretend they're you and then some people getting themselves murdered, that's suspicious enough for the Air Force."

"It's all over now anyway," Johnson said.

He looked at the lumber jacket as if the returning of it had been the big thing in the case.

"That Pete Petrolnik," the woman said, "he's always been a lucky son of a bitch. First thing he unloads that evil first wife of his without having to pay her anything and then he hooks up with a woman who inherits a whole hotel. When he told me he had got himself an heiress I thought it was just more of his talk, but what do you know, for once he was telling the truth."

"What's that?" Parker said. "Are you telling me that Mary Barch knew her brother was going to leave her the Lake House in his will?"

"That's what I said, didn't I?" the woman said. "When Pete Petrolnik was bragging about how he was going to be all set up when he left the Air Force he said his girl's brother was old and not very well. I guess he got a lot sicker. A bullet in the head makes a person pretty unwell."

Parker left Sgt Johnson and the bad-tempered redhead and drove over the bridge across the river out of Springfield and all the time he was thinking: Mary Barch lied to me, a woman like that with her hair done up nice and that pleasant ladylike manner, she was lying.

It upset Parker's new idea, which was for Joe Prew to have done it, with Joe coming to the Lake House at night to get himself some dry clothes and Gus Barch disturbing him and getting shot. Joe Prew, with his arms full of Gus's clothes, had run out of the hotel leaving Gus dead on the porch. But then Wanda, hearing the shot, had left off her amorous adventure with Hugh Styling before it had even begun and had come running downstairs after Joe Prew. This seemed a daring thing for Wanda Barch to have done but Parker reckoned Davy was right and Wanda must have been in such a temper she didn't know the danger she was in. Wanda was a bad-tempered woman, like the redhead in Springfield, and it might cloud her better judgement and get her killed.

Anyway, she ended up battered to death, and three mis-matched socks had fallen from the bundle that Joe Prew was carrying. When we find Joe Prew and find Gus Barch's clothes on him, we'll have our evidence, he thought.

When Parker had been forced to come to the conclusion that Joe Prew had done it, he was sorry. He liked Joe Prew. But now that there was this new twist in the case, with Mary Barch and Pete Petrolnik having a motive, Parker was not happy. Things were confused again. Mary Barch and Pete Petrolnik had the alibi of being together at the College Inn. But how much of an alibi was that?

Parker wondered about that alibi. Bob Blanchard had seen Mary and Petrolnik together downstairs at the College Inn, and then when he'd gone upstairs he saw a man's clothes lying on the floor when Mary Barch opened the door. Later on Dick Cleever and his wife in the next room complained about noise. Parker wondered if Dick Cleever saw the man in Mary Barch's room.

It could have been another man, Parker said to himself. But thinking of Mary Barch with her done hair and polite, careful manner, it didn't seem likely. Sgt Petrolnik also didn't seem like the sort of man who would allow his woman to entertain another man in her room while he went out to commit murder for her. But you never knew, and it could have been there was no man in the room and Mary Barch had made the noise all by herself while her boyfriend was out committing murder.

Parker thought he should speak to Dick Cleever who was a fat man who had a car agency in Holford.

Parker drove to Cleever Motors and there was Dick Cleever with a cigar in his mouth, standing out in the slush on the forecourt in front of the showrooms shouting at two men who were shovelling the snow. When he saw Parker he stopped shouting and took the cigar out of his mouth and smiled.

"Well, well, well, Boomer Daniels, as I live and breathe," he said doing a comic voice. "Have you come to turn in that old car of yours? I don't know how much I can give you on a trade-in, but whatever it is it'll be the best deal in town."

Parker's old car looked pathetic alongside the new ones in Cleever's showroom.

"That car's sad," Dick Cleever said, looking at Parker's car, "you don't want to be a sad mad loser driving a sad old car like that, Boomer."

Cleever spoke loud enough for the woman who worked in his office to hear. She looked up from her work and smiled. There was something familiar about her, Parker thought, and then he saw it was the earrings she was wearing. They were like Wanda Barch's.

"I didn't come to buy a car," Parker said. "I've come to ask you a few questions."

Once again Parker had that uncomfortable feeling he had often experienced since becoming the police chief. The feeling was accompanied by a vision of himself sitting in his dusty law office in the Park National Bank building. That life in the law office had been his real life no matter how unsuccessful he had been. He had stepped out of it and into a strange new world that didn't fit him.

"Questions?" Cleever said. "You've come to ask me questions?"

The cigar was back in his mouth but he was still being jovial. He glanced over to the woman in the office and winked at her. She smiled and then put her head down over her work with a swing of gold hoop earrings.

"What sort of questions would you have in mind to ask me?" Cleever said.

"The night of the murder," Parker said.

"Say, Boomer," Cleever said, "have you gone off your head? The murders were at the Lake House, not the College Inn." Cleever turned and winked again at the secretary at the desk.

"I guess I know that much, Dick. I want to ask you about an incident at the College Inn."

"Incident? There wasn't any incident. Except I got snowed in."

"When you got snowed in you took a room there and when you were in the room you had cause to complain."

"What the hell is this, Boomer, I thought you were busy investigating those murders? What's a pair of people screwing in the hotel room next door got to do with it?"

"Well, that's what I want to find out."

Cleever dropped his voice so the secretary couldn't hear.

"I can't see what I can tell you," he said, "or what it's got to do with anything." He looked uncomfortable, as if he were about to break out in a sweat.

"You were there with your wife?"

The question made Dick Cleever anxious. He glanced at the secretary. She was no longer pretending to work. She was turned round in her chair and was staring at Cleever with a hurt expression. Parker saw that Davy Shea had been right about her figure.

Parker said, "You heard the people in the next room making noise and your wife complained to Bob Blanchard. He had to come up."

"What's this?" the secretary said. "Your wife complained?"

She was no longer seated at the desk. She came across the room to where Cleever and Parker were. And the way her hips moved when she walked made Parker see that it was more than the gold hoop earrings that reminded him of Wanda Barch.

"Your <u>wife</u> was there?" she said. "You didn't tell me <u>she</u> was with you." She seemed terribly hurt.

"I don't want to talk about this now," Cleever said. It wasn't clear to whom he was talking.

"You're going to talk about it," the woman said. "What's this about complaining?"

"It was the couple in the next room," Cleever said," they were making a lot of noise."

"Screwing?" the woman said. "They were making a lot of noise screwing? What's the matter, couldn't that wife of yours hear her own screwing because of it? Was that her trouble?"

"Now, Shirelle" Cleever said.

"Don't give me that shit," Shirelle said.

"Don't talk like that," Cleever said.

"Don't talk like what? You told me you were all by your poor pathetic self caught in a blizzard and I felt sorry for you, and all the time you were with that tub of lard wife of yours."

Cleever went to put his hand on her to calm her down, but she said, "Don't touch me. Not after you've been with that fat bitch, don't you dare touch me. I've got to seriously reconsider my employment here."

"Maybe I should come back another time," Parker said.

"No," Shirelle said, "you stay right here and ask him what you want to know. I got to hear about this hotel room in the romantic blizzard. That's something I want to hear."

"It wasn't nothing," Cleever said. "There was noise. Ethel complained."

"Did you hear voices?" Parker asked.

"Sure we heard voices. What do you think we heard? And knocking. Knocking and banging against the wall."

"No wonder she complained," Shirelle said. "She was jealous. No one would want to bang her anymore. No one, that is, but you."

"So you did hear a man and a woman in there?" Parker said.

"I heard the woman," Cleever said.

"But not a man?" Parker asked.

"No, now that you mention it, it was the woman doing the calling out."

"Calling out?" Shirelle asked.

She had calmed down and seemed interested.

"Shouting," Cleever said to her.

"Sure, shouting," Shirelle said, "like when a woman is bored to death and has to pretend the big fat slob she's with is turning her on. I know that shouting, I know that kind of calling out."

Parker attempted to look like he hadn't heard her. "You said there was knocking or banging?"

"Yes," Cleever said.

"And you weren't making any knocking or banging yourself?" Shirelle asked.

"No," Cleever said, "no, honey, we weren't."

He smiled at Shirelle and she smiled back. He seemed to have been forgiven.

"And you never heard a man's voice?" Parker asked again.

"That's what he said, wasn't it?" Shirelle said, angry at Parker now.

Chapter 22

It was already dark by the time Parker got back to North Holford. He came into the station and found Davy reluctant to question Mary Barch and Petrolnik.

"This is another wild goose chase," Davy said. "I don't like the idea of going after more suspects when we've got a perfectly good one, armed and dangerous, hiding out in the woods somewhere."

Parker told him about Mary Barch knowing of Gus Barch's will.

"We've got to go to the Lake House and at least talk to them," Parker said.

They went out and got into the cruiser and Davy was still reluctant. As they drove through the centre of town there was a crowd going into the College Inn.

"That's where we should be," Davy said, "at Fred Skypeck's Polish polka dance having a good time. Maybe you'd meet a girl and forget that wife of yours."

They left the town centre and drove down the narrow lanes with the banks of snow still piled up, shining under a big winter moon.

Davy seemed to forget about Joe Prew. He said, "I wonder if it is Petrolnik? It could be. Maybe we're going to have trouble. He's a big guy, Petrolnik. I wonder how many shots it would take to bring him down. To tell you the truth, Boomer, I've never shot anyone, except winging Joe Prew a little."

"Has that been a source of great disappointment to you?"

"To tell you the truth it has," Davy said.

When they came into the Lake House Beverly Choquette was behind the reception desk and Parker could see the way Davy was looking at her that he had stopped thinking of shooting people.

"Petrolnik," Davy said to her, "Pete Petrolnik, where is he?"

He didn't have his gun out but he talked as if he did.

Beverly Choquette looked towards Davy as if she couldn't see anyone standing there. She turned to Parker.

"Mr Petrolnik and Miss Barch are in the bar," she said.

She turned and looked back to where Davy was and once again it didn't seem as if she saw him there taking up space.

"How do you like that?" Davy said to Parker out of the side of his mouth. "What do you think of a guy in love being treated like that?" Then he forgot about love and said, "It's spooky in here. This is a strange place."

The Lake House was empty. Even the people who were still staying there had gone out to eat somewhere else, and with Wanda's crazy furniture piled up in the lobby it looked like the hotel was being evacuated after a disaster.

But on the way to the bar someone stopped them. It was young Ed Steiger, a kid reporter from the Holford Transcript.

"Boomer," he said, "what's this I hear about the time of Gus Barch's death being changed?"

"I don't know what you mean," Parker said, trying to get past him.

Ed Steiger wouldn't get out of the way. He said, "I hear Stanley Howse isn't sure it was midnight any more. I hear he thinks it was maybe much later on."

"Where'd you hear a story like that?" Parker asked.

Steiger laughed.

"I heard it from Davy this afternoon," he said.

"It's what I heard," Davy said quickly. "It's what I heard from Stanley Howse himself. He's not too sure no more."

"Jesus, Ed," Parker said, "don't go printing that in the newspaper."

"Doesn't it make a difference?" Steiger said.

"Well, I guess maybe it will," Parker said. "But the biggest difference it will make right now is that it'll make us look like we don't know what we're doing."

"And you do?" Steiger said.

"No," Parker said, "no, we don't, but we can't let the public in on that."

"Jesus, Boomer," Davy said when they got away from Ed Steiger, "why the hell did you have to tell him that?"

"Tell him what?"

"About not knowing what we're doing. Jesus, Boomer, his father is the President of the Board of Aldermen. His uncle is the Mayor."

"Well, he's got nobody but his own uncle to blame for being stupid enough to make me the chief of police," Parker said.

"You think that's funny, Boomer? That ain't funny."

They went into the bar and the first thing they saw was Pete Petrolnik's big back turned towards them. When they moved closer they saw Petrolnik was facing Mary Barch. She had been hidden from view by the big man.

"Jesus," Davy whispered, "that must be some romance. Look at the size of him. It's amazing. How does he fit?"

Parker was thinking the same thing but he didn't say anything.

"How you going to put it?" Davy whispered. "This is a delicate damned situation."

"Mr Petrolnik," Parker said, "there are a couple of things we'd like to clear up. This involves you, too, Miss Barch."

"Oh yes?" Petrolnik said, swinging himself about on the bar stool so he faced Parker.

"I understand that you knew that Miss Barch was mentioned in her brother's will?" Parker said.

"Of course I knew," Petrolnik said. "Mary was very close to her brother. Naturally she'd be mentioned in his will."

"But inheriting the whole hotel," Parker said. "That's more than a mention. Especially when his wife was still alive when he wrote it."

"Yes," Petrolnik said, "that did come as a surprise."

"Did it?" Parker said. "I understand it didn't come as a surprise to you at all."

"Oh?" Petrolnik said, but he wasn't so sure of himself any more. "Where'd you hear a story like that?" he asked. "Who's been talking to you about me?"

Mary Barch put her hand on Petrolnik's arm to keep him calm.

"I had to go to Springfield this morning," Parker said. "I happened to see Sgt Johnson there, the real Sgt Johnson. I saw him and a redheaded woman friend of his."

"Mae Harker," Petrolnik said, "you spoke to her?"

"I guess I did," Parker said.

Mary kept holding Petrolnik down. With a man Petrolnik's size it was only a symbolic gesture.

Parker told them what Mae Harker had said.

"Yes, well," Mary Barch said, "that's the way these things go. People like telling stories."

"Is it a story?" Parker asked.

"No," Petrolnik said, "it's the truth. But what were we supposed to do? With Gus shot dead and then Wanda murdered, what would it look like if Mary said she knew what was in the will?"

"Do we have to go into all this again?" Mary said. "Pete and I were at the College Inn when Gus was shot. You know that."

"I know you were there," Parker said.

"And Pete was with me. Bob Blanchard saw him."

"Bob Blanchard saw a man's clothes on the floor of the room. He didn't see a man in them."

"This is crazy," Mary said. "What else would the clothes be doing there unless there was a man to go with them?"

"And Dick Cleever, he didn't hear a man's voice in your room," Parker said.

"What the hell's going on here?" Petrolnik said.

He started to get up but Mary held on to him.

"Who's Dick Cleever?" she said. "I've never heard of him."

"He heard you," Parker said. "Dick Cleever was in the next room. He heard you and he complained about the noise you were making."

"Oh," Mary said and she no longer looked composed like a woman behind the desk at a big Boston hotel.

"Well, listen," she said, "this is embarrassing, you going round asking people what they heard through the hotel walls."

"It's not a hobby of mine," Parker said, "I don't do it for fun."

"I don't understand this, honey," Petrolnik said to Mary, "what's going on here?"

"The man in the room next to ours at the College Inn, the one who complained, he heard my voice but he didn't hear yours."

"And the cops are making a federal case out of that?" Petrolnik said. "Maybe this man Cleever didn't hear my voice because I didn't say anything."

"Do you ski, Mr Petrolnik?" Parker asked.

Petrolnik smiled. "You know I'm from Colorado," he said. "I guess you looked that up and found I was born and raised in Aspen, Colorado. I guess you know I can ski."

"This is dreadful," Mary said. "It shouldn't be allowed."

This time it was Petrolnik who was holding her down.

"It's all right," he said. "It's nothing to get angry about, Chief Daniels is just being a hawkshaw. He thinks maybe you were only pretending to be..." Petrolnik paused and a look of comic delicacy passed across his big face. "Pretending to be with me. While all the time a big time Colorado skier like me was skiing through the blizzard down to the Lake House to shoot your brother and bash my ex-wife over the head."

"That's insane," Mary said.

"No it isn't," Petrolnik said, "it's just being a cop."

"Listen, Pete," Mary said, "you've got to stop being so nice. It's very wonderful of you, but he's been sneaking around asking questions. And can you imagine, a man in the next room had his ear pressed to the wall?"

Petrolnik patted her with a big hand. "It's all right, honey," he said.

"But the way things are going," she said. "As if things weren't difficult enough with you and me finding each other and Gus being married to that woman, and then the murders and now this."

Her blonde hair was still impeccably coiffed, but she had lost her cool manner and looked ready to weep. Petrolnik had his arm round her. "I wasn't going to mention this," Petrolnik said. "I wasn't going to tell anyone. I didn't want to get a young fellow into trouble, but there's someone here you ought to investigate."

"Oh," Parker said, "who's that?"

"The English kid," Petrolnik said. "I didn't recognize him right away. But then I thought I did and I looked up his name in the register and it was him."

"You're talking about Hugh Styling?"

"That's him," Petrolnik said. "It was such a coincidence I wasn't sure at first."

"You knew him in England?"

"Not know him. I didn't know him."

Petrolnik became embarrassed.

"It's not something I'm proud of," he said. "I watched her. I spied on her. I followed her. I knew there was something up again. It wasn't him. It was someone else. But I saw them together. And she said his name. She said she'd met a polite young English fellow and she told me his name. But it wasn't him she was having a thing with, it was someone else."

"Do you follow that, Boomer?" Davy said. "I don't follow that."

"He means Wanda met Hugh Styling in England but he wasn't the one she was playing around with. Is that right, Sergeant Petrolnik?"

"That's right," Petrolnik said.

"Jesus, what a life you've had," Mary said to him, "married to that woman."

Davy said, "Maybe Hughie wasn't playing around with her in England, but he was playing around with her here all right. We got our suspect, Boomer. You can forget screwy Joe Prew out in the woods and what Dick Cleever didn't hear through the hotel wall."

Parker had nothing to say.

When he and Davy left the bar and passed the piled-up furniture and the neglected Christmas tree in the lobby, Ed Steiger was still there.

"What's going on?" he asked.

"You heard?" Davy said.

"I heard," Steiger said.

"You shouldn't have been listening," Davy said.

"Shouldn't I?" the reporter said. "I don't see why the hell I shouldn't."

"We've got to pick him up," Davy said to Parker. "What's it going to look like, a tip-off like that in the Holford Transcript and the police don't arrest anyone?"

Parker didn't say anything. He walked up to Beverly Choquette at the reception desk.

"Mr Styling isn't here," she said. "He's gone to the dance at the College Inn with Phyllis Skypeck."

Chapter 23

Bob Blanchard was standing at the door of the College Inn welcoming people as they arrived. They stamped the snow off their shoes and glanced about for a place to put their coats, feeling obstructed rather than welcomed by the smiling manager who was keeping them from the warmth and was acting as if it were a private house rather than a hotel.

"There's my father," Phyllis said to Hugh, indicating a bull-necked man with a trumpet, and a very loud checked sports coat, standing on the bandstand with his cheeks extended with the effort of playing.

She kept talking to Hugh as if she were a guide leading a tour. It was difficult trying to make herself heard with the band playing so loud.

"Let's dance," she said and took him onto the floor.

She saw Carmen Barch, whom even mourning could not keep from a good time, standing with Duane Smek. The break that had been caused by Duane forcing her to walk home alone in a snow storm on the night of the murder was now obviously mended.

Then, rather surprisingly, Phyllis saw the Masons. Surely they hadn't come to the dance? No, they were in the hallway and barely glanced into the room full of noisy townies. The elderly couple made a stately progress across the entrance hall, completely at ease despite the noise.

Then Phyllis saw the Masons stiffen. They paused, only for a moment, and then moved on out of sight. She couldn't see the cause of this momentary setback to the placid and superior couple's progress, and then Jack Pringle came into view. Maybe he's come to find me, she thought. You know, she said to herself, maybe I'm in love with him, I could do worse, and besides I don't seem to have any choice in the selection process.

Jack Pringle stood in the entrance hall as though lost in thought, looking very handsome, even without his usual good-humoured expression'. He didn't look towards the dance floor. He hasn't come to find me, the bastard, she thought.

Hugh was out of breath from trying to dance to the polka.

"We'll sit down," Phyllis said, and led him to a table where she could still see Jack Pringle in the hall.

Hugh started talking about the murders. Everyone in the room was discussing the murders. In the future, Phyllis thought, it would be remembered as the exciting Christmas of the Lake House Murders.

Hugh had a theory that Davy Shea had done them, and, as Davy Shea was so generally unlikable, they discussed this and it was enjoyable and everyone else was doing it, talking about their favourite suspects, but they both knew it was Hugh Styling who was still the chief suspect. Everyone had heard of Wanda's red dress and sexy underwear being found in his room. Heads were constantly turning in his direction, especially female ones, but of course he was very good-looking and foreign. Phyllis would have been quite proud to be with him even if he hadn't the cache of being thought a killer. Still, he was such a kid. She couldn't keep herself from glancing over to the entrance hall to see if Jack Pringle was still there.

She and Hugh got up to dance again and when the music stopped they found themselves standing alongside Carmen and Duane. Carmen immediately started talking about the murders. She spoke out as though she didn't care who heard her slanderous remarks. It was her Aunt Mary whom she now suspected.

"Can you imagine," she said, "Petrolnik was right there, pretending to be someone else. And they're sweethearts."

Phyllis smiled at the old-fashioned word. She wondered if Duane Smek considered himself a sweetheart. Still it was suspicious about Mary Barch and Pete Petrolnik coming to the Lake House under another name. But would Mary Barch kill her own brother or, rather, allow someone else to kill him? Phyllis didn't know. Murders like that did happen. In fact she had been told many times that most murders were kept in the family.

The music started again but Phyllis and Hugh sat down. She kept looking into the lobby where Jack was seated in a fat green leather armchair in conversation with someone seated out of her sight, except for the legs, and they were a woman's legs and they were very long and beautiful in silk stockings.

Phyllis's father came down from the bandstand to her table. He and Hugh fell into conversation about the weather. She kept smiling. Jack must be able to see me, she thought, I must try at least to look like I'm enjoying myself.

She excused herself. Hugh and her father hardly acknowledged her leaving. When she got to the lobby Jack was still there, but the woman had gone.

"I'm glad you've come out," he said, "I came here to find you. They're going to arrest that English kid and I don't think you should be with him when they do."

"Don't be ridiculous." She turned and saw Hugh still chatting to her father.

"It's true," Jack said.

"What nonsense." She couldn't see the point of the joke he was trying to make.

"Who was the woman you were with?" she asked.

"A woman? What woman?"

"I saw you talking to her."

"I don't know her. She's just someone staying here."

"She had nice legs. I saw her legs."

"I didn't notice. Let's get out of here," he said, "I've been thinking about you all day."

"I came with someone. I can't just leave. Nice girls don't do that."

"You're a doctor, tell him you've been called to a sickbed."

"I couldn't do that," she said.

"Listen," he said, "you don't want to be here when the cops come."

"Will you stop that, I don't think it's funny."

"It's true, they're coming for him here."

"Who told you a story like that?"

"Young Ed Steiger."

"Him? He doesn't know anything."

"He got it from Davy Shea."

"He knows even less. Besides, Boomer wouldn't allow it. But I'll come with you all the same."

She went back and told Hugh that she was being called to a patient. She felt so excited that she was sure it must show.

"I feel a real bitch," she said to Jack as they went out.

His car started tonight and she followed him in hers. It was a long drive made longer because the roads were still bad. To get to Jack's house in Brown's Ferry they had to drive out of North Holford, over a mountain road to Holford, that city still looking grim despite Christmas lights, a run-down mill-town full of empty red-brick mills, two of them formerly the Pringles. Then up through the residential section to the old highway with the lake showing from time to time when the moonlight made the ice shine and the water glisten black where the lake wasn't frozen until they turned off the highway at last and down a country road to Brown's Ferry.

When they got in the house she was silent.

"What are you thinking about?" he asked. "Your forehead is wrinkled with the effort of thought. Are you having doubts about leaving your boyfriend at the dance?

Standing by the window she was watching clouds heading for the moon.

"Come here," he said.

"I'm waiting to see those little clouds hit the moon," she said, "and I'm also wondering about the Masons, and why they're the way they are with you."

"The Masons have had enough of me."

"They haven't had enough of North Holford. It seems strange that they should come back here, even given Mrs Mason's fondness for her old college, when they must have known they'd run into you."

"Maybe they thought I'd moved away... just disappeared like Sue did."

Sue, she had forgotten his wife's name. That's how casual this is, she thought, but it is an affair, after a certain number of times, it's no longer only simply screwing.

He was making the fire. She remained by the window, looking at the half-frozen water. On the opposite shore she could just make out a light at the Lake House.

Then they were on the floor in front of the fire. His elbow caught her hair and it hurt. She winced and squealed, which she could see annoyed him, putting him off.

"Maybe we should go into the bedroom," he said.

"Do you really not know where your wife is?"

"No, I don't."

"That's odd."

"What's wrong, do you think I killed her? And Gus Barch because he wouldn't sell me the Lake House?"

"You could have done it," she said. "You could have drugged me and skated there. Except of course the lake isn't frozen completely over."

"And except, of course, I was doing something else at midnight."

"Yes, I remember the clock chiming. I guess you're innocent."

"I'm very pleased about that."

"Of course it's not as exciting as being with a killer."

"I sure am sorry about that," he said, "I'll see what I can do."

She followed him upstairs.

In the morning she was up and out of bed while he still slept. She had calls to make.

Driving to the hospital she turned on the radio. She got the local news.

"Oh, Jesus!" she said. "Jack was right. He wasn't kidding."

She looked at her watch. She'd be late at the hospital, but she had to see Boomer Daniels and find out just what the hell he thought he was playing at arresting Hugh Styling.

Chapter 24

Parker saw the look on her face and knew what she had come for.

"Now listen," he said, "there's no excuse for shouting."

She hadn't said a word.

"Throw her out," Davy said. "She's got no business here."

"Where is he?" Phyllis asked.

She was prepared to make a lengthy speech but she stopped. Davy was looking at her. He seemed much amused. She saw him staring at her neck and it was a second before she realized what he was looking at. She had come so alarmed by the news that she had forgotten what she was wearing and the two love bites, one faded and the other new, were uncovered.

"He's here," Parker said.

"In a cell?"

"Of course in a cell," Davy said. "We're holding him on suspicion of murder. And once he's confessed we're going to charge him. Then he'll be in the county jail to await trial."

She looked at Parker.

"That's the truth," he said.

Davy was still smiling, staring at her as she turned up the collar of her shirt and buttoned it at the throat.

"I don't understand you," Davy said to her. "Why should you interest yourself in this case?"

He adopted a kindly tone as though speaking to someone much younger and unfamiliar with the ways of the world.

"What do you see in that English kid?" he asked. "I can't see what good he can do you. The only thing he can do is give you a bad name, or make you look silly defending him. You'd best stick with what you've got. Where else is someone like you going to find a classy guy like Mr Jack Pringle, even if he's twenty years older than you?"

"Seventeen years," she said, correcting him, but then she knew that had been a mistake. "What's that got to do with anything?" she asked, but she knew she was blushing. Then she pulled herself together, remembering why she had come to the poky little police station, with its two or three cells hidden out of sight behind the office.

"Why've you suddenly arrested him?" she asked Parker.

But Davy was the one who answered. "He knew her."

For a moment Phyllis didn't know who this _her_ was.

"Did he?" she said.

"Sure he did," Davy said. "All the time he was lying to us. He knew her in England. That's why he came here."

"There was a girl in Boston," Phyllis said. "He came to see her."

"Yes," Parker said, "we've located her, in Florida. That story is true enough."

"But he knew Wanda in England," Davy said, "and he came to see her. He picked up the gun Joe Prew dropped in the snow and he killed Gus with it. And then I guess he wasn't too happy when Wanda refused to go away with him after that, so he killed her too. It all fits. Remember the red dress in his room."

"And the time Carl Greene heard the shot?" Phyllis said.

"Stanley Howse isn't so sure about the time of death," Parker said.

She noticed the tone of his voice. He seemed sad about the evidence pointing to Hugh.

"I want to see him," she said.

"You can't do that," Davy said. "You're not a lawyer and you're no relation of his."

"I'm a doctor. I demand to see him. I want to see what condition he's in."

"We haven't touched him," Davy said.

"Not yet you haven't," she said. "I'm going to make sure he doesn't walk into any doors and doesn't fall down any stairs."

"We don't have stairs here," Davy said. He was standing in front of her blocking her way.

"Let her be," Parker said.

"She's got no right to visit him," Davy said.

"Let her go," Parker said. "We've got enough trouble without creating more."

Davy unlocked the door leading to the cells.

"You're going to make sure everything's OK?" she said to Parker.

"Everything will be OK," Davy said. "Strictly kosher."

"He hasn't confessed?" she asked.

"Not yet," Davy said. "He'll feel much better when he gets it off his chest."

Parker took her to the cells.

Hugh looked pale and even younger than usual.

"I'll leave you," Parker said, "although I shouldn't. You're not going to pass him a gun, are you?"

She didn't smile, but neither did Parker.

The tall, thin police chief walked back to the front office, stooping although the ceiling was high enough for there to be no danger of hitting his head. Phyllis hadn't been allowed in Hugh's cell. She stood in the corridor holding on to the bars, watching Parker's retreating figure.

She said, "I suppose Parker's all right. He didn't let Davy Shea hit you did he?"

"I thought he was going to hit me," Hugh said. "When they came to arrest me."

He spoke like someone describing a long-ago event. His face looked thin behind the bars. There was something wrong with his eyes. Then she saw that he wasn't wearing glasses.

"I'd like something to read," he said, "but my glasses were broken."

"It seems to me it wasn't a very peaceful arrest," she said.

"I didn't mean to resist. But I felt a hand gripping me. I thought it was a drunk looking for a fight."

"Did he hit you?"

"No, the glasses fell off when he grabbed me."

"Have you seen a lawyer?"

"Boomer said he'd get one."

"You should have seen one already. Don't tell them anything until you do."

"Do you think it's as serious as all that?"

"Are you kidding?" she said, but then she thought it cruel to make him worry. "When you get a lawyer it'll be all right." Once more she had the feeling that she was with a child. "It'll be OK," she said.

The pale, narrow face with the odd, out-of-focus eyes nodded.

"My mother," he said.

"Forget your mother. You'll be out of here and she'll never have to know." Not that I believe that, she thought. "So you knew Wanda?" she said. "Why didn't you say?" She didn't want to interrogate him, but she wanted to know.

"When the girl in Boston wasn't there I telephoned Wanda."

"You'd kept in touch?"

"She'd written to me — once. I didn't know anyone else in America. Once the girl in Boston had gone to Florida I didn't know what to do."

"But you pretended not to know each other?"

"That was Wanda. She told me on the phone to make believe I didn't know her. She thought her husband would be jealous. It seemed like a good idea at the time."

"She already had one man here pretending not to know her. Were you close to her in England?"

"No, I hardly knew her. I was hitch-hiking and she gave me a lift. Then she called me and asked me to show her round Cambridge."

"In the daytime?"

He didn't seem to understand the implications of the question, the difference between a daylight meeting and one at night. Then he did understand.

"Oh yes," he said, "we only went sightseeing two or three times."

"The woman in Boston, are you close to her?" Again he didn't seem to understand. "I mean," she said, "were you serious? Were you intimate?" She thought she sounded like a lawyer, or a policewoman. She frowned. "If you had a serious girlfriend in Boston it would mean you weren't serious about Wanda. Not serious enough about her to kill her. You didn't kill her did you?"

There, she had asked it and a picture of Wanda lying dead in the snow in her fake fur leopard-skin coat came to her. It was hideous and brutal, but the idea of an innocent person being charged with a murder he did not commit was terrible.

"No," he said of the Boston girl, "we aren't serious. Her mother is a friend of my mother's. They stayed with us in London."

They were silent. Phyllis had seen silences like this before. In hospital, the patient and the visitor with nothing to say to one another.

"My glasses," he said, "they fell on the floor. I don't suppose I can get them mended?"

She felt like shouting at him to forget the glasses. She wanted him to suddenly start banging his head against the bars, screaming that he was innocent.

But she said, "Stay calm, I'll find your glasses for you. If they're broken I'll get them fixed." She wanted to pat his hand as she might do with a child, but she resisted the urge.

She went out and Parker was at his desk and Davy Shea was sitting with his feet up watching a basketball game on television.

"Who's his lawyer?" she asked. "What have you done about that?"

"Say," Davy said, "what the hell's this?"

"I'm not talking to you," she said. "I'm talking to Parker, and turn that damned TV off, I want to be heard.

162

Where are his glasses? When Shea hit him they fell off. Do you have them?"

"I didn't hit anyone," Davy said. His feet were off the desk. He turned off the TV.

"I want those eye-glasses found," Phyllis said.

"Calm down," Parker said.

"Sure I'll calm down when you give him his glasses and find him a lawyer. There's something else I want to know. How did you find out he knew Wanda in England? Was he stupid enough to tell you?"

"He didn't tell us. Pete Petrolnik did," Davy said.

"Jesus," Phyllis said, "that's a good one. The chief suspect, the only one with a positive motive, tells you Hugh knew Wanda in England and you believed him."

"He admitted he knew her," Davy said.

"Sure, when you twisted his arm and hit him so hard his glasses broke and flew off his head." She went out of the door.

"What's she playing at?" Davy said.

"She's going to be trouble," Parker said.

Chapter 25

Parker walked to the College Inn to find Hugh's glasses. North Holford centre was looking pretty with the snow and with the store fronts decorated for Christmas.

He thought about his prisoner as he had last seen him, attempting to read with his arms stretched full length. It seemed a cruel and unusual punishment for a man who evidently got much joy out of reading.

Parker's own reading glasses were no longer much use. He had got them from Edgar Dupre, a North Holford optician. Parker had a reason for not returning to Dupre's shop. Before Sarah had run off with the man who had come to fix the central heating she had had her eyes and other more intimate organs seen to by Edgar Dupre.

Normally Sarah's infidelities were restricted to the Greater Boston area, but when the children were young Sarah used to spend the summers with them on the lake, with Parker travelling up from Boston at the weekends. She had fallen for the optician, but not in a big way as she had with the central heating man.

Parker could have gone to an optician in Holford, which was only six miles away, but he preferred to blink and rub his eyes and pretend that he didn't really need glasses.

Edgar Dupre's store was approaching now on the other side of the street. A giant pair of glasses was displayed on the sign of the old-fashioned store front. Parker walked quickly by.

Hugh Styling's glasses weren't at the College Inn.

"Carmen Barch picked them up." Bob Blanchard said.

"Listen," Parker said, "I'm sorry about the trouble at the dance, but we had to take Styling into custody."

"Sure," Bob Blanchard said but he didn't sound sincere.

"The other night," Parker said, "the night of the blizzard, was Mary Barch friendly with anyone besides Pete Petrolnik?"

"What do you mean?"

"Another man. Could there have been someone other than Petrolnik in the room with her?"

"I told you what I know. I saw a man's clothes on the floor, I didn't see what size they were."

Parker went back to the station, hurrying along, he didn't even glance at the store fronts. Then he drove to the Lake House.

The first person he saw there was Pete Petrolnik.

Ever since Phyllis had gone out of the station, slamming the door in anger, Parker had been worrying about something. He hadn't come to the Lake House with it in mind, but as long as Petrolnik was there he thought he'd ask.

"You've heard about Hugh Styling," Parker said. "I suppose you couldn't have helped but hear."

"Yes," the big man said, "I didn't want to get him in trouble. Not unless he's guilty of course."

"Does it seem unusual to you? I mean Wanda and a young fellow like that?"

"I suppose it does, but not really."

"But he wasn't the one you suspected? I mean when you and Wanda were in England and you knew that she was seeing someone."

"No, I told you, there was another one. I found out about him. He was someone at the airbase. Not English. An American. When I asked her she admitted it."

"But she didn't admit it about Hugh Styling?"

"I didn't ask her."

"I thought you said you did."

"I just asked her who he was and she said some English college kid who was showing her round the historic sights."

"Not sleeping with her?"

"I didn't ask. I was so upset about the other one I didn't think about the kid. But she could have been. She wasn't particular. I had a hell of a time with her. At first not knowing, and then knowing what she was up to."

"She didn't keep them secret?"

"Not her. She liked telling me, at least when she knew it hurt she did. She was probably sleeping with Styling and saving it up to tell me about it later, but I'd already had enough. We broke up."

"You realize, Mr Petrolnik, that linking Styling with Wanda is fairly damning evidence? Did anyone else see Wanda with him?"

"No one that I know of. Who else would there be? Hasn't he admitted it? I thought he had."

"He can always change his story. He's made no confession."

"And if I killed Gus and Wanda it would be very convenient having Hugh Styling here? Is that what you're trying to say?"

"I didn't say that, Mr Petrolnik," Parker said.

"Not yet you haven't."

Parker didn't say anything. He was trying to feel sorry for the man having been married to Wanda. Maybe he's found true love now, Parker thought. From Dick Cleever's description of the noise coming through the wall he had certainly found something.

Mary Barch came into the lobby. She was still in black with her blonde hair gleaming like polished metal. Parker couldn't imagine her making the sounds Dick Cleever had described. He asked her about Hugh's glasses.

"Yes," she said, "I've got them here. Carmen's boyfriend, Duane, brought them in. I'm afraid they're broken."

One lens had fallen out but it wasn't cracked.

"He wants to read," Parker said, "he can't do it without glasses."

"You're being very kind to him," Mary said. "He killed my brother, remember."

"No one's been found guilty of that yet," Parker said.

"You could get the truth out of him, if you wanted to," she said. She looked hard, almost with the hardness of Wanda. Parker wondered if there was some similarity between the two women that had drawn Petrolnik to them.

"This is a joke," she said. "I ought to complain to someone about this."

Parker didn't know what she was talking about. Then he saw her eyes on the glasses.

"Treating him like that," she said, "after what he did. He ought to be locked up alone in the dark until they take him out to shoot him."

Parker wondered if Hugh's glasses had been broken when Carmen found them on the floor of the College Inn or if Mary Barch had broken them. If she did, he thought, she would have done a better job, the way she felt.

"You don't know," Mary said, "you don't know how a person feels."

Parker stood there very tall and thin, gazing down at her not knowing what to say.

"Go give him his damned glasses," she said, "let him read his fucking books."

"Take it easy, doll," Petrolnik said.

"It wasn't your brother he killed," Mary said to Petrolnik, "it was only your ex-wife who you hated and wanted to see dead."

"I'm sorry, honey," Petrolnik said.

Parker left the reception desk carrying the glasses. Going through the lobby Carmen Barch came out to him from behind a pile of Wanda's furniture.

"You've got them?" she asked.

Parker showed her the glasses.

"Do you think Hugh's guilty?" she asked. "I'd look somewhere else if I were you. Who stood to gain? Who's got a great big dumb Frankenstein guy running errands for her all the time, a guy who'd do anything for her?"

She stood looking at Parker, waiting for him to say something.

Parker didn't say anything but he was thinking about Petrolnik being a great big dumb Frankenstein guy who'd go on errands for a woman. He wondered if the errands would include murder.

"Think about it," she said.

When Parker got back to the town centre he thought he'd better see about getting the glasses repaired.

Edgar Dupre was surprised seeing him.

"Edgar," Parker said, "can you fix these?"

"These aren't yours?" Dupre was looking at the old-fashioned frames. He was careful not to look at Parker.

"No," Parker said, "they belong to a prisoner."

"The English boy? These are English frames."

Dupre's head was down studying the frames and Parker studied the optician, trying to see what women saw in him. Parker's wife had said he was nice. When he asked her what she saw in Dupre she'd said, "He's nice. He's just nice."

"He can't read without them," Parker said, "and he wants to read. He's a young Englishman who reads books."

Dupre didn't say anything.

Parker said," I suppose he read about women like Wanda in books. I suppose that was his trouble. He should have stuck to the ones in the books."

Why am I gabbing like this? Parker thought. I ought to keep my mouth shut. I don't like Dupre, and I like him even less with him making me nervous like this.

Then he thought: There was someone else odd whom Dupre was said to have played around with. Parker couldn't remember who. He hadn't been a cop then, he was a lawyer in Boston then, he hadn't paid much attention to North Holford gossip, except he remembered being surprised by the woman involved.

"These frames," Dupre said, "they're real tortoiseshell. You have to watch out with tortoiseshell, it's fragile, the real stuff. It can snap."

"Can you put the lenses back in?"

Jack Pringle's wife, that's who it was; Parker remembered now, Edgar Dupre was said to be in love with her.

"I can do it," Dupre said. He looked at Parker for the first time now, without his eyes straying off to one side or the other. He was smiling. Then his expression changed. He looked worried. Parker thought he was going to complain about how fragile tortoiseshell was, but Dupre said, "You sure you got the right man, Boomer?"

Parker didn't say anything.

Dupre said, "I've been following the case. I've been asking myself who'd want Gus and Wanda Barch out of the way? Who was after Gus to sell him the Lake House?"

"You'd better watch what you say," Parker said, then he tried to make a joke of it. He said, "Everyone in North Holford is playing detective, even me."

But Dupre wouldn't keep quiet. He leaned across the counter.

"Where's Sue?" he asked. "What happened to Sue Pringle all those years ago? A woman like that, a lady like Sue Pringle, she doesn't just disappear without a trace. Sure people disappear. I had a girl worked in here. One day she didn't come in. There wasn't a trace of her. Then one day two years later, I got a postcard from Los Angeles. 'I finally made it to sunny California,' it said. That was all. But Sue Pringle, she wasn't a girl like that."

He turned his head to one side, as if looking into the distance and thinking of girls who disappeared to California, or thinking of Susan Pringle who wasn't a girl like that.

"Listen to this," he said, "when did Jack Pringle start pestering Gus Barch to sell him the Lake House?"

When Parker didn't say anything Dupre said, "I'll tell you when, when Fred Skypeck started digging a hole in the ground for the extension."

Parker still didn't say anything, but Dupre must have seen some expression on Parker's face because he smiled. Then the optician grew sad again.

"She was a beautiful girl," he said, "a really lovely person. I was in love with her. I suppose I still am. It's funny that, isn't it?"

Both men were silent for a moment, thinking of how funny love was.

Then Edgar Dupre said he'd have the glasses ready by closing time and Parker left. Jesus, he thought, that was some confession for a middle-aged man to make, especially to me. But he doesn't know that I know. And poor Sarah, she didn't inspire Edgar Dupre's devotion like Sue Pringle did. Sarah probably doesn't care. She could stop loving people when it became inconvenient. It was a very handy way to be.

He crossed the street to the police station. Davy Shea and young Georgie Stover were there.

"Release him," Parker said.

"Release who?" Davy said.

"Styling. We can't hold him. It's no kind of a crime having known a woman in the past."

"What the hell is this, Boomer?" Davy said. "Why'd you bring him in in the first place?"

"Maybe it was because I knew it would please the hell out of you, Davy, and I thought maybe he'd confess. You never know your luck. But it didn't work, so let him go."

When Hugh came out Parker told him that his glasses were being repaired.

"You know," Parker said, "I think it might be a good idea if you moved to the College Inn. It might not be healthy for you at the Lake House. At least I can't see Mary Barch being very friendly towards you."

"Why, what did I do to her?"

"She thinks you killed her brother," Davy said, "the same as I think also."

Chapter 26

"You were with Jack Pringle on the night of the blizzard?"

"What's this about now?" Phyllis asked.

They were in the hospital in Holford. When Parker came in, saying he had something personal to ask her, Phyllis took him into a small room which was used as an office for the night nurses.

"I meant to see you last night," Parker said, "but I couldn't find you."

"No, you wouldn't have," she said, sounding as if she had gone into another dimension. "I was with Jack Pringle. You know, the classy guy who is twenty years older than me."

"Seventeen years older," Parker said.

She smiled at his remembering the situation Davy Shea had tried to put her in.

"I probably shouldn't have come back here to practice medicine," she said. "Everybody thinks they know all about me because they know my father. They wonder who I think I'm kidding pretending to be a doctor."

"I know," Parker said.

"Well, you escaped to Boston, but then you came back."

Parker was looking at her thinking how pretty she was. I had an idea I wanted my daughters to be something like her, he said to himself, but what if they came home with love bites all over their necks and said they were seeing men twenty years older, seventeen years older?

Phyllis said, "Why are you asking me about Jack?"

"You were in his house all night," Parker said, "was he there all the time?"

"Of course," she said.

She wasn't angry, but he felt she might soon be angry.

"He didn't leave?"

"If he was there all the time he couldn't have left." She still wasn't angry. "There was a broken window," she said. "The blizzard blew it in. He got up to see to it."

She thought she might as well be honest. Besides, if he asked her he'd also ask Jack and if Jack told him about the window and she didn't Parker would think she felt there was something to hide.

"You didn't see him leave?" Parker asked.

He was embarrassed asking the question, careful not to mention the bed she had shared with Jack Pringle. Phyllis could see this so she said, "No. I woke up when he came back to bed. He told me where he'd been. And in the morning I saw the broken window."

"What time was it when he came back and you woke up?"

"About four o'clock. I asked him the time and he told me. Jesus, is this the way you go about getting Hugh off the hook, finding other innocent men to frame?"

She was angry now.

"I have to follow up all the leads," Parker said.

"Leads? What sort of lead do you have for suspecting Jack?"

Parker thought, I wonder what she'd say if I told her? Following up the off-hand remarks of Sue Pringle's former lover was not what anyone would call a clue.

"Why are you doing this?" she said.

"It's nothing for you to worry about," he said.

"Oh it isn't, is it? It sounds pretty worrying to me."

Back at the station Davy said, "Did you see her? Did she put her boyfriend in it?"

"He wasn't with her all night," Parker said.

He told Davy Phyllis's story.

"Boomer," Davy said, "you can't go round accusing Jack Pringle of killing people." He took his feet off the desk to show how serious he was. "What are you going to do now?"

"I'm going to get Fred Skypeck to do some more digging at the Lake house."

"What the hell are you talking about?" Davy said. "You can't do that to a guy like Pringle. I thought he was your pal. He was your boyhood chum, for Christ's sake, you were kids together. And he's a big guy, he's still got connections." He stood up and adjusted the holster on his belt. "It'll behove your ass to be more careful," he said.

Chapter 27

It snowed again during the night and in the morning there was an east wind blowing flurries into the cold air. Davy Shea was driving and talking. Pedestrians suddenly appeared hunched against the wind. Parker was worried there was going to be an accident the way Davy was driving.

"Pay attention to the road and stop talking," he said, but Davy kept talking.

"If the English kid didn't do it, and if Petrolnik didn't do it," he said, "then your killer's up there." He waved a hand in the direction of the mountains which were unseen behind the swirling snow.

"What about you being drugged?" Parker said.

"I told you maybe I was drugged because Wanda didn't want me to see her sneaking up to the English kid's room."

"You think Wanda would be shy about you seeing a thing like that?"

"Maybe she didn't want to make me jealous. Maybe she wanted to keep me grabbing her ass. I had a thing going with her on and off for a while."

"You amaze me. That was, of course, before you got smitten by the curvy Beverly Choquette."

"Smitten, that's a kid's word. What I feel is nothing to joke about. I got a thing for her, but she won't look at me."

"She looks at you all right. I've never seen looks like the looks she looks at you."

"Usually I see a woman, a waitress, say, in a restaurant, I don't have much trouble. What I do is ask them out to a dinner some place nice, or maybe not even too nice. What they like is sitting on their ass letting somebody else wait on them. A steak dinner with a salad and an order of fries always does it, in the winter. In the summer a nice lobster feed, hold the fries."

"You're an incurable romantic."

"Ain't it the truth," Davy said.

He got to the Lake House without running anyone over.

Fred Skypeck and his men were already there.

"You sure you know what you're doing?" Davy asked Parker.

"If we don't find nothing," Parker said, "then Jack doesn't have to know. It'll just have been Fred Skypeck continuing the excavation."

They walked up to Fred Skypeck. There was a stone-covered terrace here and Fred Skypeck had already started removing the stones.

"This isn't much of a day for digging," Fred said. "The ground's like iron."

"Well, if we don't find anything out here," Parker said, "we can start digging in the nice warm cellar."

Parker reckoned that either under the stone terrace or in the cement-covered floor of the cellar were the most likely places for a body to be hidden.

A car drove up and one of the people Parker certainly didn't want to see this morning got out and came up to him looking very angry.

"I can't believe this," Phyllis said. "I just cannot believe what I'm seeing."

"How do you know about this?" Davy asked.

"How do you think? It's my father doing the digging isn't it?"

"This is some secret operation," Davy said sarcastically when he saw Hugh Styling coming down the steps of the hotel and walking towards them. The English kid had obviously not taken Boomer's advice about moving to the College Inn.

"You can't do this, Parker," Phyllis said.

Parker pretended he couldn't hear her.

"Of course it would be of interest to you if his wife's down there somewhere," Davy said to her. "That would be the kibosh on your little romance all right."

"Fuck you, Shea," Phyllis said.

"A little lady," Davy said. "Listen to the mouth on it."

Phyllis went up the steps with Hugh and into the Lake House without saying anything more.

"Listen to that wind," Davy said, "it's like an animal howling." He looked out at the lake where the wind was swirling the snow about. "Look at it," he said. "Look out there, you can't see nothing."

Parker's teeth were chattering. He jumped about but he couldn't get warm.

"You're not made for this," Davy said to him. "You're too skinny. You ought to beef up, Boomer, then you don't feel it so bad."

"I should take some waitresses out for feeds?"

"That's right. That's the idea."

Parker spoke to Fred Skypeck.

"Can you do it?" he asked.

"It's a sonofabitch, Boomer," Fred Skypeck said. "I could use some dynamite."

He saw the way Parker was shivering.

"You don't have to be here," he said. "Why don't you go inside and get warm. I'll tell you if we find anything."

"I should stay here," Parker said.

"No you shouldn't," Fred Skypeck said. "You go inside. We find anything, we'll tell you."

"Listen," Parker said. "there's no reason to tell anyone why you're digging. Anyone asks you've just resumed work on the foundation for the extension."

"Yeah, sure," Fred Skypeck said.

Parker went into the Lake House and stood on the porch watching.

Outside Davy was talking to Fred Skypeck.

"Boomer, he's a summer guy," Davy said. "In the summer he's a swimming fool. Once he won a marathon swim the length of the lake and back. How about that?"

"I remember that," Fred said.

"But do you remember who came in second?"

"No, I don't," Fred Skypeck said. "Nobody ever remembers who comes in second."

"I do," Davy said. "It was Jack Pringle. He was a big Princeton college swimmer and Boomer beat him. They had their picture in the <u>Transcript</u>, with Pringle congratulating Boomer, shaking his hand. A real good sport. I don't think he's going to be such a good sport when he finds out about this. And what's Boomer shaking so much about? I don't think it's exactly the cold, I think he's shaking because he's nervous about what he's doing to his old pal Mr Jack Pringle."

Inside the Lake House the windows were full of the ghostly motion of the snow.

"This is terrible," Phyllis said to Hugh.

"Terrible?" he said. "You mean the weather?"

"No, not that. I mean these clowns trying to solve the murders. I'm beginning to think I'll have to find the answers myself, before Boomer and Davy make enemies of just everyone."

"Maybe I could help," Hugh said.

Phyllis looked up at him. She had always associated good looks in men with a lack of brains, but he was a graduate of Cambridge University so she thought he must have some intelligence.

"Wouldn't that show them," she said, "if two amateur sleuths solved it?"

"Like one of those classic old 'tec stories of the Golden Age of Crime," Hugh said.

"Like what?" Phyllis was unfamiliar with the expression.

"A detective story from between the wars. They wrote real mysteries then, not just some maniac going crazy with an axe."

"You think this one isn't a maniac going crazy with a deadly weapon?" she said, and smiled at him. "Come on," she said, "we'll search Milly Tencza's room again."

Hugh followed her up the stairs, talking as they went up the stairs of Agatha Christie, Dorothy L. Sayers and Marjorie Allingham, and of their sleuthing couples, Tommy and Tuppence, Lord Peter Wimsey and Harriet Vane, Albert Campion and Amanda Fitton, until he realized that Phyllis wasn't listening.

In Milly Tencza's room, there was the Sacred Heart of Jesus on the wall and a blue and white plastic figure of the Virgin on the chest of drawers. Above the bed was a crucifix.

Phyllis wondered if Milly Tencza had studied the picture of the Sacred Heart of Jesus and the statuette of the Virgin when she lay on the bed thinking of killing herself. She must have been panic-stricken, Phyllis thought, when she found her stored-up sleeping pills had been stolen. Finding the gun in the snow must have seemed a stroke of luck, or the devil putting it there for her.

Hugh didn't help searching the room. He stood on the landing looking awkward. When Phyllis came out he followed her downstairs to the bar.

Carmen was behind the bar. She looked sulky when she saw the handsome Hugh with Phyllis. "I'm not supposed to be here," she said. "It's against the law for me to serve drinks at my age. Beverley Choquette is here but she's talking on the phone to her brother in prison. When she's free, she'll serve you."

"It's too early for a drink," Phyllis said.

"Is it?" Carmen said. "I heard it was never too early for you."

Phyllis wondered what she had done to get Carmen angry with her, but then she thought maybe Carmen was jealous seeing her with the eligible Hugh.

"I'll have a coffee," Phyllis said.

"Coffee's in the other room," Carmen said. "This is the bar, this is for drinks."

"Except you can't sell them."

"That's right. It's against the law."

Phyllis tried to ignore Carmen. She said to Hugh, "What I don't understand is why you ever came here."

"Because I knew Wanda in England," Hugh said.

"That doesn't seem much of a draw."

"She was the only person I knew, once the girl in Boston went to Florida to be with her father."

"I can't really see you with the late Wanda."

"I never was with her in that sense."

"A meeting of true minds, eh? Well, forget it. You're out of it now and I don't suppose it's your fault meeting someone who gets herself murdered. And the more you tell the story, the more reasonable it seems to me."

"The more I tell it," Hugh said, "the less reasonable it seems to me."

"Maybe that's why people confess to crimes they didn't do, they simply get bored repeating the same story until they don't believe it themselves."

"And it looks like I'm going to have to tell it again, here come the cops."

Phyllis hadn't noticed Parker standing on the porch. He was partially blocked by Wanda's furniture and the big Christmas tree that was still standing there undecorated ever since the Coffins delivered it the day of the shooting at the Emperor of Ice Cream with Joe Prew in his bright red hunting cap running across the snow and then out on to the lake with the ear-muffs of the hunting cap flapping and Davy Shea trying to shoot him. It seemed a long time ago.

Beverly Choquette came in.

"About time," Carmen said.

"I got to talk to my brother when I can talk to him," Beverly said. She was looking especially curvy, even dressed warm for the weather. "He's not at no Holiday Inn," Beverly said, "he can't pick up a phone any time he wants."

"He should have thought of that before he became a stick-up guy," Carmen said.

"He never was no stick-up guy," Beverly said and she went behind the bar. "Is Davy Shea out there?" she asked. "He comes in here asking for a drink I'll give him one. I'll give him a stomach full of bleach. That's what he's got coming."

Phyllis stood wondering if maybe she'd have a drink. She had things to do but she didn't think she could leave the Lake House. Not at least until they found or didn't find what they were looking for in the frozen ground out there.

She looked at Carmen and Beverly Choquette, the former high school glamour girl, still curvy and good-looking, but for how much longer? Carmen was cute sometimes, but there was a rat-like cunning that from time to time came over her face and it was unpleasant. She wondered what Carmen's mother was like. Phyllis couldn't remember ever having seen her, not up close. I suppose she was something like Wanda, she said to herself. Men never really get far away from their destined type.

This thought made her uncomfortable. What if I'm like Mrs Jack Pringle? she asked herself. She had never seen Susan Mason Pringle, not even from a distance. She had, of course, now seen her mother and father, but she didn't think the dignified, almost stately, Masons gave much of a clue to their daughter's appearance.

Mary Barch came into the bar and broke into the argument Carmen and Beverly were having with an argument of her own.

"What the hell are you doing behind that bar?" she asked Carmen. "It's against the law you serving drinks."

"Does it look like I'm serving drinks? If I'm serving drinks, who's drinking them?"

"Well, there shouldn't be two of you there anyway. One of you should be off somewhere doing something else."

Carmen said something under her breath. Phyllis didn't hear it, but Mary did.

"You little bitch," Mary said, "saying a thing like that. You ungrateful little bitch."

I can't be like Susan Pringle, Phyllis thought, I'm nothing like the sort of daughter Mr and Mrs Mason would produce. I'm like these women here. We're all coming from the same place. Whatever Susan Pringle was like it would be nothing like me.

To emphasize the point Fred Skypeck came in stamping the snow off his boots, announcing his presence like a true proletarian with noise. He was wearing a hard hat and a bright orange all-weather jacket that was meant to show up in the dark, warning people that there were working men doing possibly dangerous things. He looked worried.

"Watch out, Boomer," he said, "there's trouble coming."

Phyllis and the others moved away from the bar. They stood in the doorway to the lobby trying to see what was going on.

"Do you think they're found her?" Carmen said. "Jesus Christ, what a fucking thing that'd be."

Mary Barch didn't tell her to watch her language. She didn't even look at her. Like the rest of them she kept looking at the porch where Parker and Phyllis's father were standing talking, in lowered voices as though what was being said was too important to speak about out loud.

Then they stopped talking and turned looking towards the door of the porch. From where she was standing Phyllis couldn't see who they were looking at. Then she saw who it was. Jack Pringle came in. Mr Mason was with him.

"How about a drink, Mr Mason?" Davy Shea said. "You'll have one won't you, Jack?"

"What the hell's going on here, Boomer?" Jack asked. "You think I don't know what you're up to?"

"I don't know what you mean?" Parker said.

"Sure you do. Bill saw you and he let me know."

It took some time before they realized that Bill was old Mr Mason.

"Christ Almighty," Jack said, "digging holes to see if my wife's buried there. Are you nuts, Boomer, are you completely insane?"

He looked like he was going to hit Parker, but then he calmed down.

"The thing is, Boomer," he said, "it's all over town that my wife is buried out there. It's embarrassing."

It was odd, saying such a situation was merely embarrassing, and he smiled after he said it.

"Hell, Boomer," he said, "you should know you can't do anything in a town like this without everyone finding out. You want to know where my wife is? I'll tell you where she is. She's sitting outside in the car with her mother." Then he turned and walked away.

Chapter 28

They could hear Jack Pringle's footsteps sounding on the wooden floor and then the glass door of the porch slamming shut.

Old Mr Mason remained standing at the bar. He looked very gentlemanly but he was embarrassed and trembling.

"Why don't you have a drink, Mr Mason?" Davy asked. "Let me buy you a drink."

"I don't think so," the old man said in a nice-sounding voice that had something of the South in it. "I thought there might be some trouble, making a trip like this, but I never imagined…" He was speaking to himself. Then he became embarrassed and stopped. "They're back," he said a few moments later and they could hear the door open and the sound of footsteps.

"It'll be all cleared up now, Mr Mason," Davy said. "You won't have nothing more to trouble you now."

"Won't I?" Mr Mason said. "I wish it were that simple."

"I know," Davy said, "this is serious business. A much-respected man's character has been maligned."

He fell silent as Jack Pringle came in with a woman, holding her by the elbow and walking slowly as though she might fall down.

The woman was very nervous. Jack got her a drink. She stood holding it as though it was another burden.

Jack got Mr Mason a drink.

"Are you all right, sweetheart?" Mr Mason asked his daughter in that pleasant voice of his.

She smiled at him. "Yes," she said, "I'm all right." She had the Southern voice too.

Jack said to her, "You remember Boomer Daniels? He's our great police chief now and he thinks I murdered you."

"Hello, Parker," she said, "it's been a long time. I'm sorry to have caused any trouble."

"Trouble," Jack said, "don't be silly, you didn't cause any trouble, Susan."

Phyllis recognised the woman's legs. They were long and slim. She had seen them at the College Inn. And then he went off with me and we made love, she said to herself. She felt herself blushing. She wanted to run out, but she remained. Sue Pringle didn't look particularly well, and Jack had certainly helped create an impression of frailty, helping her in as though she was a cripple, but Phyllis could see that she had been a beauty, with dark hair that was still untouched by grey. She didn't look all that innocent; Phyllis imagined that the woman could become very sexy when the mood took her. And then there was the voice. The Masons were from Kentucky. Old Mr Mason and his daughter had blue grass in their voices.

"I came back to North Holford to see the old place again," Susan Pringle said. "I've not been well."

"Do you see what you've done?" Jack said to Parker.

"Never mind that, Jack," Susan Pringle said. "The last thing I want is people being angry. And if you didn't tell people where I'd gone to it's no wonder they made a mystery out of it."

STANLEY REYNOLDS

"It was none of their business. Why should I tell them our business?"

She didn't answer him. She turned to Parker.

"I wasn't sure I really could go through with being here at the Lake House where I used to live. That's why I stayed at the College Inn. Of course I thought I might like to see Jack again, but I wasn't sure about it."

"I understand that," Jack said. "It was brave of you to make this trip." He turned to the others. "I guess you people can see now why I wanted to buy the Lake House. I had an idea of Sue and me getting back together and being here again."

Phyllis felt as if she had been struck across the face. She wanted to ask someone to get her a drink but she didn't trust her voice to speak properly, or her hands to hold whatever drink she got without shaking and spilling it. I mustn't draw attention to myself, she thought, and later on I can simply slip quietly away without anyone noticing.

But Phyllis couldn't stop looking at Susan Pringle. She tried to pretend she was studying her to see what exactly was the illness that she was suffering from, but she knew that wasn't true. I was just a girl for him to screw, she thought. I suppose there's nothing wrong with that. I shouldn't complain. But of course I'm complaining. Right now I'm complaining like hell.

Parker, too, was watching Sue Pringle, remembering her when Jack first brought her back to North Holford.

Mr Mason glanced at his watch. His wife had stayed out in the car, none too happy about this reunion with Jack.

Sue Pringle was still being brave. She was talking to Mary Barch and Davy Shea. She was saying, "For me

I just wanted to see a place where I had been happy, and then unhappy, a place where I had been at least alive."

"Don't trouble yourself anymore," Jack said, "I'll take you back to the College Inn."

"I'll take her," Mr Mason said in a rather firm voice.

"What a gentleman he is, that old Mr Mason," Davy said in a lowered voice, but loud enough for them all to hear.

Mr Mason led his daughter out, with Jack walking a respectful distance behind them.

"Holy Christ," Davy said, "did you hear her talking? Did you hear the way she talked? It sounded like a ghost. She sounded just like a ghost talking from the grave."

Parker didn't say anything.

"Well," Davy said, "at least now we can put this English kid back in a cell.

"What's this?" Hugh said. He was nervous and edged away from the group at the bar.

"Don't worry," Phyllis said to Hugh, "the bastard can't do anything to you. Isn't that right, Boomer?"

"I guess so," Boomer said.

Davy didn't like this.

"Come off it, Boomer," he said, "somebody's got to've killed these people."

"I thought you were still keen on Joe Prew having done it?" Parker said.

"He's a good suspect too," Davy said. He was trying to look at Beverly Choquette without her noticing him.

"Who'd you rather it be?" Parker asked him. "Which one would be your preferred choice?"

"There's no need to get sarcastic," Davy said. "I didn't ask you to go looking for any dead bodies buried in the ground. But if you're playing games I'll tell you, the English kid's a real good suspect, he's from out of town, better than that, he's a foreigner."

"You think that's a good enough reason for him to go to the electric chair?"

"He won't go to the chair, juries don't like to think of kids riding the lightning."

"Riding the lightning?"

"Yeah, sure, that's what they call the electric chair."

"You're a colourful sonofabitch, Davy," Parker said.

"You bet," Davy said, "and Joe Prew, he's a crazy fuck, and juries don't like putting loonies in the chair either. They've got their sensibilities too, Boomer, just like you. So we can arrest either of them and you don't have to worry about them riding the lightning."

"Does that make you feel good?" Phyllis said to Hugh. It was a joke but nobody laughed.

"Don't you worry, Mr Styling," Parker said, "you're not going to be arrested."

"Jesus, Boomer," Davy said, "since when have you been entitled to give free pardons to suspects. So far we've made no progress at all with this investigation."

"Don't worry, Davy," Phyllis said, "I've decided to solve this crime for you. Hugh is going to help me, then he'll write a murder mystery about it, with you as a leading character."

Chapter 29

Usually Joe Prew lit a fire only at night when the smoke would drift off unseen. But this morning with the snow being whirled about by the wind he lit one without fear of being caught. Still he was apprehensive. When he had been out gathering wood there had been a feeling of someone else present. He put that spooky idea out of his mind and thought instead of the work he would be doing if he weren't hiding out. There were jobs he had to do in town. He began to have a good time daydreaming about being in town doing those jobs.

Some time later he was sitting thinking of Priscilla, his wife, wondering if she had heard the news about him and what she thought of it, hoping that it would strike her with terror but fearing that it might only cause her to smile over what a crazy bastard he was, perhaps being pleased with herself that she had got away, when he heard over the crackle of the fire and through the whirl of wind and fall of snow the unmistakable whooshing sound of skis.

He sat dead still, listening and wondering how many skiers there were. Only one, he thought. In this wind and poor visibility it was odd someone skiing, but often a kid skier paid no attention to the weather. He wondered if it was the one he had sensed before when he was out collecting wood.

He went to the window, which was glassless, with the floor below it already piled with snow, and looked out into the whirling mist.

The skier wore a red hat, not a red hunting cap like he wore, with flaps that tied down to keep his ears warm, but a red hat that girls wore. He recognized it and the woman wearing it.

She's been good to me, he thought, she's not the kind to do bad things, not to me anyway. But she might do bad things to another man, they all do.

He watched her coming towards him through the snow and he wondered if her doing bad things to some other man was the sort of thing that should upset him.

Chapter 30

Only when she was close to the caved-in ruin of Hendrick's old ski lodge did Phyllis see that there was smoke, quite thick from wet, green wood, rising from what was left of the chimney stack. It was whirled away in the wind.

Still he's taking a chance, she thought, but it's probably for the best if he gets caught. He can't remain here forever being an old man of the hills.

At the window she saw the bright red of his hunting cap.

He had a gun in his hand, ready to shoot.

Jesus, she thought, he _is_ a loony. He could very easily shoot me, except he knows I'm bringing him food. Still, he could have fired by mistake. Or maybe not by mistake. What do I know what really goes on in his mind? Or anyone else's mind come to that? She suddenly had a picture of Mrs Jack Pringle. Pictures of Mrs Jack Pringle hadn't been far away ever since she saw her. Even with her hair still dark and good legs and the remains of sexiness about her eyes she's like a ghost, Phyllis said to herself. Davy Shea was right at least about that one thing. Except there was something wrong about it, it seemed theatrical, as though she were an actress made up to play the part of the dying heroine, and a rather old-fashioned heroine at that. By why should she do that? Unless it was to gain sympathy. If so, Phyllis thought, she'd succeeded.

And now I've got this one, Phyllis told herself, looking at Joe Prew with the red hunting cap with the long ear-flaps framing his madman's face, with the ribbon tied in a bow under his chin so that he had the look almost of a child. That was creepy, that look almost of a child.

She took her skis off and brought them inside in case someone passed by and saw them. She had a haversack with food for him.

Joe Prew seemed crazier than ever.

"They do bad things," he said.

She had no idea what he was talking about.

"Who does bad things?"

"Women."

"Yes," she said, "yes they do. I'm doing a bad thing now keeping you up here. You should go down and give yourself up to Boomer Daniels."

She bent over Joe Prew, taking the bandage off his wound to see how he was healing.

"It's coming along fine," she said. "You've no right to be in such good shape."

She opened the haversack and took out the food she had brought, seeing his eyes look eagerly for the possibility of whisky. He didn't whine about its absence, but she saw the look of disappointment.

"Doctor," Joe Prew said, showing his seriousness with the formality of her title, "do you think the folks down in Hartford, Connecticut will have heard the news of me shooting up the ice cream parlour and folk thinking I killed Gus and clubbed Wanda?"

She knew that he was talking about his wife who had run away. It's amazing, she thought, the extremes of love and the astounding variations it takes.

"I'm sure they have," she said.

That seemed to relax him. He lost the nervous pointy look of a hunted creature, but he still looked insane.

"I'd like to go down," he said, "old Mrs Brooks on Hadley Road, I took down her screen windows in October, I do them every year. I promised to mend them. They've frames of some of them have gone, they're very old. The old style and fragile now. Her son used to come over from Clairmount to do them, but he's getting on himself and no longer young."

His voice had the tones of a child when he spoke of repairing the old woman's screen windows, like a Boy Scout talking of a good deed. She looked down at him sitting on the snowy broken boards of the floor, with the flaps of his red hunting cap tied under his chin, shoving the food she had brought into his cracked face, and he seemed to her a very sad case.

That settles it, she said to herself, he's got to go in. If he's shot anyone or killed Gus and Wanda they won't execute him because of it, they'll put him some place where he'll be safe. Even Davy Shea had said that.

She stood there trying to think of the sort of words that would convince him to give himself up. She couldn't think of any right off and before any came to her he said, "I got to ask you a question."

Good, she thought, he's going to ask if he should surrender.

"Bad people," he said, "they ought to be put down?"

"Not always."

"I think they should," he said, "I think they should be put down."

Jesus, she thought, he _is_ crazy as hell.

"Women," he said, "they're more bad than men, the things they do."

Christ, she thought, and I was thinking I could talk him into going down with me and giving himself up.

"They smile at you. They smile at everyone. But then they do wrong things."

"I guess they do," she said.

"I should have shot her," he said, "if I'd shot her it would have been a long time ago and by now it would have been forgotten."

"Do you still think about her?"

"I do."

"That must be awful."

"It is."

"Time is a great healer."

"Is it?"

"Oh, yes. Time heals all wounds."

He took in the cliché as if it were a totally new idea.

"It don't," he said.

"Probably you're right," she said. "I don't have much experience."

"I seen you kissing."

She couldn't imagine where he'd seen that.

"With Pringle in the snow behind the Lake House I saw you."

"Oh that," she said. "That was nothing."

"You were dancing."

Of course, she thought, he was watching. He was there waiting for Milly Tencza to bring him something to eat.

"When Milly came out," he said, "you'd gone. I heard my name being called but it wasn't her."

"Who called your name?"

She wondered if it could have been Gus, if Gus had seen him and come out calling his name Joe Prew could have shot him.

He smiled as though he had a great secret.

"The cat," he said.

"The cat?"

"He said Prew."

"Oh, I see. That's a good one."

"It is."

He was sitting on the floor smiling over the joke of the cat calling his name, evidently he had forgotten about women doing wrong things.

"You stay here for a while longer," she said. "Old Mrs Brooks' screen windows can wait."

She went out, bending double to get through the hole in the wall where a window used to be. I'll tell Parker, she thought, I'll confess that I've been feeding him. Maybe Parker won't do anything to me about that, but he'll bring Joe Prew in, hopefully with no shooting.

Chapter 31

When Phyllis came down from the mountain she was convinced she was going to tell Parker about Joe Prew.

There was a police car parked outside the Lake House and she went in to tell Parker, but Davy Shea was the only cop there.

"Where's Parker?" she asked.

"He ain't here, he's over at Brown's Ferry, not with your boyfriend or should I say your ex-boyfriend now that his lovely wife is back, but to see the vet. That little dog of his got something wrong again. That's the trouble with Boomer, we got a crazy man with a gun on the loose and an English guy who looks very much like a chief suspect and Parker leaves them alone to see to that dog of his."

Phyllis looked around. It was hard seeing who was in the Lake House with Wanda's furniture piled up like a warehouse.

"Your other boyfriend is in there," Davy said.

Phyllis could see Hugh. He was standing at the reception desk talking to Beverly Choquette. He saw her and waved. As she went over to him, she heard Beverly Choquette saying, "Watch out for Davy Shea, he's a sonofabitch, if he can't pin those murders on you he'll get you for something else. Look at him look at the way he's looking at you now."

Hugh looked over at Davy and Phyllis did too. Beverly Choquette was wrong. Davy wasn't looking at Hugh, he was looking at Beverly.

Phyllis said to herself, She probably doesn't know what everyone else knows, that Davy's mad for her. That's often the way.

But then she suddenly saw that Beverly was possibly that way about Hugh. You can tell, the way she looks at him, Phyllis thought, and she wondered if that was the way she looked at him too, but when someone was as good-looking as Hugh there was nothing peculiar about wanting to look at him.

I don't want to make a fool of myself with people thinking I'm after every man I see, she told herself, even if I'm acting just like that.

Once again she blamed all the years she'd spent studying hard to become a doctor while other girls her age were getting all that stuff out of their systems. But of course that meant you believed it ever gets out of the system, which didn't seem to her to be very likely.

"Davy," she called out, "how can I get in touch with Parker?"

"Why don't you call him Boomer, like everyone else does?" Davy said. "Parker's too ritzy for him, a big serious name like that. Unless you got the hots for him, too. Is that what's up?"

"I've got to speak to him."

"Well, he ain't in a police vehicle, he's in his own car so he's got no phone. His mobile's broke. Boomer don't get along too well with modern technology. Maybe you could call him at the vet's. Or I'll give him a message."

"No," she said, "it's all right."

She could just see Davy finding out where Joe Prew was and going after him on his own because that way he could shoot Joe down dead with no witnesses. If Joe Prew got Davy first, that was a certain murder charge.

And, she thought, when they do get Joe Prew they'll find the pen and paper I gave him for whatever he's so keen to get down for all to see. I suppose my finger prints are on the pen and the paper too. Probably they're on the food I took him. If they bother to check they'll find soon enough that it was me helping him.

"Do you know something the police should be told, Doctor Skypeck?" He used the title and her surname in a sarcastic way. "If so," he said, "you better tell me."

"It's nothing to do with you," she said. "It's got nothing to do with the police."

She walked away. She had things to do at the hospital.

"Goodbye, Hugh," she said, and as she said it she realized she'd put something extra into her voice and she blushed.

Chapter 32

In the late afternoon with the darkness drifting in from the hills Mary Barch turned on the lights in the hotel and sent for Milly Tencza.

She was hoping that Milly would be incapable of coming down the stairs to the little office where Gus used to do his accounts. If Milly were too feeble to leave her room, Mary's point would be proved, the point being that the Lake House was a hotel and not a hospital and that Milly should leave and go some place where she could get proper medical treatment.

Mary thought that she'd have to make some gesture towards continuing to pay Milly, at least at first, but then she was surprised to learn that Milly Tencza was paid by the hour and at the minimum rate. Mary smiled when she discovered this. It showed that her brother was not the philanthropic figure she had feared. The room Milly had free of charge was of course an act of charity, but it was not a room that you could put a paying guest in, and it kept her on call for any sudden dirty jobs that had to be performed.

Mary smiled again as she waited in the well-lighted room as Milly failed to appear.

The desk were Mary sat was by a window. She turned and gazed at the woods in the snow in the fading light. She thought she saw someone moving under the trees, but when she looked again she couldn't see anyone there.

She decided that she had waited long enough. She'd go upstairs to Milly's room and tell her that she should go somewhere else to be sick. Naturally she'd be polite. But how polite could you be when you had to write it down so the woman could read it?

There wasn't any necessity for politeness. Milly didn't have any family to get angry about rough treatment. She was alone in the world and could be treated just as roughly or politely as a person chose. But there was Carmen who was a little whore and who would love to have a story to tell about how nasty Mary was; and there was Dr Phyllis Skypeck who was, apparently, another whore and drank too much and had too much to say for herself and was always, evidently, butting in. Mary would be polite to Milly — but firm.

She was all set to go upstairs to Milly when she heard footsteps outside and then a knock at the door.

Mary got up and crossed the room and opened the door. Then she quickly went back to the desk and sat down and attempted to smile as Milly Tencza walked in.

Milly was feeling better. She waited, like someone pausing to listen closely for a footstep in the dark, for the bad feeling to come back. It didn't. She waited all day for it to return but it didn't.

She stood smiling at Mary Barch, wondering how Mary would attempt to communicate with her. If she looked directly at her and spoke clearly, then Milly would be able to read her lips.

Mary was sitting up very straight and her lips formed the word "hello".

Milly nodded her head to show that she understood. Mary said, "I've...been... meaning ... to ... talk... to... you."

Mary's lips formed the words as if it was a great effort.

"You'll..." Mary said. She paused for a time. "Have to..." she said, forming the words slowly. "Go," she said.

Her mouth opened very wide and she said something that Milly could not understand. Then she went face down on the desk and there was a red hole in Mary's white blouse and there was a hole in the window where the glass had been shattered.

Chapter 33

Phyllis came into the Lake House. Parker Daniels was there.

"I had to call you," he said. "You're the only one I know who can do the sign language."

They went to the little office.

What guests there were left at the Lake House were standing in the hallway looking dumbstruck. Beverly Choquette was there and Davy Shea was near her, but Beverly did not cast any looks of hatred at him. Like everyone there she was too shocked to bother about anything else.

"Nobody saw anything," Davy said."I don't know where Carmen is."

"I'm here," she said. "What's happened? We've only just come in."

Duane Smek was with her.

When Davy told her that her aunt had been shot dead Carmen didn't say anything. Duane Smek stood as though waiting to catch her if she fainted or to put an arm around her if she started to cry, but she didn't faint or weep.

"Where were you?" Davy asked her.

"Out."

"I know out. Where out?"

"Just around."

"Jesus, there's been a murder, stop talking like a goddam kid."

Carmen turned to Parker. "Do you think I done it? I was with Duane."

"And where was Duane?" Davy asked. "Out and just around too I suppose."

"That's right."

"Jesus."

"We were at Oscar's Auto Body," Carmen said.

"That's some romance," Davy said, "hanging round watching him do panel beating, that's trés romantique."

"It's better," Carmen said, "than going out to dinner with you and listening to you eat."

Beverly Choquette laughed, then she said, "Sorry."

Mary Barch's body was still in the little office, slumped face down on the desk. The door of the office was open and from the hallway they could see her. It didn't seem right for anyone to be standing around making remarks that might cause laughter.

"There's no reason for all of you people to be here," Parker said.

"Just a minute," Davy said, "I'm not finished yet."

Parker didn't say anything. He was standing there in a wrinkled shirt with a frayed collar looking tall and thin and puzzled.

"Listen," Davy said to Carmen and Duane, "did anyone see you at Oscar's Auto Body?"

"See us?" Carmen said. "We weren't doing anything wrong."

"Jesus, how thick are you?" Davy said. "I mean do you have a witness who can place you there at the time of the murder?"

"What are you saying? Do you really think I might have done it?"

"What time was it done?" Duane Smek asked. "It depends on what time it was whether we got a witness or not."

"Milly Tencza will know what time it was done," Davy said.

"I can't believe this," Carmen said to Duane. "I can't believe what I'm hearing. What's that cop Shea doing asking us where we were?"

"It'll be all right," Duane said, "we don't have anything to worry about."

Dr Stanley Howse was in the office. They could see him through the open door. He looked sober, but his face was deadly white.

Three murder victims, Phyllis thought, I guess it's getting to Stanley.

"The boss came in," Duane said.

"Oscar Picard?" Davy asked.

"That's right, the boss. He asked if I'd be around tonight. I said I'd take Carmen home and then I'd be around."

"What time was that?"

"I don't know. It was getting dark."

"Say, listen," Carmen said to Davy, "what about Petrolnik?"

"What about Petrolnik?"

"He went back to Westover Air Force Base. But did he go? Is he there?"

"You think he shot your aunt?"

"He could. Maybe now that she's an heiress with a hotel she told him to get lost."

"A man could do that," Davy said. "It's a motive, but it's not much of a motive. You're the one with a real motive."

"What are you talking about?"

"She's dead. You're the heiress now."

Until Davy said it the idea that she now owned the hotel had not seemed to have occurred to Carmen.

Davy, and some of the others, looked at her to see if she'd smile about owning the Lake House or if she'd look worried about having a motive for the murder, but her face didn't show anything.

Phyllis said, "I suppose this lets Hugh Styling off?"

"Does it?" Davy said. "I don't see that it necessarily does that. What do you think, Boomer?"

Parker didn't speak. He still seemed far away, lost in thought. Davy repeated the question.

"I don't know," Parker said.

"I do," Beverly Choquette said. "I know where he was, he was standing by the reception desk talking to me when we heard the shot."

Davy said to Phyllis, "The murder of Mary Barch may be completely unconnected with the other two. Where is he now, this innocent Englishman?"

"He's in the bar having a drink," Beverly Choquette said, "like anyone with any sense would do in a place like this with the average life expectancy falling all the time."

"Can I go now?" Duane Smek said. "I'm supposed to be working. With the roads still icy there's plenty of accidents."

"Do you want him anymore?" Davy asked Parker.

Once again Parker looked like he was thinking of something else and didn't hear Davy. After what seemed a long time he said, "He can go."

"We're going to check the time," Davy said to Duane. "You better make sure Oscar Picard saw you and the new hotel heiress at the right time."

Beverly Choquette was back giving Davy dirty looks. Davy was thinking how beautiful she was, but he had an idea that he wouldn't be too happy about the thoughts she was having that made her beautiful.

Then she spoke to him and he found out he had been right.

"At least my brother didn't do it," she said. "This is a crime you can't pin on him."

"Let's forget about that," Parker said. He was wide awake again. "For the time being let's put that aside."

"You can forget," Beverly said. "I can't."

"I know," Parker said. "I promise you, I'll go into it, the first chance I have."

Beverly said to Phyllis, "He thinks my brother killed Geep LaMay. My brother could never kill anyone. That Davy Shea framed him for the liquor store. My brother never held up anyone."

"What about Haywood's?" Davy said. "He robbed Haywood's Rental and Repair."

"That was kid's stuff. He was a kid."

"And the Seven Eleven on Dwight and Appleton?"

"He was just a kid."

"He had a gun."

Parker said, "Go away some place else and argue that between yourselves."

"Him?" Beverly said. "I'm not going no place with him."

She walked off towards the bar. Davy watched her go and Parker watched Davy watching her.

Stanley Howse came out of the office. Ever since he had changed his mind about the time of death he had been reserved with Phyllis. He nodded to her but he didn't speak.

"Phyllis," Parker said, "will you try to talk to Milly now?"

Milly smiled at Phyllis. Her hands and fingers moved.

"What's she saying?" Davy asked.

"She wants a drink. She wants Scotch."

Phyllis could see the look on Davy's face, and on Parker's too. They thought people with afflictions should live like saints. A deaf-mute woman drinking whisky didn't fit in with that.

"I'll get her one," Carmen said, staring at her aunt's dead body, mesmerized by it.

When Carmen left the room Davy said, "I don't think she done it, but you never know. Duane Smek, he's a wise guy. He might have seen an opportunity for himself."

Phyllis was talking to Milly. She wasn't going to wait until Milly had a drink.

"What are you saying?" Davy asked.

"I'm asking her how she is."

"We know how she is. Ask her what she saw?"

Phyllis was worried about making Milly go through it again. But she was all right except her hands were trembling a bit. It was like a woman who had just seen another woman shot dead in front of her trying to talk about it and her voice wobbling.

Milly's hands and fingers moved, telling Phyllis about Mary Barch sitting at the desk smiling at her and telling her she'd have to leave the Lake House, and then Mary Barch's mouth opening wide and her face falling on the desk.

She hadn't heard anything. Of course she hadn't. And because of that she didn't know right away what had happened.

It seemed incredibly frightening to Phyllis, this tremendous violent act happening in complete silence, the woman slumping dead, the hole appearing in the window as if by magic. The wind was blowing now through the hole, making the room chilly. Phyllis shuddered, but not entirely from the cold. Of course that spooky silence is natural to her, she thought, she doesn't know anything else and we lack the imagination to sympathize.

"What's she saying?" Davy asked.

"Did she see who fired the shot?" Parker asked.

She had seen someone. A person running.

"A man? A woman?" Davy asked. He was still thinking of Carmen.

Phyllis, sitting in front of Milly, turned her head towards Parker and Davy.

"A man," she said.

"This's good," Davy said. "This's a break."

"Did she recognize him?" Parker asked, but just then Carmen came into the room carrying a bottle of whisky and one glass.

"Leave that now," Davy said to her. "Ask her," he said to Phyllis, "does she know who it was in the woods?"

Phyllis's hands asked the question.

"She couldn't tell," Phyllis said. "It was dark."

"Not completely dark," Davy said.

"Dark enough."

"Was there anything at all?" Parker asked. He wasn't his usual laid-back, day-dreaming self now. He leaned forward as though seeking a clue to the man's identity in Milly Tencza's face.

"What's going on?" Carmen asked, still holding the bottle of scotch and the glass.

"Quiet," Davy said.

Phyllis's hands and fingers moved.

Milly seemed reluctant to answer.

"What the hell's wrong with her?" Davy said.

"Ask her again," Parker said.

Phyllis did.

Milly's fingers spoke and Phyllis knew why she had been reluctant to answer.

"Jesus," Phyllis said.

"What is it?" Parker asked.

Phyllis got up. Her hands were the ones that were trembling now. The man Milly had seen had been wearing a red hunting cap with long flaps that tied under his chin.

And I let him go, Phyllis said to herself. I hid him from the law so he could kill again.

Chapter 34

"I know that cap," Davy said. "Everyone knows that cap."

"I'm afraid they do," Parker said.

"What do you mean, afraid?" Davy said. "We've got our man now. I guess we had him from the very beginning only everyone started playing detective."

Phyllis hadn't said anything since she told them what Milly had seen.

"Parker," she said, "can I have a word with you?"

The tall thin chief nodded his head and they stepped out into the hallway, where a young policeman named George Stover was on guard to keep the curious away.

Parker spoke to him and he went off leaving them alone.

"I've got to tell you something," Phyllis said.

"I think you do."

"You knew about it?"

"I had a suspicion."

"What'll you do?"

"I don't know. I'll have to wait and see."

"I feel awful."

"I'll bet you do."

She could see Joe Prew's cracked face, see him shoving food into it, and then she heard him talking the crazy talk about his wife, wanting her to read about him in the

Hartford, Connecticut newspaper or hear about him on the radio or TV and feel afraid, be full of fear that he would be coming to get her.

"You'd better tell me," Parker said.

When she told him they went back into the office.

"What's going on?" Davy said.

"We've got to get Joe," Parker said.

"But where is he?"

"I think I've got an idea," Parker said.

"Oh," Davy said and he looked at Phyllis. "Do we need help?" he asked. "How many of us do we need?"

"Get George Stover," Parker said, "he's a good boy. Tell someone else to guard the scene of the crime."

Davy went out. Parker said to Phyllis, "Hendrick's old ski lodge. I didn't know it was still there." Parker wasn't a skier. He was a swimmer and a sailor. "Just where is it?" he asked.

"I'll show you."

"No you won't. You'll tell me."

"I'm coming. It was my fault. Besides, someone else might get shot. If they do I'll be there to treat them."

"I hope it won't come to shooting. I'll try to talk to him."

"With Davy Shea there? With him just panting to shoot someone? Anyway, if Joe Prew is ready to listen to anyone talking it will be me."

Parker shrugged. "It's your funeral," he said.

As they started out towards the mountain, Davy said, "Is she coming with us?"

"Yes," Parker said.

Davy didn't question this. "I see," he said.

The moon was up in a clear pale sky and they didn't need lights.

"Which way?" Parker asked.

"This way," Phyllis said.

She hadn't been in the lead but she went out in front now.

"I see how it is," Davy said again. Then he said, "She was breaking the law, Boomer, she shouldn't get away with that."

Parker didn't answer him.

They came into the trees with the snow not very deep underfoot. It was beautiful under the fir trees with their boughs covered with snow so that the tops of the trees glistened in the moonlight.

"Not since I was a kid," Parker said, "have I been out in the woods at night. It's a good time to take a walk."

"Shouldn't we be quiet?" Davy said. He was nervous already and his voice was higher than usual.

"There's a long way to go yet," Phyllis said, and she heard her own voice sounding edgy.

They came out from under the trees and the wind was cold.

"We can see better now," Parker said.

"But can he see us?" young George Stover asked.

"I suppose that's what we'll have to worry about," Parker said almost as if it were a joke.

"There's a dangerous place over there," Phyllis said.

She spoke in a whisper. She pointed to where the mountain fell away. There were cliffs with a sharp drop. In daylight a person could look down and seen the tops of the trees and then the road that ran round the lake with the tops of the telephone poles showing, but at night there was the danger of stepping over the edge by mistake and falling two hundred feet to the rocks below.

"You know this place pretty good," Davy said. "You been up here a lot lately?"

They walked on with no one saying anything until they saw the outline of the collapsed roof of Hendrick's.

"No wonder we never thought to look here," Davy said.

They stopped and tried to see a sign of Joe Prew but nothing moved inside.

"What are we going to do, Boomer?" Davy asked.

"I'll speak to him."

"Is that a good idea? He'll start shooting."

"I'll speak to him," Phyllis said.

"Yes," Davy said, "maybe you should. I figure you've got real friendly with him lately." He turned to Parker. "What we should do is call out to him to surrender and then open fire when he don't."

"I don't know," Parker said. "What do you think, Georgie?" George Stover had been a soldier in the infantry.

George said he thought someone should go round to the back of the lodge to make sure Joe Prew didn't slip off.

Parker sent him to the rear of Hendrick's. He was nervous about losing George Stover because he was steady and Davy wasn't. He couldn't see Davy's face but he could feel him being nervous and ready to shoot anything that moved. Parker had a sudden dreadful vision of Davy shooting down young George Stover by mistake.

"OK," Davy said. "I guess Georgie must be in place now. You going to ask Prew to surrender?"

"I'll do it," Phyllis said.

"OK," Parker said. "You do it."

"Mr Prew," she shouted, "this is Phyllis."

"<u>Mister</u> Prew?" Davy said. "Whenever was Joe Prew mister?"

Phyllis shouted again. "You must give yourself up," she said.

There was no answer. She tried several times more.

"Come on out, Joe," Davy shouted. "You're surrounded."

"I'll go see," Parker said.

He stepped out and was an easy target.

"At least bend down," Davy said.

Phyllis watched the tall, thin figure walking casually towards the broken down lodge. For the first time she noticed that Parker had no gun.

"He's crazy," Davy said. "Three murders there's been and look at him."

"I'm going," Phyllis said.

"Where to?" Davy asked. He thought she wanted to go back down the mountain.

She stepped out into the moonlight and started after Parker.

"Jesus Christ," Davy said. This wasn't the scene he had imagined. He had thought Joe Prew would run out of Hendrick's lodge and be shot down.

"Mr Prew," Phyllis was saying, "it's Phyllis, Fred Skypeck's daughter, I'm coming in to see you. I've got Boomer Daniels with me."

There was the sound of someone moving inside the lodge. Phyllis began to think that maybe Davy Shea had been right to stay behind.

"Joe?" she asked. She could hear her voice sounding very nervous.

"It's me," a man said.

Young George Stover's face appeared in the hole in the side of the lodge where a window had been.

"He's gone," George said.

He turned his flashlight on and swept it round the empty room. Parker bent double and clambered through the hole in the wall. Phyllis followed him.

"You came without a gun?" George asked.

"I forgot it in the excitement," Parker said. He, too, had a flashlight. He shined it about the room.

"Did he leave in a hurry?" he asked. "Did he hear us coming?"

"I guess so," George said.

They saw the food Joe Prew had left behind.

"I wonder how he got that?" George said.

"He must have come down and stolen it," Parker said and he looked at Phyllis.

"There haven't been any reports of that sort of robberies," George said.

"Maybe they don't know it's missing," Parker said.

"Or someone's been helping him," George said.

"Who'd do that?" Parker said. He didn't look at Phyllis this time.

"I wonder if he'll come back?" George said.

"I shouldn't think so."

"He'll come back," Phyllis said.

"Why? For the food?"

"For this," Phyllis said.

She pointed to something on the floor.

Parker looked at her and shook his head for her not to say anything in front of George Stover.

"I guess we might as well go back down," he said. "Tomorrow I'll come up and have a better look around."

Davy was outside. "What's the story?" he asked.

George Stover told him.

"He'll be long gone," Davy said. "We've missed the bus."

Going down in the darkness under the fir trees Parker was walking behind Phyllis.

"What about the pen and paper?" he asked.

"He wants to write something. He wants to put down his side or leave a message for his wife."

"Before he kills himself?"

"That's right."

"You keep quiet," Parker told her. "You keep your mouth shut and don't mention this. Does anyone else know?"

"Milly Tencza."

"Jesus," Parker said, "but at least she won't say anything."

They could hear Davy talking in a loud voice to young George Stover.

"Cripes," Davy was saying, "I was anxious. When I saw you people in the hut with your lights flashing around I thought Joe Prew would come busting out of the woods and shoot you. That's why I kept back, waiting in case he came out and I had to shoot him."

"That was quick thinking," Parker said but he didn't sound convinced.

Jesus, Phyllis thought, Davy Shea's no damned good, Parker wouldn't be able to count on him if some real trouble comes, and with three dead already it looks like real, real trouble's coming.

Chapter 35

After two days Parker stopped watching the mountain. The thinking was that Joe Prew was miles away by now.

Phyllis got this news from Davy Shea who stopped her in the street in the town centre and kept smiling at her while he spoke as if he knew all about her connection with Joe Prew and might at any moment arrest her.

Davy produced his obnoxious grin. "If you're looking for your English boyfriend, you're not going to find him at the Lake House," he said. "He's elsewhere." Davy grinned some more. "Oh yes," he said, "he's got himself a new little friend."

What's this idiot think that's got to do with me? she thought. "How nice," she said.

"She is. Very nice. You'll find him with her now in there." They were standing outside the College Inn.

The last thing Phyllis was going to do was ask Davy Shea who Hugh's new friend was.

But later on she went to the College Inn and saw Hugh in the bar with Edgar Dupre's daughter who was home from Smith for the holidays. Cathy Dupre was a pretty girl and only nineteen, with an earnest face and a cute figure. Phyllis saw them together in the bar and could see that Hugh didn't need any further female company. She turned and was leaving when Bob Blanchard stopped her.

"Are you coming to the carol singing?" he asked.

There was to be carol singing outside the College Inn. They had it every year and every year Phyllis came to it, but Bob Blanchard was anxious about the latest murder at the Lake House cancelling Christmas.

"Of course I'll come if I can," she said.

"You should try to get out and about," Bob Blanchard said. "You're only young once."

She could see from the way he was looking at her that he was thinking she was a woman who didn't have much luck with men. With Jack Pringle back with his wife and Hugh in a corner of the bar with the cute Dupre girl, Phyllis could see why Bob Blanchard might think that way. She thought it too. She wondered who she was going to get involved with next, as if it was something like a force of nature which she really had no control over. The first man who came to mind was Parker Daniels, but this was probably because he was acting as her protector now and that gave her a good feeling. Still, she could sometimes see herself with him. Mostly she put that down to something maternal she felt for the man who never seemed to have an ironed shirt. But she thought now that she would be comfortable with Parker. He was a cosy sort of person. She could see herself watching television with him at night, if, that is, he ever got his TV fixed.

But romance wasn't her chief worry at this moment. The death of Mary Barch was what troubled her.

It was my fault, she said to herself, Mary Barch wouldn't be dead if it wasn't for me, and if Parker Daniels wasn't protecting me I'd be in jail now for aiding and abetting Joe Prew.

And how could she be sure that Parker would remain silent? Or, she thought, she herself might confess, unable to keep the guilt of it in. I might very well do that, she told herself, I can often be that kind of sucker.

She drove to the Lake House to see Milly Tencza. I've got to find out how she's feeling about it, she said to herself, tell her she doesn't have to confess to helping Joe. Milly's got enough problems without being an accessory to murder.

When Phyllis got to the Lake House she could see a kid out skating on the ice. It was Artie Barch again, he was incorrigible and the ice wasn't safe, there was still the great slash across the middle where the water hadn't frozen.

Phyllis went out on the ice to bring him in. She took the kid by the hand. "Artie," she said, "if you're going to skate keep close to the shore."

That's good advice for life, she thought. I should have told myself that a long time ago.

"Aunt Mary's dead," the boy said.

She wondered what all this trauma was doing to him.

"I saw it," he said.

"Don't be so silly, Milly was the only one in the room. You shouldn't tell stories."

She didn't want to be rough on the kid, but he had to learn.

"I was outside," Artie said.

"You saw Mr Prew?"

"It wasn't Joe Prew. He had the same hat but it wasn't him."

This was something different if he was telling the truth.

"Is this another story, Artie? Who was it if it wasn't Joe Prew?"

"I don't know. He had the hat, but he didn't have Joe Prew's walk."

Joe Prew had a crazy walk. She had forgotten about that. It was something kids imitated.

Suddenly Phyllis became worried for Artie's safety. After all, there was a killer loose and Artie had seen him in the woods.

"Listen, Artie," she said, "don't tell anyone what you saw."

Artie seemed to be taking this in and then he said, "How far out on the lake can I go?" He had forgotten about murdered aunts, he was thinking about skating.

"Keep close to the shore."

"How close?"

She left him and went into the Lake House. The big Christmas tree was still standing undecorated in the middle of Wanda's piled-up furniture, which was junk and not in any way antiques. Someone had kidded Wanda about the furniture, or, more likely, she had kidded herself. Anyway, it would never be used now, she said to herself. She couldn't see Carmen running a hotel, not even with outside help. The Lake House was spooky. There was something sinister about it, with the furniture and the bare tree and the sullen Carmen. Also three corpses.

When Phyllis got to Milly Tencza she forgot about what Artie Barch claimed to have seen.

"We did a bad thing," Phyllis said to Milly. She used her hands but also spoke out loud so that Milly could read her lips.

"How?" Milly asked.

"Protecting Joe Prew."

Milly's hands and fingers were still, like a long silence.

"I'm not sure," she said.

"Not sure?

"That it was Joe Prew."

"The hat?"

"Yes. The hat. It was what I saw. But there was something else not like him."

"His walk?"

"Yes, he didn't walk or run like him."

"Who?"

"I don't know."

"Or you won't say?"

"Whatever."

"You're afraid of being wrong again?"

"Yes."

Phyllis kept asking her, but she wouldn't say anything other than that she was not entirely certain it was Joe Prew.

Phyllis left Milly's room and found Carmen at the reception desk talking to the gloriously curvy Beverly Choquette.

"I'm going to the carol singing," Carmen was saying. "Why shouldn't I go? I've got to have some Christmas, don't I? I can't just sit in here in the dark all on my own thinking of people getting murdered."

Phyllis went by them without speaking. Outside, Artie Barch was still skating. He was not keeping to the shore.

"Artie," Phyllis called to him. "Come here."

The child pretended he couldn't hear.

"Artie," Phyllis shouted, "I want to ask you something."

But he skated further away.

Forget it, Phyllis told herself. But if it wasn't Joe Prew, who was it? And now more than ever there was the danger of Joe Prew being shot down out of hand by Davy Shea.

Chapter 36

Parker telephoned the Air Force base at Westover. He knew he should have done this right away. As soon as they found Mary Barch dead Parker should have checked out the boyfriend's whereabouts. But it had seemed so obvious that Joe Prew had done it. There was, after all, the red hunting cap with the long flaps that tied under the chin.

As it was Pete Petrolnik hadn't been informed of his girlfriend's death until five hours after the murder. In five hours Petrolnik could have shot Mary Barch and then taken a very leisurely drive back to the house in Springfield, which is where he was when Parker finally got through to him, telling him the sad news and hearing him at first cursing in disbelief and then choking and gasping trying to keep back the tears. To Parker, Petrolnik's sobs and gasps on the phone had sounded authentic. But he knew it didn't take an Oscar nominee to choke and gasp convincingly over a phone. It was the long silences between that did it. The silences were what would have won the Oscar, they were so convincing. But over a phone you never knew what the person was doing while you were listening to those heartbroken silences.

Of course it was not exactly obvious what motive Petrolnik could have for killing Mary Barch. In fact there did not seem to be one.

Now, when Parker finally got put on to a colonel at the Air Force base, he found out that Petrolnik didn't have the opportunity. He had been in an airplane hangar when Mary Barch was shot, doing whatever sergeants do in hangars, which was, Parker thought, probably eating jelly doughnuts while the corporals repaired the airplanes.

"Thanks," Parker said to the colonel, and Parker was thankful. Waiting all that time to check out a more or less obvious suspect was the sort of police work Parker's enemies would expect from a police chief who was only an invention of the mayor's, but he wasn't going to be caught out, not this time at least.

"That's that," Parker said when he put down the phone.

"You should have done it two days ago," Davy said. "Where are you going now?" he asked as Parker put on his coat and headed for the door.

"To Brown's Ferry, to the vet's."

"Oh, yes, the poochie. How is he?"

"She," Parker said. Davy was the sort of person who always refer to dogs as he and cats as she.

"She's OK," Parker said.

Parker went out to his old car. The sky was mostly blue but there was a patch of charcoal grey over the mountain where the weather came from. It was cold and it felt like snow. There was also a wind picking up from the North East, from over the mountain, and so if there was snow up there it would be coming pretty soon.

He thought of the State Troopers out searching for Joe Prew. That was cold work. Cold work also for Joe Prew hiding out in it. He'll be heading back this way, Parker thought. If he's not thinking clearly his footsteps will take him back home. He'll find he's run in a circle. It was nearly magic — mysterious anyway — the way a man left on his own without a map or compass will travel in a circle.

He wondered how good the State Troopers were. Most of them were city boys. Parker didn't think they knew the woods and what a man would do in them. I gave up the watch on Hendrick's too soon, he said to himself, Joe Prew will be heading back there. Even if he doesn't realize it himself, that's where his footsteps will take him.

Parker heard his American Staffordshire terrier Moll barking as soon as he got to the vet's and opened the door to get out of the car. She knew it was him. The vet's was on the old Route 5 and there was heavy traffic going by and several cars stopping and people getting out to go into Dinny's Donuts next door to the vet's, but still Moll heard him. And I heard her, too, he thought, I know that's her bark, though there are other dogs barking.

Moll was full of herself. Parker took her out and put her on the back seat of the car and he hadn't driven very far when she came into the front seat and started barking at him to stop and let her out for a call of nature.

They were still in Brown's Ferry. He saw Jack Pringle's house.

He wanted to apologize to Jack Pringle. He pulled up outside Jack's house. They were old friends, in fact friends didn't come much older. If they had drifted apart they hadn't drifted very far, they couldn't in a small town like North Holford. Jack had been rich and Parker had been poor and that had put a gap between them when they got old enough for that sort of thing to matter, but they had still been boys together.

Moll was going on Jack Pringle's lawn.

"I guess that's adding insult to injury," Parker said to the dog, "now Jack's got another reason to dislike me."

Parker went down the side of the house to the back door. Old friends called at the back door. Moll followed him.

The lawn behind the house went down to the lake. Jack's house here was small compared to the Lake House, still it was a good house. Parker couldn't see why Jack Pringle couldn't be perfectly happy there. It was much more suitable for a man on his own than the big place across the water. Even if Sue Pringle was well enough to return to him it was plenty big enough. It seemed crazy to Parker that Jack should need the Lake House again to give his marriage a happy ending. But of course it wasn't Jack's money. Old Mr Mason was the one who was putting up the money to buy the Lake House to please his daughter, to make her as happy as she could be with whatever was wrong with her.

Parker heard a car pulling into Jack's drive. He turned and was surprised seeing Sue Pringle's long legs getting out of it. He hadn't thought her well enough to drive a car.

She came down to him, walking perfectly well on her long, beautiful legs and smiling, a warm Kentucky smile, at Parker and Moll, but mostly at Moll, and not looking in the least unwell.

I've got to watch myself with women, Parker thought, I'm much too easily swayed by a pretty face, at least I am when it's smiling at me. He thought of Phyllis Skypeck, hiding Joe Prew out and then his not arresting her for it.

"Parker," Sue Pringle said, "I'm so glad you and Jack have made it up. Where is he?"

The big smile was still there, and added to the long, beautiful legs were the sexy eyes.

"I don't know," Parker said, trying not to look too closely at those eyes. "I only got here a minute before you did. Jack and I, we haven't made it up yet."

"I'm sure you will," she said, as if Jack and he were only small boys.

Then she turned and looked towards the lake.

"What's going on out there?" she said.

A man was running out from this side of the lake to whatever was going on in the middle. The running man was carrying something. He was dragging it along behind him and at first Parker thought it was a sled, but then it flashed in the sunlight and he saw it was a metal ladder.

"It's Jack," Sue said.

So that's it, Parker thought, that's how it was done.

He couldn't see at once what was going on. Then it was clear enough. There was someone broken through the ice. Parker could see a head and struggling arms. It was a child.

Parker and Sue watched as Jack laid the ladder down across the big gash of water until each of its ends rested on solid ice. Then Jack crawled along the ladder and pulled the child from the water.

It was Artie Barch.

Jack was on his feet, carrying Artie to the Lake House across the ice.

"That was heroic," Parker said. "I guess he must have seen the kid go through and he grabbed the ladder and went out."

But Sue wasn't listening. She ran away up the lawn on her long beautiful legs towards her car.

How do I prove it? Parker asked himself. And a small voice inside him rather hoped he wouldn't be able to.

Parker caught up with Sue Pringle.

"What's wrong?" he asked.

He was holding her. Even with those beautiful legs of hers she looked like she might fall down.

"You can't drive like this," he said, "come into the house and sit down."

She was in no state to argue. She was white and the sexy light had gone out of her eyes and she looked like she'd never smile again.

Parker helped her to the open back door. They went into the house. There were logs on the kitchen floor, thrown down as if someone had been carrying them and suddenly let them fall. It was cold, colder than it should have been simply because the back door had been left open.

Sue sat down at the kitchen table. Her face was white and her hands were trembling. Parker's terrier came in and sat looking at her.

"I don't suppose it matters," Sue said, "there aren't any children."

Parker didn't know what she was talking about.

"It's terribly cold in here," he said.

"Yes," she said, "I was going to come over earlier today. I telephoned Jack but he said the central heating was broken and he was going to try and start the old coal furnace but I shouldn't come over until he did."

Parker looked at the logs on the floor. "He must have been trying to light a fire, but then the drama happened on the ice," he said.

"Yes," Sue said, and the tone of her voice and the expression on her face, made it seem like Jack had done something terribly sad.

"Listen," Parker said, "I could take a look at the boiler. There's no use sitting here in the freezing cold waiting for the hero's return. In recent years I've taken a keen amateur interest in central heating systems." He saw her begin to smile. "Oh," he said, "someone has told you my sad story."

"I'm sorry. It was the first thing Jack told me about you when I came back."

"I'll take a look at the furnace," Parker said.

"You don't have to."

She was nervous again and really didn't look well.

"It's no trouble," Parker said.

"Forget it," she said. "Jack'll do it when he gets back."

"Nonsense," Parker said.

He walked to the cellar door.

"You don't have to come down," he said.

"I don't mind."

Her face still didn't have any colour and the sexy look was still gone from her eyes.

Moll followed them down to the cellar too.

There were two boilers, the new oil-fired one and the old solid fuel furnace that dated back to some time before the Second World War.

Parker examined the oil-fired furnace. It was clear why it wasn't working. It had been switched off. He pushed the switch to on. There was a few seconds delay and then he heard it ignite.

"Wonderful," Sue Pringle said. "What did you do? I can't believe the heat is on again. You're a wizard."

She smiled but somehow she still managed to look sad.

"No wizard," Parker said. "It wasn't switched on. He must have turned it off by mistake. You'd think he'd have checked the switch to see before going to the trouble of getting wood to light the old one."

She was standing in front of the half-opened door of the old furnace.

"Let's go upstairs, it's dusty down here," she said. But she didn't move. She still stood in front of the old solid fuel furnace waiting for Parker to turn and go up the stairs. She tried to close the furnace door with one hand behind her back so Parker couldn't see, but he saw something.

"Jesus," Parker said.

He didn't shout. He said it almost in a whisper as if he couldn't believe the thought he'd just had.

He walked towards her.

"What is it?" she said.

"Please get out of the way," Parker said.

She didn't move. He had to push her away from the door of the old furnace.

Her face was paler than ever and her eyes were frightened rather than haunted or sexy.

He opened the door.

Sue Pringle made another sound, a gasp of pain or fear.

There was a red cap inside the furnace.

Parker took it out. It had ear-flaps that tied under the chin. There were more clothes inside. He recognized them from the description of the clothes that were stolen from Gus Barch's room. There was also a pair of boots in the furnace. The sole of the right foot was worn away where it had been dragged along the floor for a number of years.

"You knew," Parker said. "When you saw him go across the ice with the ladder to rescue Artie Barch you knew right away. Or was it that you knew already and were frightened that I'd see the way he got to the Lake House that night to kill Gus Barch?"

Sue didn't say anything, but she had more colour in her face. And her eyes weren't fearful or haunted any more. They hadn't gone back to being sexy. They were full of hate now looking at him.

"Of course," Parker said, "Jack set it up to incriminate Joe Prew but me and the others went too quickly up to Hendrick's. We got there before Jack could plant these clothes. That meant Jack had to destroy them. Gus's missing clothes would have remained a mystery. The old furnace was the easiest place to get rid of them and to put off suspicion he turned off the oil-fired central heating and made up a story about it being broken."

"He should have let that damned kid drown," Sue said.

She didn't say it loudly. She was speaking to herself.

Then she looked like she was about to faint. Parker looked for a chair for her to sit on. There weren't any, but there was a packing case. It was covered with dust and he wiped it off and gave it to her to sit down before she fell down.

"Thanks," she said.

For a while then no one spoke. Then Parker said, "I never thought it could be him."

"Even when you started digging at the Lake House looking for my dead body?"

She smiled at him, forgiving him for thinking she might have been a dead body so unceremoniously dumped in a makeshift grave.

"I suppose it was Phyllis being here the night of Gus's murder that made me fail to really suspect him," Parker said.

"You suspected him enough to start digging at the Lake House," Sue said.

"That was Edgar."

"Edgar?"

"Edgar Dupre."

"Oh," she said, "<u>that</u> Edgar."

"Jesus," Parker said.

Once again he only whispered it, amazed at what he had just heard. There were two Edgars in this.

"Edgar Geep LaMay," he said. "He's the one buried at the Lake House."

"Yes," she said, "that's why I ran away from Jack. I couldn't continue living with him, and I couldn't inform on him. I was his wife. Jack said it was an accident and I suppose I wanted to believe him."

"You were into Geep LaMay for a lot of money?"

She smiled, a real smile, it was amazing seeing it.

"No, not so much. But I did use Geep LaMay to bet on the horses. I'm from Kentucky. I've got to follow the horses."

"Christ," Parker said, "it was them having the same name. He got killed for that?"

Her eyes were incredibly sexy, and she smiled as if she had a secret that was very humorous, that he would die laughing at when she told him.

"Jack got them confused. He knew I was having an affair, but he didn't know who with. When he asked me I was frightened the way he was. I thought he was going to kill me. A big handsome man like Jack, he'd had it all his own way his whole life. He couldn't stand the idea of a wife being unfaithful to him. He gripped me by the throat. He asked who the man was. I said Edgar. I could hardly breathe. He took his hands away from my throat. 'Geep LaMay?' he said. I didn't know what to do. I could see how angry he was. I didn't want him to hurt Edgar Dupre. I let him think it was Geep LaMay. I thought, being a bookie, he could look after himself. I didn't think Jack would kill him. I wanted to protect Edgar Dupre. I loved him. I think I still do. That's why I went away. I didn't want Jack to find out about me and Edgar Dupre. I never got in touch with Edgar again after that. I couldn't take the chance of Jack finding out."

"And you knew Geep LaMay was buried at the Lake House?"

"What?"

She glanced up at him, annoyed at being called back to murder after the beautiful story of her sacrifice for love.

"You knew the body was buried there?" Parker said.

"Of course."

"And you didn't say anything?"

"What was he, Geep LaMay, just a cheap crook? Of course he was good-looking, in a flashy way, Jack could just about believe my story."

Parker watched her. When she told her story about saving Edgar Dupre she had looked terribly sad and self-sacrificing. He had believed her. I'm a real sucker for these women and their tales, he thought.

"You're some woman," Parker said, "letting a man get murdered to save your lover."

His voice sounded angry and that was the way he wanted it to sound.

"What are you going to do?" she asked.

"I'm going to arrest Jack, and I'm going to arrest you."

"Me?" The sexy eyes went big with amazement. "Why me?"

"Because you knew a man had been killed and you didn't do anything about it."

"Geep LaMay? I can't believe you're getting so angry about Geep LaMay."

"Don't worry, you'll get off. Jack was your husband and the jury will like you standing by him. They might even like you protecting Edgar Dupre. Of course up here they might not appreciate a rich Southern girl being so off-hand about a low-rent guy like LaMay getting himself murdered by mistake. You might suffer some inverted snobbery there, but you'll most likely walk free."

She sat quietly on the packing case in the dusty cellar. Parker thought he didn't have anything more to say until she glanced up at him and he saw something in her sexy eyes.

"Of course," he said, "Jack may have a different story. Maybe Jack'll say you killed Geep all on your own and he's been covering up for you. He could say that, and it might even be true. It's a wonderful story about Edgar Dupre. I think people will weep in court when they hear you tell it the way you told it to me here. And the high-price lawyer your daddy buys for you might even work up a few extra dramatic tricks for you. But if Jack turns against you, and we learn that you were into Geep for a lot of money which Jack wasn't too happy about paying, maybe you won't walk."

"You bastard," she said. "You know I'm not well."

"I know that sometimes you don't look well, I haven't seen a doctor's report, but we don't let people off with murder because they're feeling peaky."

"You're not the way I remember you, Parker, you used to be rather noble and chivalrous for a Yankee."

"Let's go upstairs," Parker said. "You can use those eyes on me and I'll try to look noble and chivalrous while we wait for Jack to come home."

They went upstairs and Parker started to worry that he didn't have a gun. It was the sort of stupid thing he would forget to have on him when there was a murderer on the loose.

I suppose, he thought, if Jack comes bursting back in here and finds me with the evidence he might not think twice about doing away with me. He's already gone on a killing spree, I don't see why he should stop with me.

Parker used the telephone in the kitchen. He kept glancing toward the lake, expecting Jack to appear.

He got through to Davy at the station.

"I'm at Brown's Ferry," he said, "is there anybody in this area?"

"In Brown's Ferry? Why should there be anybody in Brown's Ferry? What's up, Boomer?"

"I need a man here."

He told Davy why.

"Jesus," Davy said, "this is something. Hold on. Georgie Stover is at the Mohawk Trailer Park on a domestic. I'll call him."

The Mohawk Trailer Park was just down the old highway. Parker waited while Davy tried to reach young George Stover.

He looked at Sue still sitting being sad at the kitchen table. He wondered if he should smile at her the way people do when they're on the phone and there is a pause and someone else is in the room waiting. He decided a smile wasn't appropriate. And then Sue smiled at him but the smile didn't reach her sexy eyes.

Parker was thinking of Jack leaving Phyllis Skypeck fast asleep in bed and going across the ice in a blizzard and shooting Gus Barch on the Lake House porch while Davy Shea was asleep only a few feet away. And then Wanda, who must have been in it with Jack, who had indeed drugged Davy, had come down with the clothes to make it look like Joe Prew had broken in to steal something dry and warm to wear. Then something had happened. Something that made Jack and Wanda fall out and he'd killed her in a sudden rage.

He waited for Davy to get in touch with George Stover at the Mohawk Trailer Park and he thought about how Jack might at any moment come bursting into the kitchen and do something unpredictable.

"I got Georgie," Davy said. "He's on his way."

"And you," Parker said, "go to the Lake House and pick up Jack."

Parker sat down now, opposite Sue Pringle, but then he realized his back was to the door. That, he thought, was another stupid thing. He got up. He felt like asking Sue if there was a gun in the house that he could borrow. It would be embarrassing asking the wife of a murderer if he could borrow something to possibly shoot her husband with, but then he asked her anyway.

Chapter 37

As Davy Shea drove to the Lake House he wondered if he was at last going to have the opportunity to shoot someone properly. It did not seem beyond the promise of the American Dream for him to have the chance to gun someone down. He was, after all, a cop. When kids, when women, when anybody, found out he was a policeman they always sooner or later got round to asking if he had ever shot anyone. It always made him feel like less of a cop to have to tell them no. At least that was the way he felt when he admitted the truth. When he didn't say no, when he shrugged and said "Sure", he could see their eyes light up and he knew what it must be like to be a real tough guy cop who had been in shoot-outs and lived to tell the tale, except a tough guy didn't talk about them and only shrugged and said "sure" and then went silent as though deep in thought about the terrible places he'd been and the awful things he'd seen.

Of course Davy couldn't put on a show like that with anyone from North Holford, at least with no grown-ups in North Holford, only with kids and very, very inexperienced girls. The others knew that nothing ever really happened in North Holford. Except now it did. It was happening and happening, and, he guessed, it was going to be happening some more real soon.

It's my rite of passage, Davy told himself. He'd heard that expression, rite of passage, and he'd liked it, there was a dramatic sound to it that appealed to him.

There was, however, one difficulty and it was a big one.

Jack Pringle had been killing people; in a few days before Christmas Jack had been putting them down one, two, three — a bullet right straight in the face, a head bashed in, and another corpse with a bullet in the back.

Jack certainly wasn't fooling around. It didn't look like he would go quietly. When Boomer said "Go to the Lake House and pick up Jack Pringle" it sounded like a very routine sort of thing. But Jack Pringle was proving himself not to be a very routine sort of guy. Davy couldn't see him coming quietly. The rite of passage that he had been looking forward to experiencing now changed into something else. It might be a *baptism of fire,* which was another great phrase, it sounded real good, but was perhaps one of those things that was best left missing from a policeman's CV. He'd be like a cop in New York going up an alley with a shooter waiting for him. But that cop, Davy thought, always had back up. There wasn't any back up now. There was only goofy Boomer Daniels waiting across the lake in Brown's Ferry in case Jack Pringle returned home. That was no help for Davy going into the Lake House with the possibility of a shooter waiting there.

Davy called Georgie Stover on the car phone.

"This guy's a shooter," Davy said. "I need back up."

George Stover didn't seem surprised by Davy's language.

"I'll come," Georgie said. "I'm taking Mrs Pringle into the station and then I'll come."

That didn't seem very urgent to Davy. That didn't seem like back up and he was already pulling up to the front porch of the Lake House and it was standing there looking dark and ominous in the fading winter sun.

Cripes, he said to himself, I've got to go in and I don't know what the fuck's there.

He picked up the phone and called Georgie again.

"I'm going in," he said.

"Okie dokie," Georgie said, "I'll be dropping off Mrs Pringle real soon."

Georgie sounded to Davy like someone who was running a taxi service. Okie dokie wasn't the sort of response Davy had been looking for.

He took out his gun. It was a .38 Smith & Wesson with a two-inch barrel. A real big city cop's piece, but it only had five shots. Also he didn't know how good a two-inch barrel would be for hitting a target that was any sort of distance away. Not very good, he thought.

"Jeez cripes," he said as he opened the car door and got out. I'm a perfect target, he thought, one hell of a perfect target for any crazy goddam sonofabitch shooter who wants to shoot.

He went up the steps of the Lake House and pushed open the door. Holy shit, he said to himself, this is it.

There wasn't anyone there. Only Wanda's crazy furniture piled up and the big undecorated Christmas tree.

"Hello," Davy said.

No one answered.

He walked through the stacked up furniture.

"Hello?" he said again, hearing his voice sounding frightened and a bit too polite for a cop coming into a room that might hold a killer.

He didn't know what he expected, maybe Jack Pringle to pop out with a gun in his hand.

"Oh, it's you," a voice said.

He knew the voice. He knew the nasty tone in it.

Beverly Choquette came out from behind the reception desk.

She was still dynamite. Even in the state he was in Davy noticed how dynamite she was.

"What's all the shouting about?" she asked.

She glanced down at the Smith & Wesson. She didn't seem very surprised to see it in his hand.

"Where's everybody?" Davy asked.

He had an idea that Jack Pringle might be there, that he maybe had a gun trained on Beverly Choquette and had told her to get rid of Davy or he'd shoot them both.

"Carmen and Duane have taken Artie to the hospital," she said. "Artie fell in the lake only he got rescued. Then they're going to the carol singing at the College Inn. I'm the only one here and I'm not staying. I'm leaving Milly in charge. Who's going to come here with people keeping on getting killed? Is there anything else you want to know?"

It was the longest speech Beverly Choquette had ever made to him.

"Have you seen Jack Pringle?" he asked.

"Jack? Sure I've seen him. He rescued Artie. He came across the lake and pulled him out of the water,"

Davy had his finger on the trigger. Anytime now, he thought, I might have to start shooting. Five shots, he wondered if that would be enough. Jack Pringle was a big rugged guy. He'd take a lot of killing.

"Is he here?" he asked.

"No," Beverly said, "he went skiing. He borrowed some skis and he went skiing."

"Skiing?" Davy said. "He went skiing?"

That didn't seem like something a crazed killer should do.

Davy could see himself reflected in the glass of a framed poster of some hotshot skiers from long ago. He didn't think he looked very hotshot. He thought he looked real dumb standing there with his gun out and his mouth open.

Chapter 38

Parker was sitting in Jack Pringle's kitchen when Davy called to say that Jack wasn't at the Lake House because Jack had gone skiing. There wasn't anyone at the Lake House, Davy said, except Beverly Choquette who, Davy said, was leaving herself any minute now.

"Skiing?" Parker asked in a disbelieving tone.

"Skiing," Davy said.

"You sure you got that right?"

"That's what she said. I asked her three or four times and that's what she always came up with. What am I supposed to do now, Boomer?"

"Go after him."

"I can't ski."

"I don't suppose you have to."

"On my own?" Davy asked. "I'll get lost up there."

Davy had lived all his life in North Holford surrounded by woods and mountains but he never went into them. He sat instead watching TV and dreaming of being a big city cop with nothing around him but skyscrapers and pavement.

"Wait for George Stover," Parker said and he could hear Davy sigh with relief.

Parker went back to waiting in the kitchen for Jack to return. Parker had a shotgun on his lap. Sue Pringle had displayed no emotion when she showed Parker where Jack kept his gun. Then she went off with Georgie Stover with only one look back at the house where her husband might possibly get himself shot down.

The central heating was back on and the house was beginning to warm up. It seemed incredible to Parker that Jack would suddenly have an urge to go skiing.

Jesus, Parker said to himself, Jack's a cold-blooded bastard. When Gus Barch wouldn't sell the Lake House the opportunity came along for Jack to get rid of him when crazy Joe Prew shot up the Emperor of Ice Cream and dropped one of his guns as he ran away and Jack strolling through the woods found that gun. Jack's a quick thinker, Parker thought. In no time at all he talked Wanda Barch into going along with him. He must have been playing around with her too, with her daydreaming of getting rid of Gus. He was also going out with Phyllis Skypeck, and all the time without either Wanda or Phyllis knowing that he was working on reconciliation with his wife because she was the one who had the money to buy the Lake House. Jack Pringle was a smooth item, Parker had always known that, and Jack was also a man who could act on the spur of the moment, able to take advantage of a situation when it came along.

Jesus, Parker thought, he's going to kill Joe Prew. He doesn't know I've found the evidence. Or that Sue told me about Geep LaMay. Jack thinks all he has to do is kill Joe Prew and make it look like crazy old Joe, full of remorse for killing Gus and Wanda and Mary Barch, has committed suicide, and then Jack burns the evidence in the furnace and he's in the clear.

But where was Joe Prew? Why should Jack be able to find him? Parker couldn't find him and neither could the State Troopers.

Then Parker said to himself, I know where Joe Prew's gone: But the trouble is Jack also probably knows.

Chapter 39

Phyllis couldn't stop thinking about what Milly Tencza and Artie Barch said about the man in the red hat.

She drove out of the town centre and up into the woods as far as the car would go without getting stuck in snow.

There were snow boots and ski pants on the back seat and she took off her skirt and put them on without any fear of someone coming along and seeing her undressing.

She put on her red hat, pulling it down tight and pushed her hair under it. Then she started to walk.

She was going the same way she had led Boomer Daniels and the other cops the night they had gone to find Joe Prew. There had been a fresh fall of snow and there was no sign of their tracks. Once out from under the trees it grew colder and the wind was so strong blowing up whirling snow that she thought she might walk too close to the edge of the mountain where it fell away into sheer cliffs.

She reached the top. It was snowing now, it wasn't simply the wind blowing it up off the ground. She had trouble seeing. Then she saw the outline of the lodge. There was a man standing in front of it. She couldn't tell who it was. She went closer, moving with difficulty where the wind had created drifts.

"You!" the man said and there was something odd about his voice. He was peering at her through the snow and then turned his head and glanced back towards the hole in the wall of the lodge.

When he turned to look at her again she was close enough to see who it was. She was glad to see him. She had been half expecting Joe Prew to shoot her down.

"What's wrong?" she asked. "What are you doing here?"

The wind dropped and she could see Jack's face quite clearly. He looked like he was seeing a ghost.

"Phyllis," he said, "I've been meaning to talk to you."

It wasn't much of a setting in which to meet an ex-lover who had dumped her to go back to his wife, but he was smiling that old smile that she knew from before, the slow lazy smile of seduction, and she'd always been a sucker for it.

"I'm looking for Joe Prew," she said. She ran her tongue over her lips, feeling where they were chapped. Then she tried to wipe them dry. "Let's go in," she said, "we don't want to stand around out here."

He had skis with him. They were standing upright where he had poked them in the snow.

"I don't want to go in there," he said.

He looked like he was going to put on the skis and go away. I guess I was wrong about the seduction, she told herself.

"Is Joe Prew here?" she asked.

"I don't know," he said. "I've only arrived."

She was bending down ready to step through the hole in the wall where the window had been.

"Are you coming?" she asked.

She stepped through the hole.

"Jesus," she said. "Jesus Christ Almighty."

Joe Prew was lying dead on the floor. He was wearing his red cap with the long flaps that tied under his chin and there was a gun in his hand and a big hole in the cap where a bullet had gone through.

"Christ," she said, "come in here and look at this."

"What?" He was still outside.

"Old Joe Prew, the poor bastard," she said, "he finally did it."

Jack came in and stood beside her peering down at Joe Prew.

"We better report this," he said.

He was anxious to leave and who wouldn't be, she thought. But she still stood there gazing at Joe Prew.

"The poor loony," she said, "he kicked off a horrendous chain of events when he got the idea to shoot up the Emperor of Ice Cream to get the attention of his runaway wife in Hartford, Connecticut."

"I guess that ends it," Jack said.

"Yes," she said, but she still stood looking at Joe Prew.

Then she squatted down next to him and touched his face. It was warm and blood was still trickling down from under his cap. He hadn't been dead long.

She searched the floor around the body.

"Where is it?" she asked.

"Where's what?" Jack was anxious to go. "Leave it to the police. We shouldn't touch anything."

He seemed to her to have more confidence in Parker Daniels than he used to have.

"Here it is," she said.

She found the paper and pen that she had lent to Joe Prew and with which he was going to write his final message to the world, or, at least, to his ex-wife.

The paper was blank.

"That's odd," she said.

"What is?"

She didn't answer him.

She knelt on the broken boards of the floor, many of them simply lying loose, and she stared at the blank pieces of paper and she knew that Joe Prew had not killed himself.

She glanced up at Jack and then she looked away.

There was something wrong with Jack's face. There had been something wrong with his face when he first saw her in the half-blinding snow outside. His mouth had been hanging open as if he was seeing a ghost. "You!" he'd said and his voice had been full of fear. My red hat, she thought, that was what he was seeing. Coming out of the snowstorm all bundled up he couldn't see it was me. He only saw the red of my hat and it gave him a shock because he had just shot the red-hatted Joe Prew.

That's a bit fanciful, she thought. But there was the blank sheet of paper, and the bullet hole in Joe Prew's cap was wrong. People don't blow their brains out holding a gun up so high on their heads. When a man is committing suicide he picks up the gun and places the barrel against his temple. When people talk about shooting themselves they pretend to be holding a gun and place their index fingers to the side of their heads. Or they put the barrel in their mouths.

Chapter 40

She looked at Jack and she thought, he knows I know.

It sent a wave of terror through her. Her hands were trembling.

This is crazy, she thought, he wouldn't kill me. I've slept with him, I was his girlfriend, he said I was the most wonderful thing in the world.

She looked at the gun in Joe Prew's hand. Rigor Mortis wouldn't have set in yet. The fingers round the gun wouldn't be too stiff. She might be able to grab it.

She decided to play dumb.

"A gun like this," she said, "it'd make a lot of noise. Didn't you hear anything?"

She wondered if that seemed innocent enough. It didn't seem it to her. It sounded like a police detective questioning a suspect.

"No," Jack said. "I didn't hear anything."

He's playing dumb too, she thought, and his play-acting isn't any better than mine.

She tried something different.

"You didn't tell me about your wife. What'd you think? Did you think I didn't have any feelings? I was crazy about you. You really gave me a shock, suddenly producing that wife, I can't tell you how that made me feel."

"I'm still crazy about you, Phyllis," he said.

He didn't sound any more real than she had. Of course, a love scene over a corpse was a difficult one to play.

"Susan's very ill," he said.

"Yes," she said. She attempted to look sacrificial, on the verge of tears.

"There's no reason why she should come between us," he said. "Of course, we'll have to be more careful."

He assumed a sad expression, as though stricken with thwarted love.

"We can be together lots," he said. "And then..."

He paused. He meant when the illness had finally conquered Sue.

"I love you, Phyllis," he said.

Jesus, she thought, he'll make it look like Joe Prew killed me before committing suicide. Stanley Howse, even without the befuddlement of a couple of belts inside him, wouldn't be able to tell the differences in the times of death.

She picked one up one of the loose boards on the floor and hit him with it.

She got him across the face and blood flew out. She could feel it hot on her own face and she could see it all over his. She couldn't imagine what had caused that much blood and then she saw there were three nails sticking out of the board.

He wasn't down. She hit him again. He went down this time. There was more blood. She was used to seeing blood, it shouldn't trouble her but it did.

Before she knew what she was doing she was out of the lodge standing in the cold with the snow falling and the wind blowing it up all around her and she didn't know what to do.

Jack's skis were there. She thought she could put them on and boom down the mountain free as anything, but she'd have to adjust the clamps to fit her boots. That would take time and Jack might come out and shoot her.

She ran in the blinding snow not sure of where she was heading.

I should have picked up the gun, she said to herself. When he went down after the second time I should have broken Joe Prew's fingers if I had to and got that gun. But would I have used it? That would have been something totally out of character. And was hitting a man across the face with a board with nails sticking out of it in character? I guess it is now, she told herself.

She stopped running and stood trying to catch her breath. If he gets up and comes after me on those skis, I won't be able to outrun him, she told herself.

The cliff, she thought, he can't come skiing after me down the cliff. But can I get down it? In this snow and with all this wind?

There was no alternative.

She made her way to the cliff edge and looked over.

He'll never think I went this way, she thought. Only a complete lunatic would try something like this.

She had done it before. When she was a girl she'd come up the mountain that way. She couldn't remember if she had gone down the same way. Anyway that had been in the summer a long time ago without snow or wind and with nobody after her with a gun.

She went over the side, her toes digging into cracks and her fingers clutching at any holds in the rock.

The snow stopped. She could look down and see the tremendous fall she would take if she slipped. She could see the tops of trees and, a little way out of the woods, the telegraph poles on the edge of the road that ran round the lake. A couple of times her foot slipped and the rock crumbled away as she gripped it and she almost toppled over before she got another hold.

The wind came up again and although it made things difficult she was glad about it because the swirling snow would make it hard for Jack to see her.

There was a fall of rock above her head. Several small boulders came tumbling down near where she was hanging on to a ledge. Then more followed.

She knew what was happening. Jack was up there. He had spotted her on the cliff face and was attempting to dislodge her.

The stones stopped falling.

She went sideways across the rock face, making for a place where she could let herself go and drop down to where the snow was piled in a bank that would cushion her fall.

She was almost to the end of the ledge when she heard him. He sounded close.

She looked up and what she saw then frightened her so much she nearly fell.

He was peering over the ledge not fifteen feet from her.

He had a white handkerchief tied round his face where the nails had caught him. The handkerchief was stained with blood.

She turned on the ledge so her back was to the rock. There was nothing to hold onto. She glanced down to the piled snow. It didn't look so safe now. She could see places where big boulders showed through the snow.

She pushed herself off the rockface. For a moment she thought she was going to die and then she came down hard. There was no rock under the snow. She landed on her backside and started to slide. She tried to stop herself but she was going too fast.

She shot in under the tall fir trees and a tree stopped her. She hit it hard enough to shake the snow off the boughs. The breath was knocked out of her. She lay wondering if anything was broken.

Then she stood up. I did it, she said to herself, I jumped off the mountain and I'm all right.

The way ahead led straight down under the cover of the trees to the road that circled the lake. She started to walk. It was getting dark. When there was a break in the trees she could see the ice on the lake. In the houses across the lake there were lights coming on. The Lake House Hotel wasn't far away. Even if no car came along to give her a lift it wasn't much of a walk to the Lake House.

But Jack Pringle wasn't going to leave it at that. He's after me, she thought, I'm not clear yet.

Chapter 41

There was something wrong with the Lake House. There was only one light on and when she came up the porch and into the lobby with the bare Christmas tree and Wanda's piled-up furniture, there was no one there. She thought, They've all gone to the carol singing at the College Inn, she said to herself.

But where was Milly Tencza? A carol concert wouldn't mean much to Milly. She should be in the hotel.

"Milly!" she shouted. Then she thought, that's real thick, shouting for a deaf woman. Besides, Milly might have gone to the concert to see the Christmas lights and smiling faces.

Phyllis crossed the lobby to the telephone at the reception desk to call the police. Sooner that's done the better, she said to herself.

Then she saw the snow on the floor. Someone had only recently come into the hotel with snow on his boots.

On the wall in front of her was the old-fashioned poster advertising a ski holiday sometime about 1937 with handsome guys and glamorous women in baggy slacks and expensive knitwear puffing on cigarettes before taking to the slopes. It was covered with glass and in the glass she could see Jack Pringle's reflection with half his face still covered with the bloody handkerchief.

He was standing staring at her. He wasn't moving towards her but she knew there was no way she was going to reach the phone and make a call.

She tried to act as though she hadn't seen him. She didn't know how this would help, but it might give her a few more seconds to figure out what to do.

She stood very still, holding her breath, and then she ran in under the cover of Wanda's furniture and crouched down behind a big wardrobe, wondering which was the best way to make it to the door and, if she could make it to the door, what she was going to do once she got outside.

I've been stupid again, coming here, she told herself, I didn't think. Jack knew I'd head for the nearest place, which was the Lake House. She thought, All he had to do was go back for his skis and then, a good skier like him, he'd get here before me and then he only had to wait.

"Hi," he said and it sent a chill through her.

She couldn't see him now. Can he see me? She asked herself. No, it's a trick. He wants me to answer so he'll know where I am.

"Why'd you hit me?" he asked in a conversational tone of voice as though there was nothing really wrong between them. She still couldn't see him.

"What did I do?" he asked. "Was it because of Sue?"

His tone was warm and chatty although his voice was strange because of the wound to his cheek.

"I could explain about Sue," he said. "You should be able to see about Sue."

He didn't sound far away.

"Are you there?" he asked. "What's wrong with you? Can't you see the position I'm in with a wife who's ill?"

She kept quiet, trying to hold her breath.

"Christ," he said, "this hurts like hell, where you hit me. Goddamn it, Phyllis, you're a doctor, you should take a look at it for me. What the hell's wrong with you? What have I done? Come out and at least talk."

She stayed in the dark, hidden by the big Christmas tree and two piles of Wanda's furniture stacked on either side of her.

She could see across the lobby to the stairs that led to the upper floors. She could see the turn of the stairs and a bit of the railings on the next floor. There was someone moving there. She wondered how Jack had got there without her seeing or at least hearing him. Then she saw Milly Tencza's face.

Milly was hidden where the stairs turned and went up to the next floor. She spoke to Phyllis with her hands.

"He's behind you, on the left," Milly's hands said.

That cut off any chance Phyllis had to run to the front door.

"They know about him," Milly signalled.

Phyllis wondered if she had read this correctly.

"Who?" she asked

"The police," Milly's hands told her. "The police are looking for him. Davy Shea was here. They know he killed them all."

Jack doesn't know this, Phyllis thought, he wouldn't be after me if he did. He'd be trying to get away.

She signed to Milly. "Where are the police?"

Milly signed back that she didn't know.

That's good, Phyllis said to herself with heavy irony, that's dandy. Well, she thought, if I wait here, if I can stay hidden here long enough, they're bound to come.

"He's moving," Milly signed.

Phyllis could hear him. Then she couldn't. She held her breath. Her eyes were on Milly's hands. They said, "He's on the other side of the wardrobe."

Phyllis didn't dare move.

"He knows you're there," Milly's hands said.

Oh my God, Phyllis thought. For a moment she thought she should try to run to Milly on the stairs, but then she jumped to her feet and threw herself at the big wardrobe. It went over, bringing down several lesser items of furniture and the Christmas tree with it.

There was a loud bang above the crash of falling furniture.

He's got a gun, she thought. Goddamn Milly didn't tell me about a gun. It must've gone off by accident when the big wardrobe suddenly fell on him. I hope he's dead, she said to herself, I hope the furniture cracked his goddamn skull wide open.

Her ears were ringing with the explosion. The falling furniture and toppled Christmas tree blocked her way. She had to climb over it to get to the door. She was pushing through the branches when she saw Jack Pringle.

He was lying half under the wardrobe and half under the tree. She was actually stepping on him.

He's dead, she thought.

She turned, still standing in the middle of the branches of the big tree, to sign to Milly.

Milly wasn't there.

Phyllis bent down to take a better look at Jack. She thought the wardrobe must have fractured his spine.

Then she went stiff with fear. He was looking at her. His eyes were open and he was watching her.

He grabbed her leg. She tried to kick him but he pulled her leg and she went down among the branches of the tree.

Jack pulled himself out from under a branch of the Christmas tree which had taken the brunt of the wardrobe's fall. He stood up.

He was pointing the gun at her. It wasn't the big one that had killed Joe Prew. It was only a small gun but it was pointing right at her and he was smiling with the half of his face that wasn't bandaged.

Jack leaned over and pulled her to her feet. The gun was pressed against her.

"Jack," she said, "the police know you killed Gus and Wanda and Mary. You'd better give yourself up."

"Who told you a story like that?" he said.

"Milly."

"When did she tell you?"

"She told me here."

"Here? When here?"

"Just now."

He glanced around, looking for Milly.

I've done wrong, Phyllis thought, I've put Milly in danger.

"Call her," Jack said.

"Call her? She's deaf."

The barrel of the gun pressed against her so hard it hurt.

"With signs. Call her with signs," he said.

"What should I say?"

"Say I'll kill you if she doesn't come out."

Phyllis made signs. She didn't say what Jack had told her. She told Milly to get out of there and get the police.

Nothing moved in the dark hotel.

"Tell her again."

"I'm trying to, but I can't see her."

He still had the gun pressed hard to Phyllis' head.

Milly didn't appear. Phyllis waited for the gun to go off.

Nothing happened. There was an unnatural silence.

"She's not here," Jack said. "You were making it up." He pushed her towards the porch. "Outside," he said, "we're going outside."

When they came down from the Lake House porch he shoved her towards the lake. What's he doing? she thought. Then she knew what was going on. He doesn't believe about the police knowing he's the murderer and he's looking to create an accident. He's going to drown me under the ice.

They were walking towards the big gash in the ice. The water looked very black in the moonlight where the pale shining ice stopped.

Far in the distance there were two people skating.

If she was going to do anything she had to do it now. She started to run along the road, heading towards the two moonlit skaters. He won't shoot, she thought, not if he wants to make it look like an accident. But the road was slippery, covered with black ice.

She was drawing near the skaters. They hadn't noticed her but she could see who they were. One was Hugh Styling, and Cathy Dupre was the other, skating round him, holding him by the hand. Phyllis struggled to get a foothold on the black ice, trying to run, and shouting to Hugh Styling.

And then there was an explosion and she saw Hugh Styling's face, with his glasses reflecting in the moonlight, turning to look at her and then she didn't see or hear anything else.

Chapter 42

When Parker Daniels heard the gunshot he knew what he was hearing.

He was sitting in the dark in Jack Pringle's kitchen, with Jack's shotgun across his knees, and he went to the window which was partially covered by frost but still had a good view of the moonlit lake. He could see a man on the ice.

"Stay here," he said to Moll.

He went out the back door into the now silent night, stumbling several times even though there was the light of the moon. When he reached the lake shore he saw that Moll had come with him.

"Be quiet, girl," he said to her.

The man was on the ice, quite close, just beyond the big gash of dark water where Jack had crossed over. The ladder was still there. He saw two other people further out on the ice across the lake. They were some distance away, but he could see the blades of their skates catching the moonlight. About halfway between the skaters and the lone man, there was something lying on the ice, something dark and still.

Parker walked out on the ice, with the terrier behind him. "Go back, sweetheart," he told her, but she stayed with him. "Oh, well, come along then," he said, "but don't blame me."

He reached the point where the ice ended and the ladder straddled the black water. He recognized Jack Pringle, even though there was something covering half his face.

Jack Pringle had a gun.

Parker said quietly, "You've been a fool, Jack, better give yourself up. We know about Geep LaMay. Sue told me where he's buried."

Jack didn't say anything.

In the moonlight Parker could make out colours. He could see that the person down on the ice was wearing a red hat. He thought it was Joe Prew, but then he saw the female outline.

"Jesus," he said to Jack, "that's Phyllis over there. Let me go to her. Let me help her."

Jack stood with the gun pointing at Parker and didn't say anything.

"Stand back," Parker said. "I'm going to Phyllis."

He started across the ladder.

"Why don't you stay right where you are?" Jack said. "I don't want to shoot you, Boomer. There's no reason for this. Just go away and let some real policeman have the bother of catching me."

"You're not going to shoot me," Parker said.

"Don't bank on it," Jack said. "Just because we were boys together I wouldn't count on that."

Jack didn't shoot and Parker knew it didn't have anything to do with them being boyhood chums. It was the shotgun he had pointed at Jack with his finger on the trigger that kept Jack from firing.

"I had her," Jack said.

Parker thought he meant Phyllis.

Then Jack said, "I had her and Edgar Dupre had her too. There were plenty there before the man who came to fix the central heating. A goofy guy like you, with your high-water pants and night school law degree, what'd you expect?"

Parker knew then that Jack was talking about Parker's wife but he didn't say anything. He was still moving across the ladder over the gash in the ice towards Jack.

Jack said, "You never did have any luck with women, but then neither did I. Did that bitch wife of mine really tell you about LaMay? Edgar Geep LaMay, can you imagine her going with a low class guy like him?"

"You killed the wrong man," Parker said, "it wasn't Geep LaMay. You got the wrong Edgar."

"What?" Jack said.

"Drop the gun," Parker said.

He had crossed the ladder and was standing close to Jack, who had his revolver right in front of him. He's waiting till he can't miss, Parker thought, and he can't miss now.

Parker had trouble breathing. He had to gasp for breath, he could feel his heart beating and even in the cold night air he was sweating.

"I don't want to shoot you," Parker said and he whipped the butt of the shotgun around and batted the gun out of Jack's hand. It went skidding across the ice. He had an idea it might have gone in the water. He didn't have time to see. Jack was gripping him and he was strong, Parker had forgotten how strong Jack was. He was attempting to wrestle Parker down on the ice. Christ, he's going to drown me, Parker thought.

He could feel his feet sliding on the black ice as Jack pushed him towards the hole. Then he went into the freezing water. Jack had one hand on the top of Parker's head and the other on a shoulder and he was pushing him down. The water was freezing. Parker kicked, trying to keep himself up, but Jack's powerful arms kept forcing him down. Take a breath, Parker thought, get a real deep breath. He stopped trying to climb out of the hole. He took a deep breath and reached up and grabbed Jack by both ankles and pulled him down off the ice and into the water.

Parker moved fast, taking Jack by surprise.

Parker dived, holding Jack and swimming down. He didn't know how much air Jack had been able to take in before he pulled him over but he didn't think it would be much. He had a grip on him and kept diving.

It was completely dark under the water. Parker felt Jack pulling, trying to go up. Then the pulling stopped. Parker didn't let go. He kept swimming down to the deep lake bottom. Jack wasn't struggling any more.

Then he felt Jack's hands on his face, clawing at his eyes. It was terrible the way Jack thrashed about trying to free himself. Then he stopped and was still.

Parker had no time to carry him to the surface.

He came up to the surface alone and the stars were out. He hadn't noticed the stars before, but now he had trouble seeing, there was blood running into his eyes where Jack had gone for them.

He was near the ladder and pulled himself out. The clothes started sticking to him, freezing on him. He couldn't feel his legs or feet. He tried to see where Phyllis was, but he couldn't see. He wiped the blood out of his eyes with the back of his hand. He saw her and the two skaters standing beside her.

He started across the ice to them.

"Is she all right?" he shouted.

They didn't hear him.

He wanted to run but he had trouble walking and the blood kept getting in his eyes.

Parker could see the lights of an ambulance and men running across the ice to where Cathy Dupre and Hugh Styling were.

Davy came across the ice to Parker.

"You got him," Davy said. "I saw two figures go into the water and then only one come up. I was all ready to shoot until I saw it was you."

"Is she all right?" Parker asked.

Someone had put a blanket over Parker's shoulders. It didn't seem to make any difference.

"You got your man," Davy said, "that must have been one hell of a fight. Underwater, Jesus."

They were putting Phyllis in the ambulance.

"Is she going to be all right?" Parker asked.

A paramedic stood looking at Parker. "You better come too, Boomer," he said. Parker didn't recognize him. He was trying to see if Phyllis's face was covered up.

They shoved Parker in the ambulance. Davy got in too.

"Here's a drink, Boomer," he said, "you'd better have a drink."

Parker was looking at the blanket trying to see if her face was covered.

The ambulance door was still open. There was someone standing there. Parker couldn't see who it was with the blood dripping into his eyes.

"Get that dog out of here," the paramedic said.

Hugh Styling was standing there with Moll in his arms.

Davy pulled Hugh and the dog into the ambulance. "You're a witness," he said to Hugh. "You got to come."

"What's wrong with your eyes?" the paramedic asked Parker.

"What about Phyllis?" Parker asked him.

The paramedic wiped the blood from Parker's eyes.

Parker could see Phyllis's face.

"She'll be all right," the paramedic said.

Phyllis's eyes were open but she didn't seem to be seeing any better than Parker. One of her hands was outside the blanket. Parker thought someone should hold her hand but he thought his own hands were freezing and wouldn't do her any good.

"Hold her hand," Parker said to Hugh, "hold her goddamn hand."

Hugh didn't move.

"Jesus," Parker said, "give me her hand."

Phyllis said something but Parker couldn't hear.

"What's that?" he asked.

Phyllis spoke again.

"What's she saying?" Davy asked.

"I don't know," Parker said.

But he had heard what Phyllis said. She'd said, "I think I love you, Boomer."

And then, in spite of his ice-cold fingers, he felt the faint pressure as she squeezed his hand.

Three days later they took Jack Pringle's body out of the lake and two days after that they unearthed the remains of Edgar Geep LaMay from the cellar of the Lake House. Beverly Choquette's brother was released from prison, but it didn't make her stop giving dirty looks to Davy Shea.

Somewhere about this time Parker was up and about again and he went to see Phyllis Skypeck at the hospital. He didn't know what he expected to find and when what he found was Phyllis with Hugh Styling by her bedside and Phyllis kissing Hugh rather passionately, Parker wasn't surprised.